Ceridwen of Kilton:
Book Two of
The Circle of Ceridwen Saga

Ceridwen of Kilton

Octavia Randolph

Ceridwen of Kilton is the second book in The Circle of Ceridwen Saga by Octavia Randolph.

Copyright 2001 Octavia Randolph This print version 2014

Pyewacket Press

ISBN: 978-0-9854582-5-6

Bookcover design: DesignForBooks.com

Photo credits: Landscape image, iStockphoto©Irene1601. Birds and moon illustration, texture, graphics, photo manipulation, and map by Michael Rohani.

The Circle of Ceridwen Saga employs British spellings, alternate spellings, archaic words, and oftentimes unusual verb to subject placement. This is intentional. A Glossary of Terms will be found at the end of the novel.

To the one who cut the quills for my pen, and to the one who prepared so many sheets of parchment.

List of Characters

Ceridwen, formerly the Kingdom of Mercia, aged sixteen when the book opens

Gyric, son of Godwulf of Kilton in the Kingdom of Wessex, her husband

Godwin, Gyric's older brother

Edgyth, wife to Godwin

Modwynn, Lady of Kilton, mother to Gyric and Godwin

Godwulf, Lord of Kilton, an ealdorman of Wessex, husband to Modwynn

Ælfred, King of Wessex

Ælfwyn, a lady of Wessex residing in Lindisse, now controlled by the Danes

Sidroc, a Dane

Cadmar, once a warrior of Wessex, now a monk

Contents

Ceridwen of Kilton

Ceridwen of Kilton

Preface

There is power in words, and power is the root of fear; and I have cause to fear for what I am about to tell. But in words there is joy too, and greater power than that of fear; and as my heart speaks so must my hand follow.

I am Ceridwen, wife to Gyric of the famed stronghold of Kilton; but before that I called myself Ceridwen, daughter of the dead ealdorman Cerd of the Kingdom of Mercia. Early in the year 871, I met the Lady Ælfwyn of Cirenceaster, a true sister in kindness to me, and travelled with her to the conquered keep of Four Stones where she went, an unwilling bride, to the Dane Yrling, for the Danes were ravaging the kingdoms of the Angles and the Saxons. In the damp cellars of that place we found a young nobleman of Wessex, cruelly blinded by the Danes; and to save him from death I rode off with him. We journeyed in danger far to his home at Kilton, and with him I knew love. And his people, thinking him dead, rejoiced at his return, and treated me with every honour, and rejoiced the more when I found myself with his child. And in that same Summer did I reach my sixteenth year.

Chapter the First: A Return

The Year 872

"WE have had naught but war with the Danes for six years, and for six years they have exacted huge sums of silver from us."

The young man who recounted this was Ælfred, King of Wessex, come himself to stand as God-father at the naming-feast of my son. The King's light blue eyes flicked from face to face around the high table of Godwulf, Lord of Kilton. "Lindisse, Anglia, and Kent they now control. Egbert of Northumbria will not last long; his Kingdom too shall fall. Only Wessex and Mercia remain."

For the naming-feast the oaken board had been massed with all the early Spring bounty the burh of Kilton could provide, and our first cup had been precious wine from Frankland. We had feasted on crackling-skinned rock doves, bitterns, and grouse, and bowls of thick browis, steaming with leeks and turnips; and then taken bright ale with platters of dried apples and cherries stewed in tart ver-juice. All was of delicious savour, and as I was always hungry now that I was suckling Ceric, I ate my fill and more.

But jesting talk was over, and Ælfred had set down his golden cup and spoke so that all at the table might hear. Godwulf sat at the King's right side, and at the old lord's right, his eldest son, Godwin; and the faces of all others at that table were turned unto these three.

"Now, as of last Summer we have peace with them," Ælfred went on, "but a watchful, restless peace, for they only grow stronger as they raven off the richness of the kingdoms they have conquered."

Godwulf's pale eyes had never left Ælfred's face during this speech. Now the old man roused himself, stood up, and rasped his answer. "You are the bringer of our peace," he said, and gestured to the King's golden dragon banner, "a peace purchased not only with our silver, but bought dear by them at the points of our spears. Let them buy peace from Wessex at the price of their blood!"

A cry went up from the men at the table, and they hooted and stamped their feet in acclaim at Godwulf's words, so that all in the hall looked up at us.

"It will take both silver and spear-points, to drive the invader from our borders," said Ælfred. "If we are steadfast in our courage, and steadfast in our faith, God will not forsake us to the heathen horde."

"I am steadfast in my steel," echoed Godwulf, with his hand upon the hilt of his seax.

"And no man's steel I value more than yours," returned Ælfred with a grin, at which every thegn of Godwulf's cheered. The King looked over the hall at the faces turned towards his. "I thank God that I was entrusted to lead a people such as you." He took up his cup again. "Therefore I drink to you, that we might all be brothers in this great task before us."

It was easy to salute such a man, and to honour him as King. We lifted our cups in gladsome tribute, and I felt, sitting in that strong-hold filled with the finest thegns in the realm, that no harm could come to Wessex as long as Ælfred ruled.

I looked at Gyric at my side, and watched the tilt of his head as he listened to the talk of the table. He had not raised his voice during the meal to address his King; he no longer claimed the right now that he could not back up his words

3

with deeds on the field of battle. Yet no one seeing the two young men together could be unmoved, or unaware, of the honour and love that Ælfred held in his eyes for his companion since boyhood. Gyric knew this as well, for Ælfred had showered a hundred kindnesses upon him since learning of his return alive to Kilton, and these kindnesses extended even to me, and now to our babe. But to Gyric no token of loving-kindness from his King and former battle-mate could dispel his gloom at being rendered unable to fight for Kilton, and for Wessex.

Towards the end of our meal the massive oak door at the end of the hall was pulled open by one of the thegns, and a slight figure, a boy or young man, began picking its way through the press of tables and benches. This visitor was alone, and wrapped in a plain dark blue cloak like unto those pilgrims wear. Tho' the hall was bustling, I watched him approach, thinking it might be a monk about to beg shelter. Modwynn, ever generous, saw him too, and by her attentive gaze made ready her welcome. Halfway through the hall the visitor paused and pushed back the hood which shrouded his face. To my surprise, it was no man at all, but a woman who smiled up at us.

"Edgyth," said Modwynn, with real pleasure, and stood up to greet her other daughter in law.

Edgyth nodded her head and continued to the table, stopping at the very centre before Ælfred. "My lord," she began, and curtsied deeply, "forgive my disturbing your repast."

In answer Ælfred reached his hands across the narrow table and took both of Edgyth's in his own. "Edgyth," he said. "In faith, how good it is to see you again."

Now Gyric too had risen, and as he spoke her name extended his hand through the space to his brother's wife.

4

She turned her eyes upon him, grey eyes beneath a pale brow, and her lips parted but she spoke no word. She let go the King's hands and took that which Gyric offered, and enfolding it touched it to her lips.

"Dear brother," she said.

These two words and the tenderness with which she spoke them told me much.

She came around the end of the table, and Modwynn and Godwulf embraced her. Then she turned to her husband Godwin, who kissed her upon the brow. He spoke some word of welcome to her, what I could not hear, and gently pulled the cloak from her shoulders. Beneath she wore a grey wool gown of fine weaving but the simplest make. No thread-work embellished it, no jewel was pinned at throat or shoulder, nothing but a thin strand of amber beads about her neck lent any colour. Her hair was covered by her headwrap, and only a few light, ashy strands showed. Her lips were full but pale. Her whole expression was one of pleasant quietness. She was of middle height, no more; slight and straight. She was fully twenty-six, no longer very young, and tho' her face was unlined any beauty which it once held was faded away.

Having thought this thought, I kept looking on her, for tho' there was nothing in her face or form to lure the eye, once caught it found pleasure there. There was the simple grace with which she walked, which made her seem more akin to Modwynn than I thought woman ever could be. She had a lovely way of moving her hands, and their gentle gestures gave fullness to her soft words. She was ready and well spoken to all, greeting each at the table with some special remembrance or little jest.

Modwynn led her to where Gyric and I stood waiting. Her grey eyes turned to me, and took me in as fully as I did her. I was nearly a hand-span taller; my round breasts and

5

hips now those of a suckling mother. My strong nose, chestnut-gold hair, and mossy-green eyes made my face as vivid as hers was pale. I wore one of my two finest gowns, sewn of yellow silk, for it was Easterweek, and the King with us. Circling my brow was the narrow fillet of gold which I wore every night at table in the hall. Around my waist was tied the sash upon which I had worked in linen thread two flying pheasants, bright with gay colour. Looped over this sash hung the ring of keys, given me by Modwynn, which opened many of the store-houses and treasure hoards of Kilton; the very keys which once Edgyth had worn.

Edgyth saw all this, and did so, I thought, without judging or gauging.

"What beauty you have!" were her first words to me, and the sudden sweetness of this declaration left me tongue-tied.

Modwynn laughed, and took my hand and pressed it into Edgyth's. "Yes, Ceridwen is beautiful, and better than beautiful, clever; and better than this, good."

Now I laughed too, for this fulsome praise stung my cheeks with warmth.

"Welcome," I told Edgyth, and regretted it at once, for who was I to welcome she who had lived at Kilton for six years back to her rightful home? But I went on, "I have wanted so long to know you," and this I tried to say with the truth I felt.

Edgyth took me into her arms and embraced me, and then turned to Gyric and pressed him to her breast. She kissed his cheek, and her eyes closed as her lips brushed the linen wrap he wore; save this there was no sign of grief.

"How glad Ceridwen will be for your company," he told her. "How glad we all will be."

But at this Edgyth lowered her eyes. Still holding onto Gyric's hand she told him, "I cannot stay. I am on my way to Glastunburh, and my men and I will leave again when our horses are rested."

A foundation of Benedictine nuns was at Glastunburh, this I knew. Modwynn's quick glance spoke her question to Edgyth, but Edgyth shook her head. "I think it best to spend some time there," she said deliberately. "To help me think," she finished.

Modwynn nodded her head. "We will speak of it later," she invited. "Now, come sit and eat."

Edgyth took her place, more than a year empty, next to Godwin at the table. For the first time I saw him share his plate with another, and watched them as they spoke together. I could not read Godwin's face; he treated her with courtesy, but I had seen him treat all women thus. Nor did Edgyth's calm visage betray any unease, or especial joy, at being once again back at Kilton's high table. I lifted my eyes and was caught in my staring by Godwulf. Godwin sat, as always, just next his father, and the old lord himself may have been watching Edgyth, for as his eyes met mine I thought he too wondered what would happen.

When the last dishes were set upon the table, I said to Gyric, "I think I will go back to the bower house. Ceric may be hungry now."

I rose and went to bid Good-night to Ælfred, Godwulf, and Modwynn. As I did so Edgyth stood and said to me, "And may I see the babe?"

"O, yes," I answered. "Please come."

So Edgyth and I walked together to the end of the hall, and out through the smaller oaken door on the side that led to the pleasure garden. The noise of the hall fell away behind us, and the roaring of the waves upon the rocks below rose to fill our ears. "The sea," said Edgyth in a low tone. "How I have missed it."

Then we were before the round bower house, in which she and Godwin had lived, and which he had given up to his brother and me when we had arrived last Spring. Now it was our house, Gyric's and mine, even to the carved dragon bed within it, which Godwin had had made so many years before for his own new bride. I did not think Edgyth could look upon these things unmoved, and in fact, I watched her pause a moment as we stepped inside. I went from cresset to cresset, lighting more oil lamps that we might see. Edgyth moved to the cradle.

"Ah, a lovely child," she said, with true warmth. I lifted Ceric from the cradle, and Edgyth's hands rose in faint echo of my movement.

"Will you hold him?" I asked. She nodded wordlessly, and as she took him Ceric yawned, his tiny red mouth opening and shutting.

"He is not hungry after all," I laughed, as Ceric snuggled into Edgyth's arms. We sat down together at the table, and Ceric closed his eyes again.

"Do not let him get too heavy," I told her. "He grows so quickly. Put him down whenever you like."

"He is not heavy," she said softly, peering into the pink face.

I knew enough to be quiet. Some little time passed, and we, tho' nothing was said, grew closer in our knowing of the other by the silence.

At last she laid the babe down in the cradle. She stretched her now-empty hands upon the table, and looked over at me. "I have heard much of you," she said in her mild voice.

I was quiet, and she went on. "How blest Gyric is to have you."

"I am blest to have him," I returned.

She nodded. "That is as it should be; that you might both think so." She shifted in her chair, and the room fell quiet.

"You were very kind to Gyric in the hall," I offered.

She moved her hands in a little gesture of acceptance. "How could I not be? He is so dear to me. Gyric could always make me smile; he was always mirthful and teasing."

I said that which would be hard for her to say. "He is greatly changed."

She searched my face. "Yes, greatly. Last year I left Kilton in mid-Winter, at Candlemas. I knew nothing of Gyric's capture. Then a rider came, sent by Godwin, to my parents' hall. He told us Gyric had returned, as from the dead. This message was also a Fare-well, for Godwin meant to ride after the Danes who had wounded Gyric." Her voice dropped to a hush. "I knew Godwin did not expect to survive the avenging."

The starkness of her words recalled those sorrowful days to me, but from Edgyth's vantage alone. "You feared Godwin would be lost to you."

9

Her hand moved slightly in assent. When she spoke it was in steadier voice. "But through the grace of God, it has all turned out well. Gyric lives, and Godwin lived to avenge him."

She went on, with something like a smile, "And you have taken your rightful place at Kilton."

"My place is to be with Gyric. That is all I ever cared about."

She answered with gentleness, but with resolve. "Your role is a far greater one than that. You have wed the second son of the most powerful ealdorman in Wessex. There are many rights, and also many bounden duties, with that role. You are fulfilling them all. Not one year into your union, and you have already borne an heir for this heirless hall. Godwulf's gratitude to you will be endless."

I was too surprised to speak, and she went on. "Forgive me for the frankness of my speech. It was a quality that Godwin always valued in me."

"I am honoured that you speak to me thus."

She smiled, and then bit her lip for a moment. "You have doubtless heard something of me," she prompted.

"Yes, indeed," I answered, and thought of the first thing Godwin had ever said about her. "The morning Gyric and I arrived at Kilton, Godwin told me that you would like me."

She almost laughed, a gentle sighing laugh. "But that is really about you, is it not?"

I felt abashed. "Yes, you are right," I admitted.

She shook her head, and with her gentle fingers pushed a wisp of hair back under her head wrap. "Forgive me, I am just being cross-grained. A fault of mine. Go on."

I tried to tell the truth with care. "He told us that you had gone home to your shire, but that there was no trouble between you, and that you were a good woman. Then I told him that I was sure you were a very good woman, and that I hoped you would come back to Kilton soon so I might meet you. That is when he said he thought you would like me."

She nodded her head. "And that is all that you have heard?"

"No," I confessed. "Gyric told me when we were upon the road, making our way here, that you had been wed to Godwin for six years, and that it was your sorrow not to be able to bear a live child."

Her brows drew together, and her voice was low. "I fear that is the sum total of my story: 'Poor Edgyth.'"

Our eyes met, and she went on in the same low but steady tone. "Now it is nearly seven years," she ended, "tho' I have seen so little of my husband this past year."

"Why did you leave Kilton?" I made bold to ask.

"I had no choice but to leave."

"Godwin sent you away?" I could not believe it.

"No, no. He would never send me away. I had no choice within my own heart; I could not stay. It was too painful to stay."

"Because of...this sorrow?"

"Yes." Her voice was even softer. "Godwin wants, and needs, an heir. In six years I was gotten with his child eight

11

times. At first, as soon as I was certain I was with child, there would be an issue of blood, and I would lose it. Months would pass, and I would again conceive. I tried every remedy to keep my babes, even to making myself sick with draughts of burdock. But nothing would allow me to bear a quick child. Some I lost at three months, some at five. Twice I bore the babe right to the eighth month."

"How terrible for you," I said. I wanted to take her hand, but did not have the boldness to do so. Her eyes, tho' gentle, held within them a distance, as if she spoke not of herself, but of another.

"Yes," she murmured. "It was very terrible, for me, and for Godwin. Terrible for a great source of pleasure to become a great source of sorrow."

I thought of all the nights and mornings of love spent with Gyric, and how I should feel if these fleshly joys be lost to us.

"But...he still cares for you," I offered.

Her answer was quick, but the voice still low and mild. "He cannot bear to look at me. Not that I ever was a feast to the eye. What little looks were mine have been bled out of me with my lost babes. There has been too much pain between us. Every glance seems a reproach, from Godwin, from all of them. Even Modwynn."

I could hear naught against her, and began to speak, but Edgyth lifted her hand.

"Modwynn is too kind to reproach me, even with her eyes. But her pity is even harder to bear."

I had no answer for this. I had learnt much about pity, I thought, for I saw it in the eyes of all when they looked upon Gyric. Of all those in Kilton I thought I was the only one who

12

did not pity him, for I was the one who never knew him whole. I had found him, blinded, filthy, and near death, in the cellars of a keep far from here, and had carried him away that he might live. On our journey to safety I grew to love him, and loved him as he was, and could never know what he had been before. With him I first knew desire, and the great joy of passing from maiden to wife; and now the fierce sweet bond of motherhood. All my world and happiness lay within him and what he had given me. Pity was no part of my love.

Edgyth spoke again, with words that were awful to hear, and worse to speak. "I am nothing more than a dried relic of a love that was once warm and strong."

My protest died on my lips; the sudden earnestness in her grey eyes stayed me.

"That is why I travel to Glastunburh, to think on this. Godwin could be released from the marriage vows, and take a new wife, and have the joy with her that you and Gyric feel now. We could in law dissolve our marriage, and his vows would be annulled."

"His vows? And what of yours?"

"My vows to him will never be null; say whatever bishops or law-code will. But if we jointly agree to dissolve our union, or if I take the veil, he will be free to wed again."

"You love him this much?"

She dipped her chin the slightest bit. "Is there truly a choice? If I stay wedded to Godwin, I will force him into the bed of another woman, and that I could not bear. He will turn to the village, and get himself a son there easily enough, and no one will blame him. There is no shame in being a lord's bastard." This last word hung on her pale lips.

13

"Do your parents, and Godwulf and Modwynn, agree with all this?"

"Yes; and no. Godwulf and Modwynn have been aggrieved at my barren marriage, but their loyalty to me and my folk runs deep. Then there is the matter of treasure. My dowry was a rich one, for my parents greatly wished this match for me. They in no wise want this union to end, but should it, they will sue for its return, or at least for much of it. Godwin will not find it easy to part with so much silver. Whatever I do, there will be a price to pay."

"And what of Godwin?" I asked, almost fearing to know. I did not want to think less of him in any way.

"He will neither ask me to stay, nor bid me go." She looked straight ahead for a moment. "So I go to Glastunburh, and there will seek an answer." She studied her hands, flat upon the tabletop. "Perhaps I will find a vocation, some ghostly guidance. I have some skill at herb-craft, and would learn more; there are nuns there known for their leech-craft. At least I will find a measure of peace, away from the urgings of my parents and the longings of Godwin."

I thought of the foundation of Glastunburh, and of all the great ladies that must be holy women there, and all the learning and books stored up between peaceful walls. There might be solace there for Edgyth. Then I thought of my own life, and early yearnings for I knew not what.

"I was Priory-raised," I told her, "and there is peace in that life, for some. I was not one of them."

"Fate brought you here instead, to our beloved Kilton." She ended, "And tomorrow I fear Fate may lead me away from it, forever."

14

The crunch of gravel underfoot told me that Gyric was come. I rose and opened the door to him, and holding his spear in his hand as a staff, he stepped within. Edgyth came to his side and in her low and calm voice spoke.

"Brother, if ever a man was worthy of good wife it is you, and as further blessing God has given you a son both fine and lusty. Recalling you three will serve as a most happy remembrance in the days before me."

She kissed us all and so took her leave of us. Ceric started to fuss, and then to cry, and my breasts, heavy with milk, began to flow in answer. I dropped the front of my suckling-shift, and settled in my chair. Ceric's sobs ceased as his seeking mouth found my nipple. The babe pulled strongly at my milk-swollen breast, its hardness softening quickly under his greedy mouth. His tiny hand splayed against my skin, and his body relaxed against mine in contentment.

I was safe and well, and greatly loved, and had a healthy babe as part of that love. I had in full measure that which was denied Edgyth. Her name meant 'gift of happiness' but little happiness had she given, or received. Even the house in which I dwelt and the bed in which I lay had been denied her, and as I sat there I wondered why Fate had dealt thus with us.

Gyric spoke not, just listened with intent to the gurglings and sighings of his infant son. He reached with his hand and found the little one in my arms. His fingers gently touched the linen veil and stroked the babe's head. All the dark birthing hair had fallen away, and now Ceric's head was as pale and smooth as the egg of a goose.

"He has hair," said Gyric after a moment. "I can feel it."

I moved my own hand to touch the babe's crown. "You are right, I can just feel it too, tho' I can see nothing; it is that fair."

"I am thankful we will not have a bald child," said Gyric.

"He is only as bald as you and Godwin were," I answered, glad to be playful. "Your mother says Ceric looks just as you two did, and you grew hair in abundance." And with a little tug I pulled at a lock of Gyric's red-gold hair as it lay upon his shoulder.

"Are his eyes still blue?" ventured Gyric in a low voice.

"Yes, dark blue; but Modwynn says the eyes of all new babes are thus. They will come to their true colour soon enough."

"They will be green," said Gyric. "Like yours...and...all of us."

"Yes," I said, keeping my voice light. "I am sure he will look just like you."

He nodded his head, and then found my free hand and pressed it to his lips. "It is as Edgyth said. You are everything," he murmured.

"I am part of everything, everything that is good and loving in your world," I told him.

"You are my world," he answered gravely.

I wanted to counter this, but as gently as I could. "No, my love, do not say that. Not when you have so much to give."

"Without you I would have been dead these twelve months."

"Without you none of these joys would be mine. The joy of being your wife, of our child, of all the comforts and pleasures of life here at Kilton." I thought of Edgyth, so gentle, so learned, and so unhappy. I touched his face. "You have given me so much."

He nodded his head, but with no real conviction. The set of his mouth, the angle of his head, the slightest gesture of his hand, told me he could not believe my earnest words.

Chapter the Second: A Parting

HARVEST that Summer was so bountiful that Godwulf ordered new grain houses built hard upon each other within the burh yard. In these were stored bushels of rye, wheat, and oats which rolled through the palisade gates after our first-fruits feast on Hlafmesse. The village folk gained precious coin in return for the sale of their excess to the grain merchants who visited Kilton then, and even the humblest hut holder prospered in the sudden bounty. But Godwulf sold none of the burh's grain, tho' ready silver was put before him many a time, but filled the store houses, old and new, to bursting.

Likewise at the end of Summer he sent many men into the forests that fronted Kilton, who returned with their ox-pulled wains laden down with the trunks of oak trees. These logs were straight, clear-grained, the kind loved by joiners, and were set to dry in a roofed shed against the palisade wall.

One morning in the yard I saw Godwin speaking to the foreman who oversaw the unloading of yet another wain of this timber. When he was done he turned and saw me, and I gestured to him.

"Is this for even more grain houses?" I asked him, and then jested, "I know it cannot be only our Yule fires that Godwulf is providing for."

Godwin laughed and shook his head. "No to both. It is for building, tho'. To be held in case of need."

"Need?" I echoed, looking around at the bustling yard, ringed with store houses.

The laughter left Godwin's face, but his tone was still light. "Yes. Should the folk need to leave the village and live within the burh walls for a time, this will provide timber for housing them and penning their beasts."

The thought of all the village folk crowding into the yard made me blink.

"It has happened before, and since it may happen again, it is best to be prepared," ended Godwin, in an easy voice.

I nodded, and forced myself to smile. Nothing but fear of attack would drive the village folk away from their huts and crofts and into the burh yard. Now I understood Godwulf's refusal to part with any grain. In a siege, he would need every kernel to feed those dependent upon him. Another thought came to me.

"And the new landing stage?" A path, steep and treacherous, led from the pleasure garden down to the sea rocks below. Nearby coves held the few small boats kept by Godwulf. In the water, at the pathway's end, was a wooden landing stage, that one might swim, fish, or launch a boat from.

Godwin nodded. "Yes, that too is part of our defence. The new one will be much smaller, and anchored to the rocks by just two iron pins, which can be pulled out by one man and so prevent the Danes from landing at our backs."

He moved his head in the direction of the garden. "Our archers would pick them off one by one as they climbed the path. If they were bold enough to attempt our swift current and steep tides."

This last was said only to calm my fears. I thought I knew as well as any man at Kilton the boldness of the Danes; in fact, better, as I had lived amongst them. In their daring

19

they had crossed the whole of the Northern Sea to reach our lands. The channel upon which Kilton lay would prove no barrier to their seamanship.

My face must have said these things, tho' my lips were silent, and for a moment Godwin would not look at me. Then he shifted his weight from one foot to the other.

"I will let you get back to work," I said lightly, and turned to the hall.

Two days after the Feast of St Matthew, on a morning marked only by its ripe fairness, Gyric sat with his father in the pleasure garden. The day was so mild that I had brought Ceric out to join the two men as they sat in the Sun, for now the babe was old enough to sit upright Godwulf delighted in taking him upon his knee. It was near noon when I carried Ceric back to the bower house to Hrede, the young girl who had charge of him. I had put him back in his cradle when I heard Gyric cry out.

From the door I could see the standing Gyric, his arms extended before him. "Father! Father! Help!" he cried, and then fell to his knees.

I could not see Godwulf as I rushed into the garden, Hrede at my heels. Part of my view of the pleasure garden pavilion was blocked by the still-green shrubberies. Gyric called again, in anguish, and I found him crouched on the gravel, his hand pressed over the chest of Godwulf, now laying slumped against the seat of an overturned bench.

Men were now come from out the hall, thegns running in answer to Gyric's cries, their eyes wide, hands gripping the hilts of their seaxs. They crowded speechless round the old man, one of them freeing an arm twisted behind him, another stretching to support his head. I had reached Gyric, and had my arms about his neck as he still pressed his hand over Godwulf's heart and wailed.

Godwulf's eyes were open, and in them was a look of utter amaze. His lips were parted, but he spoke not, tho' a tiny bubble of spittle lay upon them. Perfect stillness was his. If Death had touched him, His touch was quick indeed.

Now Modwynn was come, skirts gathered in her tightly-clenched hands. The thegns parted as she fell upon her knees and buried her face in the snowy beard and hair. She did not sob or speak, she was silent as her husband himself, and only Gyric's soft cry of "Mother?" opened her lips. Then she took Gyric's hand, and laid it upon her face, and breathed forth a long, low lament.

Tears spilt from my eyes, and I dug my fingers into Gyric's shoulders as he cried out, and Hrede clung to my gown and bawled. The thegns stood, stunned and dull-eyed as more folk from the hall ran out and then stopped in unbelief at what they saw. Serving men and kitchen women and thegns' wives with spindles still in their hands clustered at the door, gaping into the garden. Then Godwin came.

He ran out to us, and stopped before the prostrate form of his mother as she lay upon the old lord's chest, and seeing this all colour fled from his face. Then he lowered himself to the ground at his father's head, and laid his right hand upon his father's brow, and with that hand gently closed the pale green eyes forever.

He knelt this way for a long moment, and Modwynn turned her face and reached up and took her eldest son's hand in her own, and kissed it.

21

Godwin rose. He stood, as he did, separate from us all; but his eyes were fixed upon the face of his father. Then did Wulfstan, senior most of the thegns of Godwulf, step before Godwin.

Godwin's eyes went to the face of the trusted thegn, and Wulfstan dropped on his knees before Godwin and drawing his seax from its scabbard offered the hilt of the sharp blade in homage to his new lord. And Godwin, in his first act as ealdorman of Kilton, took the offered hilt in his hand for a moment and so accepted the works of that seax as a vow of fealty.

Then did each of these picked men of Godwulf, his most favoured warriors, become the picked men of Godwin, for each and every one of them knelt before their new lord and offered fealty to him.

Now Gyric spoke, and called his brother's name, and still kneeling by their lifeless father drew his seax into the air over the dead man; and Godwin touched the hilt and took his brother's hand in acknowledgement of his pledge.

And above all this I heard the hungry crying of my son Ceric, left alone in the bower house and wanting to suckle, and I rose and tore myself away from Death to Life.

That was a day without seeming end. We went about the needful tasks that Death demands, moving together as in a dream-walk. In late afternoon Modwynn and I together washed and dressed the honoured body of Godwulf. I saw for the first time, as she had seen every day, the story of battle upon his body. The pale arms and chest, flecked with white hair, were creased with scars from spear-point and sword blade, fighting thrust and hunting mishap. Yet he died, this warrior of great renown, the straw death of one who ends his days in the safety and fellowship of his own home, and despite the suddenness of it, his widow rejoiced in this.

Modwynn gathered from wooden chest and treasure box the richest clothing that was in Godwulf's store, and these we dressed him in. She placed on his wrists bracelets of twisted gold and on his tunic pins of gold and of silver studded with emeralds and garnets. With her own carved comb of pear wood she combed the long white hair and smoothed the beard.

Left untouched, and still upon its loom, was stretched the binding sheet she had laboured over for so many years, its spiralling border and leaping stags picked out in brilliant thread-work. Tomorrow would the old lord be buried, and tomorrow would she wrap the beloved body in this shimmering cloth for its final resting place.

I left her alone and in peace. The hall was quiet and near deserted. On the platform where each night the high table was set up waited the scop, keeper of the word-hoard, standing alone with bowed head, tears upon his face.

The afternoon was now far gone, and long shadows slit the golden light in the pleasure garden. Passing from the hall to the bower house, I saw Godwin and Gyric, sitting together upon the bench on which their father had last sat. Gyric's face was covered by his hands, and his brother's arm was about his shoulder; but Godwin's face still wore the blank look of unbelief.

"Modwynn waits for you in the treasure room, Godwin," I said softly, not wanting to startle them. Godwin nodded and rose and moved slowly away from us. I sat down next to Gyric, circled him in my arms, and pressed my lips to his temple. His chin was lowered, his jaw slack, and he shook his head the smallest bit, as if denying some unsaid charge.

"Will you come to the bower house and lie down?" I whispered.

He did not turn his head, and spoke as if to himself. "I could not find him. We talked of the harvest, and then were quiet for a few moments. I heard an odd sound, and spoke his name, but he answered not. I reached for him. I could not find him. He had fallen -" Gyric's voice broke off, and his shoulders shook with sobs. I clutched him tighter to me, but he went on, his voice rising in agony, "I could not find him!"

I grasped both of his hands in mine and squeezed them, and spoke with all the force I could, tho' my words were hoarse with my tears. "My love, my love, there is nothing you or anyone could have done; nothing. Come now, Gyric, come and rest."

His answering words were swift and cruel. "I am cursed, and cursed be this day that I live, a useless cripple, and Godwulf, best of lords is struck down!"

Now I sobbed, felled by the force of his unhealed grief amidst his new mourning. I bent over his hands, still enfolded in mine, and kissed them as my tears rained down upon them. "Gyric - my love - my husband - never say that. I love and need you. You have a son who needs you, and a loving mother. And Godwin - Godwin will need you more than ever - now..."

I could not go on. My heart ached, and my head swam, and I wanted only to get to the bower house to my little babe, and give to him the solace and comfort that I myself yearned for, and could not give to Gyric.

24

I pulled him by the hand, and he rose and let me lead him away. I took Ceric and lay down upon the great bed with him curled in my arms, while Gyric sat alone and in silence at the table.

That night all the folk of the burh, even unto the slaves, and all the village folk, and all gamesmen and snaresmen and woodcutters of the forests, all who had been within the call of horns or sounding of bells or hurried cry from swift riders; these all filed into the timber hall at Kilton. There before the fire-pit heaped with fresh logs, brightly burning, stood a single table. Upon this table lay the great Godwulf himself, gorgeously arrayed, his golden-hilted sword at his side, his silver-wound seax on his belly, and over his chest the black painted shield of stout linden wood centred by its iron boss. His helmet of polished steel lay by his head, and all walked by and looked upon the warlord in his glittering war-kit. And all of his thegns stood behind him, keeping watch; and the chief of these was his own son Godwin, who stood unmoving hour after hour. Crouched at the foot of this table was the scop, tears streaming from his eyes, his painted harp laid out upon the floor, and every string broken. Gyric stood apart, locked in his double grief; and Modwynn stayed in solitude behind the closed door of the treasure room, hemming with tiny stitches of linen the hallowed binding sheet.

Outside the hall smoked a small fire of new-cut holly boughs, so sacred that it never be burnt save in remembrance of the funeral-fires of our heathen fore-folk, for it was the tree of Hel, mistress of the underworld. And this fire was laid and tended through the long night on the order of Godwin, ealdorman of Kilton.

Chapter the Third: The Dance of Life

The Year 873

HIGH Summer's Day dawned fair and warm. As befits a high holiday, all but the most vital of chores was laid aside, and by ones and twos the folk of the burh, thegn or workman, stable-boy or washing-girl slipped out the broad gates and headed down the red clay road to the village.

I too had made preparation, in the pennon I had made for the High Summer fire. On a background of undyed linen I had sewn a large circle of yellow-dyed linen. The light brown undyed cloth was the symbol for our ripening wheat, and the circle the Sun. From this circle I had added in red wool thread-work long rays, and beneath it, many green shoots reaching up.

The ash branch Gyric had readied for my pennon pole was long and smooth, the whiteness of the peeled wood almost akin to birch. I pulled the pennon on the tip of it through the narrow sleeve I had sewn, and waved it aloft. Godwin stepped out of the hall and came towards us as I was doing this. He stopped and squinted up at it against the morning Sun.

"You did fine work," he told me, and I could not keep this praise from pleasuring me. "We have not had such a banner before." He took the pole from my hands. "Are you ready?" he asked, looking at us both.

Gyric sat at the pavilion carving a small block of wood. Hrede, who spent her young days caring for Ceric, knelt upon a patch of woolly thyme with the boy, and she looked up hopefully. Gyric turned his head. "Go, Ceridwen," is all he said.

"Will you not go with me?" I asked, coming towards him.

He shook his head. "You have made a fine banner; take it so that you see the folk enjoying it."

I turned to Godwin. "I will stay here. Thank you for taking it for me."

Godwin set the end of the pole down in the gravel. "Will you not come, Gyric? You know it is important to the cottars."

For answer Gyric shook his head.

Godwin looked around. "Mother is mourning; she will not come."

Gyric spoke not.

Godwin went on, "We are the family of Kilton; we must show ourselves at festivals," and a rare note of impatience found its way into his voice.

Now Gyric stood up. "I do not want to 'show myself,' brother. I know they point and stare. I will not serve as part of the day's sport."

I hung my head at this, and Godwin too looked away for a moment.

"I want you to go, Ceridwen," said Gyric after a moment. The edge had left his voice, and he reached his hand out to me. As I took it he said, "Go; I want you to." He squeezed my hand and said softly, "I recall your gladness last year when we went."

I brought my lips close to his ear. "I want to stay with you, my love," I said. "Or for us both to go."

He stiffened. "No." He took a breath and said again, "Go; I know you want to."

"I do want to," I allowed, and searched his motionless face. "If you are certain." He nodded his head.

I kissed his brow. "We will not be long; I will just stay for the lighting of the fire." I looked to Hrede. "Next year Ceric will be old enough to come," I told her. "Take him to Lady Modwynn for his nap. You can watch the fire from the ramparts."

I turned back to Godwin. "I am coming," I said. He furled the pennon, and we walked out towards the stables.

As we swung up into our saddles Dunnere the priest walked by. We greeted him, and his eyes fell upon the pennon held in Godwin's hand. I had never offered to make anything to adorn the chapel, and felt this with some keenness as he looked upon me. And too, it was he who prepared the parchment for all of Kilton, and I was his greatest user. He said nothing, but his snapping black eyes met mine for a moment.

Godwin took the pennon and laid it like a spear across his saddle, and we set out side by side. A thin high haze made the Sun seem even more intense as it climbed in the sky. A few people were upon the road, like us headed for the mowed field in which the fire was laid, and they bowed their heads to us as we rode by. A knot of village girls, their loose hair crowned with wreaths of new-plucked flowers, walked hand in hand, giggling and whispering. A group of young men, both cottars and workmen from the burh, swaggered before them, looking back over their shoulders. Beyond the village we could see the gathering folk, even then circling the base of the waiting wood pile.

The withy-work man, woven from the supple boughs of the willow, and emblem of Summer's flowering, lay upon the ground before the fire-pile. Each year he was crafted anew, a green and ancient symbol of fruitful abundance. Men and women both swarmed around it, twining flower stalks and leafy branches of hawthorn, Summer's tree, through the slits in the withies. Each in turn pushed out of the crowd, stepping forth with some living token of greenery to dress the figure, that each might have their share in the coming asked-for abundance. The withy-work man was twice the length of a mortal man, and the fire on which he would burn was the greatest I had ever seen, for the bed of it was whole trunks of trees, laid over with pallets of charcoal saved from last year's burning, and topped with a small mountain of dry branches.

Withy-man and fire-pile lay in the centre of a mown rye field, its early grain gathered save for a shock still standing before the pile. We left our horses at the edge of the field and walked, Godwin carrying the pennon on its pole. Once off our horses, we became almost part of the crowd, tho' those near us dipped their heads and stepped aside to let us pass. All the folk of the village were there, and nearly everyone from the burh. I smiled at the thegns' wives and daughters who spun or wove in the hall by day, and ate there at night; and smiled too on the kitchen women who were wont to boil my broth and bake my bread. Those who had fine clothes wore them, but even the poorest was adorned, be it only with some token of flowering greenery, or a sprig of the herb verbene.

The noise of the crowd was everywhere, filling the warm air; talking, boasting, shouting, and children either crying or laughing. The Sun pennon waved ahead on a slight wind as we made for the withy-man.

The crowd parted when they saw who held the pennon, and Godwin stepped to the figure's side. The whole of it was now obscured in greenery; no trace of the underlying withies could be seen, even to its outstretched arms. With one hand Godwin parted a cluster of leaves, and then grasping the pennon pole in both hands, drove it deep into the framework. Those around us gave out with a shout of assent. A young man pushed through to Godwin, one of the plough-men I gauged, by the size of him; and with a grin made bold to thrust a leafy hawthorn twig into Godwin's hand. Godwin laughed and took it, pulling it through the studded belt that held his seax scabbard.

The word was given, by whom I could not tell, but the young men upon the pile began to climb or jump down from it, and the crowd moved back. Other men moved about the base of the pile with lit oil torches, their flames feeble in the bright day. Every few paces they thrust a burning torch under the fretwork of charcoal, until the base of the pile was punctured with the ends of torches sticking out towards the circling folk.

The crowd quieted, waiting. A sizzling hiss, like that of charcoal cakes in a brass brazier, but a hundred times over, seeped out from the pile. There was no smoke, nor smell of smoke, but the bright hiss of the flame licking at the readied charcoal told us fire was there.

We stood, near all the folk of Kilton, under the blue sky, with eyes fixed upon the pile. Then, almost at once, it lit, and the hissing of charcoal was joined by the crackling of oil-soaked brush. Plumes of flame, barely seen but felt almost at once, arose from four or five places in the pile.

We looked not at the fire but the sky, for the Sun was nearly overhead. We stood as one, watching and waiting as She crossed the heavens.

Now four men took up long poles, and with them picked up the withy-man under his outstretched arms, and as they strained to lift him into the air, we called out in wonder at the great green man.

They hoisted him aloft, staggering under his weight and struggling to guide him. The Sun pennon I had made stuck out of his body at an angle, as if he held it himself.

The carriers lunged to the edge of the fire, and held the withy-man above the very top of it, and lowered him into place upon it. The Sun beat down, directly over the withy-man, the fire, the folk.

We shouted, all of us.

Now stepped a slender young woman from the crowd, whose flowing yellow hair was as fair as the few tassels of rye that stood in the shock of unmown grain. She moved to a young man, in face and form as comely as she herself, firm-fleshed, open-faced, the glow of youth and strength fast upon him. With both hands she pulled him towards her, then twisted from her flowering wreath a budding white rose, which she slid into his yellow hair amongst many other blooms already tangled there. She turned with him to face the unmown shock of grain, and other maids and youths, flower-bedecked and smiling, took their free hands and circled round the bit of standing rye. They began to dance, moving slowly in a simple grapevine step, one leg crossed over, dipping, crossing, circling round and round the rye shock. Again and again they circled; three times, and then three times three, the crackling of the great fire growing behind them. Then she who led them freed one hand, holding fast with the other to her chosen, and spun to face the fire. The youth thus freed caught up another with his hand, who caught up a girl, who took the hand of a man, who pulled an old woman, who brought a small boy; and the boy took the hand of another, and another, and another.

We moved back, to make room, but others pushed forward, ready; reaching for the free hand of the last dancer. The line grew and grew, snaking round the fire, circling it, more than circling it, doubling back upon itself, dancer facing dancer as they spiralled Sunwards. I saw each thegn and thegn's wife and child as they clasped hands with goatherds and goose girls. The hissing of the charcoal and cracking of the branches grew louder, and dancing yellow flames mirrored those who moved in the shimmering heat. The withy-work stood still untouched, a great green man with outstretched arms, bearing the banner of the Sun, and looking down upon the throngs weaving in circle round the base of the fire.

Godwin and I had moved back, driven off by the heat thrown by the growing fire; and others, unready to join the dance, moved with us too. We stood together, unspeaking, our gaze fastened on the withy-man above us. Now the rising heat was withering some of his leafy dress, and the same heat made my pennon wave in eerie motion. He was Summer, and Summer's abundance. Today, the year's longest day, and the first of Summer, marked also the death of the Sun, for even as the grain grew and ripened the Sun's light diminished from here to Winter's Yule. The green man echoed the Great God, bringer of bounty to his people, who in ancient days danced the spiral dance with the Goddess. The God sacrificed himself to bring abundance to his people, just as in later days Kings willingly offered their lives to feed and defend their folk.

I was jostled from behind as the line of dancers now wove amongst the few pockets of folk still unmoving. Near everyone now danced, sweating faces glowing as they twined round and round and back again in ever-growing spiral. A woman, last in the line, was pulled alongside Godwin, brushing against him and then starting as she saw who she had bumped, her eyes wide above her outstretched hand.

Of a sudden Godwin grabbed my wrist, and pulled me as he lurched after the line. He caught her up, and held tight my hand as we stepped, leg over leg, dipping and twisting as we weaved past doubled-back lines of dancers. A man took my other hand, and another after that, and a woman beyond him; until I could not see anymore.

We swung in and out, turned our faces and then our backs to the flames, grew so close that the heat watered my eyes, swung away again. We passed the unmown shock of rye, now trampled down beneath our feet, returning seed to giving Earth. Some of us were laughing, and some chanting wordless songs, and some panting from breathlessness and heat. Someone stepped on the back of my shoe, so that I almost lost it, and I could feel one stocking rolling down my leg. My linen head wrap was slipping from my hair, my ribband-less braid undone and spilling over my shoulders. The shift beneath my thin wool gown was sticking to my damp body. At one point I stumbled, and Godwin slid his hand up on my arm and caught me. We laughed at each other, never stopping in our dance. We could not stop if we wanted to, for we were pulled along by the stream of bodies before us.

The fire was ablaze, the withy-man's greenery curling and smoking. My Sun pennon, crisp and blanched, burst into flames on the end of its ash pole, glowing like a tiny Sun. The withy-work was crumbling now, and one arm sank down into the licking flames. Those of us watching cried out, so that all lifted their eyes as we danced, waiting for the toppling of the Green Man into the hungry fire.

Then it came. The figure twisted forward, pinned by the fallen arm, and sunk face down into the flames. The God had died; we would live.

We shouted, all of us, and staggered to a stop, some falling spent upon the field. Godwin pulled me to him and we laughed again and took each other's hands. Around us those who had danced long lay sprawled upon their bellies or sat slumped against each other's backs. Not far from us stood the yellow-haired girl who had begun the dance, her wreath gone, her pale gown slipping off one shoulder as she stood locked in embrace with the yellow-haired youth she had chosen.

At the edge of the field tables were set up, bearing stout tuns of ale. Godwin, still holding my hand, led me to them. They swarmed with thirsty revellers, but as we grew closer a man dipping crockery bowls into an open barrel saw us. He passed a bowl to a boy, gesturing with his hand. The boy scampered to us, spilling not a little, and handed the bowl up to Godwin. He took it in both hands and held it to his mouth and drank from it, and then passed it to me, and I drank deep of the sweet ale. Then, in unthinking action, he took it from me and drank again, as does the bride-groom at the bridal feast

Behind us the fire blazed forth; I could feel it on my sweating back; and around us as folk slaked their thirst with ale, young men and women crept off into the unmown fields to slake another deeper thirst.

The Sun had moved from overhead; I was gone far longer than I thought. I straightened my head wrap. "I must go back," I told Godwin, and began to turn to the trees where we had left our horses.

"I will go with you," he said.

"No, stay," I said. "I can easily ride alone. If no one is at the stable I will let my mare into the daming pen."

He looked around the field. Folk remaining would either drink long into the night, recalling earlier days, or slip into the tall fields of grain together. Godwin would do neither.

I felt the colour come into my face, but then the heat of the fire and the dance was still upon me. He said nothing, just led me to our horses.

When we reached the deserted walls of the burh he took my mare for me, and I went straight to the pleasure-garden. Gyric sat alone, near where I had left him. I called out his name as I opened the gate, and he turned his face to me.

I put my still-damp face next to his and kissed his cheek. "Where is Ceric?" I asked.

"In the hall with Modwynn. I sent Hrede off to the fire." He touched my neck, wet with sweat. "Did you dance? You are soaking."

"Yes, with Godwin. It was a grand fire, Gyric, even greater than last year's."

He nodded his head. I sat down next him and gently opened his hand. In it was a small wood bird with folded wings, like onto a dove. Gyric's carving knife sat upon the table, and on the gravel beneath lay a pile of shavings.

"O! Is this what you were working on when I left? It is beautiful," I praised, and meant it.

"Yes," he answered quietly, "it is for Ceric. A bird for our little Chirp."

He did not often use Godwin's name for our son. He fingered the head of the carving. "I tried to make eyes. Are they on straight?" He set the bird upon the table, where it rocked slightly back and forth.

"Yes, perfectly spaced. Ceric will love it." I looked at his fingers, punctured with tiny knife marks.

He nodded his head again and was silent. I picked up his hand and kissed the little blood spots on them. He moved his hand to stroke my cheek, and I took one of his fingers into my mouth and sucked upon it.

He placed his other hand on my breast, the wool of my gown damp, the linen shift beneath soaked through.

He slowly drew his hand from my face and I pressed my mouth to his. He leant towards me, his hand clutching at my breast, and slipped his tongue into my open mouth.

"Come, come into the bower house," I whispered, when I could speak.

We rose and I led him to the open door. The little house was bright and warm; light flooded through the glassed casement and spilled unto the wooden floor. I shut the door. Gyric went to the bed and leant against one of the tall carved dragon posts and unlaced his boots. I took a basin and poured out water, stripped off my damp clothes and soiled stockings, and splashed my heated face and breasts.

Gyric came to me, his hands outstretched, and met with his reaching fingertips my naked skin.

"Your skin is so hot," he murmured as he pulled me to him. He ran his fingers down the hollow of my spine, and I arched my back against him as he lowered his head and found my breast with his lips.

I felt aflame, as if the Summer's fire had entered me. The heat of that blaze was in my bones, and in my blood, and rose within me with all the desire I had ever known.

It kindled Gyric, too, and he unbuckled his seax belt and let the weapon drop to the floor, and pulled off his linen tunic. Now he wore naught but his leggings, and I grasped them at the waist with both hands and pulled them down, freeing him.

I stood again, raised up on tiptoe, straddled his rigid prick with the furry thatch between my legs. He gasped and pulled me tightly to him, his arms low against my back. I leant back again against his strength, and he pressed his face to my throat.

He led me the few steps to the bed. He fell back upon it, and pulled me astride on top of him. I loved to see him thus, his red-gold hair falling upon his white shoulders and touching his lean arms. He turned his head, and the linen wrap about his maiming moved slightly, showing the top of the burn mark upon his right temple. I leant forward and kissed that mark of fire, as I always did. His hands were everywhere, stroking my breasts, smoothing my hair, grasping at my nape, curling in the silky floss beneath my arms; this was how he saw me, through his fingertips, and his hands travelled from my lips to my thighs in endless caress. The heat from my damp body rose and mingled with my woman's odour. I bent over him, brushing my breasts over his chest, and he pressed lightly on my shoulders. I lifted myself, and grasping his prick in my hand guided it within me.

His hands slipped down my body and rested upon my hips, and he held me fast. He spoke no word, tho' his lips were parted; and by the movement of his beautiful mouth I read the pleasure that he felt.

Later, at Sundown, we stood together at the open gate of the burh wall. Ceric was in his father's arms, and the boy held the carved bird in his hand, teething on it. Gyric placed his arm around my back as we stood there, sniffing the mingled

37

smells of burnt charcoal and green wood. Across the expanse of the village of Kilton the still-smouldering fire glowed redly in the late dusk.

Well-come Summer, and well-met, I said within me; and knew joy.

Chapter the Fourth: The Letter, and the Lady

GODWIN was gone most of the Summer, gone to Ælfred in direct service to his King. We had heard that scattered bands of Danes raided at Wessex's edge, or even made bold to sail around the coast and land, taking what they could and fleeing in their swift sharp-prowed ships. Because the bands were small, with many leaders, a treaty made with one was not honoured by another. There was peace in our shire, but a peace made fragile by constant threat of attack.

It was war-work that Godwin went on; for Ælfred had decreed that every ealdorman and reeve and a third of their trained men come join the King's fyrd for three months standing, so that his army for the defence of the land be always strong and fresh. The fyrd travelled all about Wessex, moving with the young King; but save him, each man's service was but a season's length. In this way no man, whether great lord or young thegn, was gone from home so long that he began to fear for the livelihood of kin or crops.

When he turned for home at harvest, Godwin sent a rider ahead, that we at Kilton might know of his return. With joy the hall set to preparing a feast to welcome him and the two score thegns who had shared his journeys. They arrived late the following day and rode through the palisade gates as scudding clouds spattered huge drops of rain.

Gyric and I stood on the oak threshold of the great door to the hall, Modwynn in front of us with Ceric clutching at her skirts. The jingling and stamping of over forty heavy-laden horses mingled with the constant sounding of the brass horns from the watches on the ramparts. Waiting men stepped forth to take the bridles of the weary beasts as the

39

men in the forefront reined up before the hall door. They were filthy, masked in grime, and the raindrops left streaky marks as it hit the dust on their faces. Women and children who glimpsed their men now rushed to their horses in welcome. Godwin swung down from his grey horse, his copper-gold hair falling bright across the shoulders of his blackened iron ring tunic.

Ceric, frightened at the noise, clung to his father's leg. Gyric reached down and pulled the boy into his arms. Godwin crossed to the door, his teeth flashing white in his dirty face as he grinned at us.

Modwynn, never grudging a grimy son, clasped him in her arms. "Welcome, and God bless you, Godwin," she greeted, and we all crowded round him.

The returned men were now pouring into the hall, laughing and jesting, and dropping their saddle bags and war kits along the walls. Cauldrons of hot water were ready waiting for them, and the men began to take themselves off to the washing sheds.

The serving man who bore Godwin's saddle bags passed us, and Godwin said to me, "I have something for you," and bade the man halt. He unlaced the smallest hide pack, pulled out a few cloth items, and then drew forth a rolled piece of hardened leather, such as are used to protect parchment scrolls.

"A letter for you," he said, and placed the roll in my hands. "From the kingdom that was Lindisse." The smile had left his lips, for who could know what news, good or ill, lay within? He went on, "Ælfred took it from a monk on pilgrimage whose path he crossed, knowing I could get it to you faster."

The roll was short, not longer than my hand, and so light to the touch that it might be empty, but the sudden knowledge that its contents would bring me joy or sorrow made it feel a hundredweight.

The hall was loud with men and their families. Modwynn glanced about. "Come into the treasure room. The light is good there and you may read in peace."

We all went, and Modwynn shut the door behind us and lit the cressets. I poked my fingers into the roll and felt the edge of the furled parchment, and eased it out.

I unrolled a small piece of virgin parchment, well-prepared and well-inked, for the letters flowed in smooth and graceful hand upon the creamy surface.

I read aloud; I do not think I could have borne whatever news lay within in silence.

GLORY BE THE NAME OF THE FATHER,

And the Son, and the Holy Ghost, and blest the day that I, the humble Wilgot, Priest of Four Stones bears greeting to the noble Lady Ceridwen of Kilton from the noble Ælfwyn, Lady of Four Stones. Lady, know that your letter through God's great mercy found its way to Lindisse by the priest who scribes these words. And this was in the Passiontide of this year. I rejoice in your life and that of your lord's. I come to Cirenceaster at the Feast of St Matthew to visit the grave of my father. By the leave of your King Ælfred I travel thus. If I and my party may visit Kilton, send message to Cirenceaster for your loving

ÆLFWYN

41

No one spoke, nor could I speak again for a moment. I lowered the letter and pressed my hand over Gyric's. "She lives," was all I could say.

He nodded his head, and Modwynn came to me and touched my shoulder. "How happy I am for you," she said. "And St Matthew's Day! It is scarce a week away. We will send a rider tomorrow to Cirenceaster to bring message to her to come."

I could barely speak. "Thank you, Modwynn. She - she lives and is well." I put my hands to my face, and tried to take it all in. "I will see her - in less than two weeks she will be here!"

Modwynn laughed a merry laugh. "Yes, and at last I will see the shining ideal that is Ælfwyn."

I found my voice and started all in earnest. "She is everything I said of her, and more," and then stayed my careless words. I looked back to Gyric sitting at my side, now clutching Ceric so tightly that the boy was kicking to be loose. Gyric lowered him to the floor, and he scampered off to Modwynn.

Now Godwin spoke. "Cirenceaster." He shook his head. "I recall what a hall her father kept. She will find nothing left but ashes."

All the tales Ælfwyn had told me of the beauties of her parent's hall, of the numbers of their fine sheep and herds of cattle, flooded back to me. "She says she will visit her father's grave," I said, again reading the words. "How will she ever find it?"

Godwin shifted his weight against the wall he leant against. I turned to him as he lowered his ale-cup. "One of

42

the folk of Cirenceaster who lived must have found him on the field of battle, and buried him," he answered.

Godwin had been there when a band of Danes led by Healfdene had attacked Cirenceaster. He was not there to join the fray, but rather in hopes of catching Yrling, the Dane who Ælfwyn had wed by her father's wishes. Ælfsige, her father, had been no true friend to Godwulf or Ælfred, but the loss of the keep and driving off of its livestock had been a blow to the resources of Wessex.

Modwynn's voice was thoughtful. "A young widow, of good birth but family now dead. I wonder if she has come back to Wessex to dedicate herself at a convent?"

A convent. Ælfwyn as a holy woman. The thought made me blink, but how could I know now, after all that had happened, what was in her heart?

Little Ceric was standing before Godwin staring up at him, and seemed at last to recall who he was. He lifted his arms to his uncle and began to cackle, wanting to be taken up in Godwin's arms. Godwin swung him up and Ceric began poking his tiny fingers through the links in his ring tunic. The boy pulled back his hand and looked at the dirt on it, and sang out cheerily.

"I am going to the washing shed," laughed Godwin, and set Ceric on the floor and left.

Modwynn came to where we sat together, and regarded Gyric's downcast face.

"Gyric," she said gently. "We know Ceridwen's friend is from the keep at which you were held captive." Gyric raised his head, leaning back from his mother's words. She went on cautiously, "Thinking on those days must bring you great pain...But this young woman, Ælfwyn, was innocent of any wrong doing. Ceridwen has told us many times she wed the Dane against her own desires."

At this even I gaped. Modwynn knew not what she spoke, but her words were difficult indeed to hear.

Gyric nodded his head sharply, and Modwynn opened her hands in a little gesture of acceptance.

"Well, I will check on the work of the kitchen yard."

When we were alone I took Gyric's hand in both of mine.

"Gyric, forgive your dear mother; she could not know what she was saying. And most of all forgive me. If you do not want Ælfwyn to come, I will send no message."

His first answer was a long sigh. "For two years you have waited to learn if she was alive, and if she ever received your letter to her," he said. "Now that she is so close, I do not see how I can ask you not to see her." He shook his head slightly. "You love her as a sister."

I reached up and touched his face, and the tears were in my eyes. "You loved her, too," I whispered.

He swallowed hard. "Yes. Once I loved her. A lifetime ago, I loved her."

He moved a hand towards his face. "Before...this."

I did not trust myself to speak. For month upon month I had waited for a letter from Ælfwyn, or a message or token borne by some South-riding traveller. Now, beyond all expectations, she was here, in Wessex, and I yearned to see her with my whole being. Most of it had to do with the friendship, sudden and rich, that had sprung up between we two in our short time together. But part of it ran much

44

deeper. If I could see her, speak to her again, then I could be truly sure that all be well in her heart concerning Gyric and me.

"Send the message," said Gyric, and tho' his voice was hoarse he spoke with firmness.

I threw my arms about him in reply.

Three days after the Feast of St Matthew, on a day so fair and warm it might still be Summer, I waited with Modwynn outside the palisade gate, in answer to the summoning brass horns of the rampart-watchers. A rider had come to us the night before when we were at table, saying that the Lady Ælfwyn was on her way. I had scarce slept that night for joy; but Gyric was as solemn as I felt gay. After dawn I looked out of the bower house to see the young thegn Worr standing outside the garden fence. Worr's father was the thegn who had keeping of all of Kilton's horses, and the son had of long been a favourite of Gyric's. Now Worr held the bridle reins of two mounts, including a fast roan horse of Gyric's. They would be gone, Gyric had told me, much of the day, and this slight forestalling of the hour when he should once again be before Ælfwyn quelled the happiness within me.

Now she was almost here. Godwin too stood with us outside the tall gates of his burh, as was meet for a lord to welcome a high-born lady of his country. It could not have been pleasant for him; he was about to welcome into his hall a woman widowed by his hand. With him stood a few of his men. As the horns above us sounded welcome, we watched the progress of a group of waggons as they wound along the dull red clay road that snaked through the village.

45

There were perhaps three waggons; and now I could make out a cluster of horsemen flanking the waggons, as well.

As they grew closer Modwynn said to me, "She has not gone for a nun; rather this is the train of a great lady."

I could do no more than nod; my eyes were straining to pick Ælfwyn out against the blur of brown horseflesh and the like-hued leathern tarpaulins arching over the waggons.

They grew closer, and little clouds of dust rolled from beneath the many horses' hooves; and then I saw her. She sat upright in the front of the first waggon, next the driver himself. The waggon was pulled by a double team of horses, and behind this waggon rolled two more, and around them all rode flanking men, fully armed in war-gear.

She wore a gown of some creamy stuff, and a veil of thin silk fluttered behind her head, showing a glimpse of her wondrous yellow-white hair.

Now she was close enough for me to see her smile, and forgetting all ceremony, I broke and ran to her.

The driver stopped the horses as we cried out each other's names, and she reached out her arms to me, and I lifted my own and took her white hands in mine and kissed them.

"Ælfwyn! Lady and true friend, welcome!"

"Ceridwen, I give thanks to God for this day of my life," she answered, and leant down so we could kiss.

For a moment we just looked at each other, I on the red clay road, clasping her hands, and she seated on the waggon-board. Her eyes, as dazzling as the best blue stones, looked out from a face even fairer than in memory's store. The face was thin, the nose long, fine and delicate, the tint of lips and cheeks the palest blush of rose. All was as I recalled from our days of weaving, jesting, and scheming together at Four Stones. But it was changed too, that face; for it seemed now a woman looked back at me. There was no girlishness left in her.

Then the jingling of one of the horsemen made me look up. One of her body guard moved forward on his horse, a great bay stallion. The rider wore a ring-shirt over a dark tunic, and strapped to his waist was a sword-belt of red-dyed leather from which hung a silver-hilted sword in a carved scabbard. His dark hair fell lankly from a narrow brow, and slate blue eyes glinted from over a curling beard. On his left cheekbone beneath the eye, a straight scar disappeared into the dark beard.

He looked down upon me, and my hand gripped at the wood of the waggon-board so I would not fall to the ground under the force of Sidroc's gaze.

His eyes scorched me; I could not move nor even blink.

When he had had his full he took his eyes from me and looked to where Godwin stood.

"You have before seen me," said Sidroc in his slow speech, heavy with the flat twang of his native tongue.

Godwin had stepped forward, his amaze on his face. The few thegns with him had closed up the space between themselves, and looked up uneasily at the war band before them.

For weapons Godwin wore naught but his seax. He placed his hand on its hilt and nodded once.

"Yes." His voice was low and grave. "On the field of battle at Cirenceaster."

47

One of the thegns backing Godwin was Wulfstan, lamed for life by Sidroc's spear thrust on that field. Wulfstan stepped forward, his knuckles white as they gripped the hilt of his sheathed seax. Godwin raised his own hand to stay him.

Sidroc looked above Godwin's head to the palisade walls and the roof of the great hall which could be seen above them.

"You are Kilton?" he asked.

"I am Godwin, Ealdorman of Kilton," he answered, with another nod.

"I am Sidroc of Four Stones, Jarl of South Lindisse. I travel with leave of your King." Here Sidroc pulled at a leathern pouch in a hide saddle bag. He slipped the pouch back and went on. "My wife is of the tribe of Cirenceaster. We came to make Offering there, and also look to buy fleece before we return home."

My Wife. The words thunked dully inside my numb brains. I turned to Ælfwyn, and she slipped her thin hand into mind and gripped it. Her face too was blank, but she nodded her head, Yes.

Sidroc turned his horse slightly. "We come in peace," he said, and then repeated, carefully, "I come in peace." Now he gestured to his sword hilt. Leading from the wooden scabbard was a stout leathern thong, which was cross-wrapped around the guard of the hilt so that it could not be drawn without stopping to untie it.

Godwin's eyes looked too at these Peace Bands. He took a step forward and said, "You and your wife and your men are welcome. I bid you enter my hall in peace."

"I thank you, Kilton," answered Sidroc, just as carefully.

He turned to his men and spoke to them briefly in their own tongue. I recognised two of the ten. One was the red-haired Jari, who had but three fingers on his sword hand, an old favourite at Yrling's table; and the other the young, fair-haired Asberg.

Modwynn came to me now where I stood at Ælfwyn's waggon, her eyes creased in warm welcome. She put her hand out to Ælfwyn, who took and kissed it, and said, "You are most welcome here, Lady Ælfwyn." She put her arm about me and went on, "My daughter Ceridwen has spoken much of your beauty and your goodness."

Ælfwyn looked upon Modwynn's face, lined by years but graced with nobility. She saw the love my husband's mother bore for me, even unto Modwynn's naming me Daughter, and she squeezed her blue eyes shut for a moment. If Fate had dealt differently with her this love and praise would be hers.

For answer her words, softly spoken, were, "You are all that I always imagined."

Modwynn laughed, uncomprehending; and then the waggon started forward through the gates, with us walking at Ælfwyn's side.

We came into the yard of the burh, and folk looked up at us and at the new warriors. Ælfwyn's eye fell on all, stables and work-sheds, armourer's forge and smith's fire, and came to rest on the walls of upright timber, taller than three men, that was the hall of Kilton.

"I knew it would be like this," she murmured.

The waggons halted, and Godwin came in courtesy to us and lifted his hand to Ælfwyn to help her from the waggon-board. He looked at her with his grave face and said, "My

49

lady," as way of greeting, but her face latched onto his and her hand froze in the air between them.

He gestured once again with his hand to take her arm, and she found her wits and let him help her down.

Now the men were off their horses, and Sidroc came to stand next to Godwin. He was taller than Godwin by a hand-span, but Godwin a bit broader in the shoulders. From the tail of my eye I saw glittering upon his right wrist the silver disk bracelet he had once given to me. I could not look at him, he was so close; and I was grateful to hear Modwynn's smooth and gracious speech. "You all will be weary from the ride. After we lift our cups in the hall, you, Lady Ælfwyn should go with Ceridwen to her bower house and rest."

Ælfwyn had thrust her hand back into mine. "My daughter is sleeping in the waggon with Burginde," she told me, and for the first time a true smile lit her face.

"Your daughter? And Burginde here?" I stepped to the waggon. "Burginde! Are you truly here?"

The tarpaulin flap in the front of the waggon opened, and there in answer was the broad plain face of Burginde, the hair more grey, but the black eyes still snapping like that of a hungry crow.

"Ach!" she scolded, but her face wore a merry grin. "You be like to rouse the poor babe, and she wakeful all night with the teething and all."

Then we were both laughing at each other, and she said, "Ach, Lady, how big and fair you've grown." This said, she burst into tears. "I be fine, fine," she sniffed, mopping her face with her apron. "But O!, your letter set my heart to rights about you," she ended, blinking away tears.

Modwynn sent serving men to work, and the waggon was driven closer to the pleasure garden gate so Burginde and her charge could more easily go to the bower house.

The rest of us walked across the broad oak threshold of the hall door. Godwin went first, and Sidroc with him, and then Modwynn leading Ælfwyn and I by the hand. The party stopped just inside, but I do not know if it was Godwin or Sidroc who halted. We looked down the length of the hall, its white-washed walls painted over with skilfully drawn birds and beasts, lit in bright day by the iron casement with the precious glass panes and by night by the massive fire-pit in the hall's centre. The floor was of stone, of pieces so closely cut and joined that no man could slip a knife-blade through the cracks; and the roof rafters, once forest kings, were carved and scrolled in spiralling designs so clever that one grew dizzy trying to find beginning or end. Sleeping alcoves pocketed both long walls, and tables and benches for four score thegns and their wives and children rested ready for the evening meal. At the far reach of the hall lie the stone step upon which each night the high table was set up, and beyond that the bound and iron-strapped door of the treasure room of Kilton.

It was a great hall, the finest, I thought, in all Wessex; and no man or woman seeing it could be unmoved. Sidroc and his men stood and stared at this show of power and wealth. Sidroc's eyes turned to Godwin, and a slow smile spread over his face.

In answer Godwin lifted his hand in gesturing welcome, but his eyes were like hardened steel. The hard-won treasure of his father, and his father's father, was now Godwin's, here made manifest in this rich hall, and the men who filled it. All of this, and the confidence spawned from this, was in Godwin's gesture, and in those hard eyes.

51

We moved deeper into the hall. Serving men bearing bronze trays massed with silver cups met us, and Modwynn took the silver ewer and herself poured out her bright ale. She took up the golden cup of Godwin's that for many years had been Godwulf's, and lifted it to her son; and then took up a cup of silver chased with gold and studded with coloured gems and handed it to Sidroc.

Modwynn flinched before no man, spoke freely to them all, and now spoke thus to this strange Dane who stood before her: "As Lady of Kilton, I, Modwynn, widow of the great Godwulf, welcome you to our hall."

Sidroc looked at this woman before him, a face of dignity and wisdom in which a vestige of great beauty still lingered. He took the cup from her hands and inclined his head to her.

Chapter the Fifth: Tell Me Everything

MODWYNN pressed a cup into Ælfwyn's hands, and we all took up cups and drank. Tables were now being set up, and cakes and loaves brought. Modwynn saw my eagerness and my hand caught fast in Ælfwyn's, and smiled at us both. "Go you now to the bower house," she said quietly. She looked over to where Godwin and Sidroc stood, eyeing each other warily. "These men are occupied enough."

So I led Ælfwyn out through the side door, back into the bright Sun and into the pleasure garden. As we stepped out her eyes rose at once to the shimmering blue water, white-tipped with the freshening wind. Her eyes travelled back from the edge of the brown rock cliffs, across the muted greens of the pleasure garden, still abloom with clustering white and gold daisies.

I read the wonder in her face and said, "When I first saw Kilton, I felt it was like unto the halls of the Gods."

She nodded her head. "Yes, just so; almost more grand than mind can allow." Her brows rose in her familiar gesture of question. "But Lord Godwulf - he is no more?"

"He died, just a year ago, in this very garden. It was so sudden, all at once he was dead. A burst heart, Modwynn thinks."

"That is a quick death indeed." She sighed. "How sad for you all. He must have been a truly great lord." She lifted my hand in hers. "And Modwynn...so beautiful a lady, so stately and so kind!"

"I know how blest I am," I said, and lowered my eyes.

When I looked up she herself looked away, and asked softly, "Where...is Gyric?"

"O," I answered with some heartiness, "he is with Worr, a young thegn of the hall. They are out riding."

Her brow furroughed. "He rides?"

"O, yes, and with Godwin swims and sails a little boat right off our rocks below."

She seemed almost not to believe these things, and said simply, "O." Then she said with sudden strength, "Godwin...he...I had never seen him. He looks so much like...Gyric."

"Yes," was all I could say.

I tugged at her hand and we began to move into the garden. From behind a tall stand of yellowing tansy stalks I could see Burginde, hands on hips, gazing down at something on the ground. Clinging to Burginde's brown gown was a girl a bit younger than Hrede, of perhaps nine or ten Summers. This girl was richly dressed, in a wool gown of soft blue colour bordered with darker blue step-weaving at the sleeves and hem. Yellow-white hair streamed down from the young one's fine veil.

We grew closer to Burginde and saw she watched Ceric who sat on a clump of thyme with a golden-haired girl of the same age. The two babes had grasped each other's hands and were now trying to stuff tufts of thyme sprigs into their mouths, but both were pulling at the same time. Hrede crouched near them laughing and urging them on.

"Your daughter? O, she is beautiful," I praised.

"Thank you." She looked down at the little golden head. "She is Yrling's daughter." The children now fell over on the

54

soft thyme, hugging each other and giggling. "Your boy, what a sweet child," she said, and turned smiling to me. "To think we truly did have babes at the same time, as I always wished."

I moved to Burginde, glad to at last be able to hug her.

"And what a great lady you have grown to," she said again, as I was caught fast in her strong embrace. "To see you here, in flush fettle! And more of a beauty as you ever were!"

"You do not know how I have missed you," I told her truly, but she only laughed.

I looked at the young girl, still clinging to her gown. She was a dainty creature, but her face was oddly still. As I looked at her, her thumb rose to her mouth.

I could see all was not well with the child, but I asked Ælfwyn, "And who is this pretty maid?"

She answered softly, "My sister, Eanflad." She said no more.

Kitchen women were now bringing trays of cakes and an ewer of ale. "Would you like to sit here in the garden, or come into the bower house?" I asked Ælfwyn.

"It is lovely here, but in truth I have been outside so much these past few weeks. And I long to sit in a real chair!" she smiled, sounding very much like her old self.

"Then come in, and we will talk while Burginde and Hrede stay here with the babes." I turned to the kitchen women, and gestured them to carry the ale within.

"No ale, please," spoke Ælfwyn of a sudden. "It makes me queasy."

I looked at her open-mouthed. "Are you -?"

"Yes," she smiled, and the faint colour deepened in her cheek. "Sidroc and I will have a babe in the Spring."

"Bring broth to us," I ordered the kitchen women, "and bread -" here I looked over to Ælfwyn, who nodded. The women left and I said, "I could always eat a bit of bread, and keep it down, when I was carrying."

I left the door to the bower house open, and we sat at the table on cushioned chairs as Ælfwyn looked about the place. Her eyes finally rested on me, and on the gown I wore.

"That is the green silk gown I gave you," she said.

"Yes, my very finest. I wear it on all high and happy days. But none so happy as this."

Our eyes locked. "Tell me -" we both began, at the same instant.

When we had stopped laughing I spoke. "You are my guest," I said playfully. "You must speak first. Tell me everything."

"Everything," she repeated, and her smile faded. "Everything will be hard to hear."

"Nonetheless, I must hear it," I told her. "And you too shall hear everything, so that once again nothing is secret each from each."

She took a breath and started. "Then I begin when you left Four Stones. I thought I should go mad with worry for you, and mad with grief for Gyric's wound. Yrling did not come back from hunting for three days, but Sidroc returned to Four Stones the day after you rode away. Not until late on that day was it discovered that Gyric was gone from his cell. Eomer and Dobbe and the rest of the kitchen folk were questioned, but all played their part well. Sidroc did not seem to care much about Gyric's escape. He did not think Gyric would...live long anyway, and so wherever he was he felt he would not get far."

A serving woman returned, and I was glad to put a cup of warm broth into Ælfwyn's hand. She took a sip and went on. "Sidroc did not yet know that you were gone, and I was able to hide the fact until the following day."

She lifted her eyes to me, and the shadow of the awful fear of those days still dwelt there. "I did everything you said, gave him back the bracelet, begged him not to follow. He would listen to nothing. He rode off that night and I half-prayed that he would find you, tho' it meant Gyric's death for sure! I could not bear the thought of another Dane catching you upon the road." She shook her head. "You might even fall prey to wolves, or ravening bears: I feared everything and could know nothing.

"Yrling came home from hunting and was angry at it all, but it soon passed. Finally Sidroc came back. He would not even look at me. I had to beg him, beg him almost on my knees, to tell me if he had found you. At last he said no.

"Then everything happened so fast: A messenger came, bearing what news I did not know. Yrling armed his men, nearly all of them, and he and Sidroc and Toki and the lot of them rode off. This was the first time Yrling had ever done this, taken both nephews with him, so I knew whatever they rode to was bad.

"Burginde and I were alone, or almost so, at Four Stones. How miserable I was! I cursed myself a thousand times for letting you go!"

Tears were in her eyes. I looked at her and said, "And so you did forbid me to go. But I went anyway. Nothing you could have done would have stopped me. You had no blame at all in what you did, and saved our lives I think, many times over. First you lied and schemed at great danger to yourself to protect Gyric and me, and then when I unpacked the saddlebags, I found the spear point, the silver-hilted seax, and all the silver coins and jewellery. How I praised your name for so providing for us!"

She swallowed back some of her tears. "Ah, Ceridwen, how grateful I am you lived! I could not bear the black mark on my soul if you had not."

She calmed herself and went on. "Yrling was gone for weeks and weeks. No rider came with a message - nothing. Then I realised I was with child. I knew Yrling would be glad, yet I felt no happiness; nothing could give me pleasure.

"One day I heard the wardmen whistling out warning from the palisade. I went down into the hall, and stood on the steps to see what was happening. The gates were opened, and in rode Toki and a few men, their horses so lathered as to be half-dead. Toki looked wild; I thought he was drunk again or truly mad. He ordered the gates shut but I could not make out what else. Then he turned to me. I was frighted at him, at how he looked and acted. I went into the hall and made to return to my chamber. He grabbed my wrist! 'Yrling is dead,' he told me, 'and Four Stones and all in it, mine.' I pulled away from him, I did not believe it. I asked him where Yrling and Sidroc were. He laughed and said 'All dead! All dead before the wall of Cirenceaster, dead like Ælfsige!'

"I nearly swooned. My father dead, and Yrling and Sidroc too? And pitched battle at Cirenceaster? Some how I got up to my room, I think Burginde almost carried me. We locked the door. I could hear Toki below, laughing and boasting with the few men there. He broke down the door of the treasure room; we could hear it. They drank a long time, and every moment we feared they would climb the stairs and force our door. We had no weapons with us, only weaving knives and shears, but even if I cut my throat with that it would be a better end than submitting to Toki."

She shuddered and clutched at her thin shoulders. "O Ceridwen, can you think what I suffered those few hours? If my father was dead, and Yrling too, I had lost everything. I was far beyond aid of any kin. I had no standing, none! Toki could use me as he liked; kill me; cast me out into the village - anything he chose!"

I put my hand over hers and squeezed my eyes shut at these horrors. I recalled too clearly Toki's face, his yellow hair and sneering mouth, and thought of the day he had caught my own wrist on the village road outside Four Stones and tried to fright me. I thought too of the drunken night he had grabbed me upon the stairs to our chamber, and how Sidroc had beaten him until we begged him to stop.

"Finally Burginde and I slept that night, huddled in each other's arms. It was not yet dawn when we heard more whistling from the gate. Men were shouting everywhere, I thought we were being attacked. From the shutters I could see into the yard. Men carrying torches were running about. Toki was yelling, and men on the other side of the wall were yelling, but it was all in their speech so I knew not what. Then the men who controlled the gate started to open it. Toki began screaming at them. Still they went on. He grabbed spears and killed one of them, but another took his place, and the gate opened. Sidroc rode in, with a good number of men, two score or so.

"Sidroc got off his horse and faced Toki. They were shouting, both of them. Then they fought."

Ælfwyn took a breath, and another sip of broth. "It was awe-ful. They did not use shields; both each took a sword in one hand and a knife in the other." She looked into my face. "It did not last long. Sidroc killed Toki."

"When I finally went downstairs I asked Sidroc if it was true about my father and Yrling. He said yes, that Yrling had heard that the Dane Healfdene was about to attack Cirenceaster. Yrling felt no one but he should have its treasure, since he had already gotten so much of it in my dowry. So he rode to fight Healfdene."

I now asked a question whose answer I feared. "Do you know how Yrling died?"

She blinked her eyes. "He was killed in vengeance for Gyric," she said, and tears flooded her eyes. "But my father, defending his own land...they say he was hacked to pieces!"

She was sobbing now, and I took her in my arms until she was ready to speak again. I forced more broth upon her, she had drunk hardly any.

"The rest is even harder to say, Ceridwen. I felt so lost. I went almost...mad." She hung her head and went on in a whisper. "Now that Yrling was dead I could not bear the thought of his child within me. I sent Burginde to the village to Wilfrede the dyer. She came back with some black rye, telling me if I ate it I would lose the babe. I ate it...It was dreadful, horrible; like riding the worst night-mare, only it did not stop! For a day and a night I was out of my head; raving and retching, but I did not lose the babe! I recall Sidroc, almost breaking down the door to our chamber; he was yelling at me and Burginde was crying...Finally the next day I was well enough to go downstairs.

"I sent a slave to find Sidroc. He came into the hall and just looked at me. He walked into the treasure room and I followed him. I stood there and told him that I wanted to go for a nun, and asked him to send me to the foundation at

Oundle. I was trembling and still sick and weak. I did not care if I lived or died."

She clasped my hand and leant towards me, our heads almost touching. "Do you know what he said, Ceridwen? First he told me that the convent at Oundle was no more, that there was war everywhere and no safe place for me to go. Then he looked at me and said, 'Stay with me, Lady, and again be the Lady of Four Stones. Yrling's child shall be as my own. I will be good to you.'"

Tears were in both our eyes now. I nodded to her to go on.

"That night...I came to the treasure room, and...vowed to him. A few weeks later we found a holy man, who blessed our marriage. Then last Spring Yrling's child was born – a beautiful girl, unharmed by that poison! I named her Ashild, the name of Yrling's mother."

"And now she will have a little sister or brother," I said, blinking back my tears.

"Yes, yes," she agreed. "How good he is to me, Ceridwen! He heard that my mother and sisters were still alive...it was not long after I had pledged to him. He left with much gold to find the Dane who had captured them. He found them and bought them and brought them back to Four Stones.

"Much had happened, tho'." Her voice rose as she recounted it. "All three of them had been ravished, many times...the first time when our hall still lay burning before them. Mother begged them to spare Eanflad, a little girl who had not yet bled! Mother has not told me all of it, even now. Eanflad has not spoken since. It is like she does not hear, either. The only one who she listens to is Burginde. At first she was even worse, and would only rock back and forth alone all day. Nothing my mother or sister or me could do helped. After some time we noticed that Eanflad watched Burginde, and Burginde always spoke merrily to her. She began to follow Burginde about, and now even helps her with her chores. Everywhere Burginde goes, Eanflad must come."

"I am glad that you brought her," I said, and shook my head. "And I sorrow for your dear mother and sisters. I do not forget that their Fate so easily could have been my own."

"Or mine," added Ælfwyn. "But mother is strong. She says that she will go for a nun once a convent is again opened in Lindisse. Until then she runs the hall with me."

"And your other sister? How old is she, and how does she fair?"

"Æthelthryth has sixteen Summers." She twisted a ring on her finger. "I do not know what path she will chose, after what has befallen her. She is doing well enough; there is much work to occupy us at Four Stones, and any of the Danes would wed her."

I nodded my head, realising that since their sister was twice wed to a Dane she could have no objection to her so marrying.

"Sidroc has rebuilt the hall, the old hall," she went on. "Of course it is nothing as fine so Kilton, but..."

"I am sure it is fine indeed, if it fits the ruins left at Four Stones," I answered. "How gladsome for you! You always hoped it would be rebuilt."

She laughed a bit. "He had no choice. When the ships came with the men's wives and sweethearts, he had no room to put them."

"They finally came! Tell me, how are the women of the Danes? What are they like?"

Now she really laughed. "Well, like us, in some ways. They wear their hair wrapped differently and their brooches come always in pairs, and some of their jewels are the oddest things - bits of broken booty all cobbled together. Anything bright they like. But they are hard workers, never fight amongst themselves," she added in fairness. "And I am learning a bit of their speech, and they mine."

"And the kitchen woman Dobbe, and Eomer, and young Mul? How do they fare?"

"All well. Dobbe is so old now, and trembles so, she directs the workings of the kitchen from her stool. But she has trained up well some of the village folk, and our food is better for it. Eomer is still hearty, and brewing good ale. And Mul is so good with the horses that he is now in charge of one of the stables."

"Remember me to them, all three," I asked her, and she smiled and nodded. "And your sheep?" I teased, knowing how important the building of her flocks was.

"The sheep do well, growing season by season. Four Stones will never be as good sheep country as Cirenceaster, but it will not be from lack of effort." She tilted her chin towards the door. "What flocks we saw, driving through your lands here!"

"It is a fat land," I agreed. "Godwulf kept it wisely, as does Godwin after him."

"How well-ordered everything is here, and bountiful. I do not think even King Ælfred lives as you do!"

"Perchance not; he could of course, save for that he must always move from estate to estate to see his people and

63

keep his fyrd in trim. I know how kindly Fate has looked on me," I said, fully aware how little I had done to deserve such abundance. "Godwulf - Godwulf made me a rich woman."

Ælfwyn lifted her eyebrows, and I went on, "In his will he left me five thousand coins of silver."

"Five thousand!"

"Yes, five thousand; they are in the treasure room now, buried in a secret space beneath the floor stones with much else. How generous a lord he was! In his will he ordered that thirty slaves be freed as his death-boon, and they all be given land and tools to make their living. To Modwynn he left life-interest in the lands of Kilton, and added to her own wealth by giving back the three hundred head of sheep she had brought him when they wed. And of course she has caskets of jewels. Gyric was given twenty thousand pieces of silver, and the contents of many chests, some of which have not been opened for a long time. Godwin, of course, he named as ealdorman and lord of Kilton, and to Godwin too went the chiefest portion of the burh's treasure. Ælfred approved this at once."

Ælfwyn had listened open-mouthed to this report, and now asked, "Godwin - is he not still wed? Gyric told me of his wife."

"He is still wed; her name is Edgyth. She too was named in the will, she received her dowry back from Godwulf's store. Edgyth and Godwin have lived apart for some time. She is at the foundation at Glastunburh and may yet forsake her marriage, or become a nun."

"Forsake her marriage?" she asked wonderingly. "To a man like Godwin?"

"It would not be her true choice if she does; she cannot bear a live child; that is her grief."

For a long moment her gaze met mine. "He looks so much like..."

"Yes. The first time I saw him, I was struck by the likeness."

We heard a little noise outside our open door and looked over to see Ashild toddle over the threshold, grasping a lidded wicker basket against her chest. A step behind her and reaching for the basket was Ceric. Hrede followed him, giggling, and Burginde with the clinging Eanflad came after.

"O!" laughed Ælfwyn. "Here is a gift for you, from Burginde."

"A gift?" I asked, looking up at her twinkling eyes. The babe was struggling to hold the basket, and I reached out my arms to her. Instead she sat down with it.

The basket jolted, and Ashild pushed it from her in surprise. It fell over, the lid rolled off, and out leapt a kitten, with strange brown markings like tortoiseshell.

"The Browny!" I called out in delight.

Burginde and Ælfwyn were laughing. Burginde put her hands on her hips and declared, "'Tis not she herself, but one of her hundred daughters. They swarm round the hall like the mice they replaced."

"All true," Ælfwyn laughed. "The Browny was your choice amongst mousers, and a good one. Burginde thought you ought to have one of her kittens."

Ceric had never been able to get close to the half-wild cats in the stable. Now he dove at the little one, who rewarded him with a solid scratch. The boy howled and dropped the kitten as Ashild looked on with wide eyes.

Burginde picked up Ceric. "Now, now little master, you must be light handed with the tiny beast," she soothed, and held up his hand and patted it against her cheek. Ashild had since scooped the mewing kitten up. Burginde bounced Ceric in her arms and directed, "See now, how the wee mistress holds it, gentle-like."

Through it all, laughter, surprise, and delight, Eanflad's thin face was still. She never let go of Burginde's skirt, and shadowed her every movement. Ælfwyn caught me looking at her.

"Look, Eanflad, the kitten," she coaxed, but the girl looked straight ahead, past the confines of the room.

Burginde swung Ceric down to his feet. "Well, we will leave you two in peace again. Come to me, Ashild, with that squawker; and Hrede, you bring the little lord."

"Burginde, other than seeing you, you could not have brought me a better gift," I told her.

Chapter the Sixth: Fate Looked Away

ÆLFWYN had told her tale, and now I must tell mine. I began at the end of it by asking, "You have a priest now at Four Stones, the one who wrote the letter to me."

"Yes, Wilgot. He is a learned man, and a comfort to my mother. I have asked him many times to give me writing lessons - I still have the wax tablet you had made for me! But he does not seem very eager to teach me. I think he likes being the only one at the keep who can read and write."

I considered this. "Sometimes it is the only power a scribe has; and being amongst the Danes cannot be easy for him. But still, he is in your train; you must order him to teach you." With a wicked thought I added, "Say it is for the Glory of God, that you be able to teach your children the Holy Book. Then he cannot refuse you."

Her eyebrows went up, and she laughed along with me.

"But you did not receive my letter until this last Passiontide?"

"That is right, it was just before Easter."

"It took that long for Ælfred to find a monk or priest brave enough to travel to Lindisse," I thought aloud.

"Until your letter, all I knew was what Sidroc told me following the battle at Cirenceaster, that the warrior who killed Yrling had yelled out Gyric's name. The warrior was an avenger, that seemed clear. From that I hoped that you and Gyric were alive, and at Kilton."

She did not add that this avenger took the life of her own husband, a man who she had learnt to respect, and even begun to care for.

"Do you...know who the avenger was?"

She shook her head, then looked at me. "Godwin. Was it Godwin?"

"I am sorry; yes. I told him before he left that Yrling was innocent of Gyric's maiming; his crime was no greater than accepting him into his cellar afterwards."

"Gyric would have died in those cellars. Except for your courage."

I shook this away. "Godwin pulled the hammer of Thor amulet from around Yrling's neck, and brought it to his brother with the other proofs of vengeance. I asked Gyric for it, and that is how I was able to send it in my letter."

"For that I truly thank you. I have it saved; I will give it to Ashild when she is older." Her voice dropped and she asked, "Did Godwin catch the man who...hurt Gyric?"

"Yes. He was the Dane Hingvar. Hingvar's brother attacked an ealdorman of Wessex who Hingvar himself had a treaty with. Ælfred and Gyric and a great number of thegns fought against the marauding brother. The fighting got too hot around Ælfred and Gyric let himself be taken captive to shield Ælfred. He knew he would be held to high ransom but it was worth it to preserve Ælfred's life.

"The Dane who had captured Gyric was Hingvar's brother, he who had broken the treaty. Hingvar was angry that his brother had fought this battle in the first place, so to prevent him from collecting the ransom he maimed or killed all the Saxons his brother had taken captive."

"Gyric was blinded out of spite?" Her voice rose in disbelief.

"Yes."

She pressed her hands to her own eyes. "But Godwin caught Hingvar."

"Yes. Godwin caught him, and tortured him to death, as he had vowed."

There was nothing more to say on this.

"The morning after we left Four Stones we found the witch-woman Gwenyth, or rather she found us. She and her son sheltered us for days in their forest camp. I do not think I could have kept Gyric alive without her help." I thought of what the sanctuary of her hidden camp truly meant. "Nor for that matter, might I be alive if I had not found her. When Gyric was strong enough to ride we began our journey. We went for weeks and weeks, always South and West, and always amongst the woods and forests, for we dare not travel upon the roads."

"How arduous it must have been for you," Ælfwyn said.

"It was, slow and very difficult. The one time we tried riding upon a road we were attacked by two brigands. Gyric had me almost run them down, and he slashed one of them with the seax. O, Ælfwyn, I wept when I found that seax in our saddlebags, fearful that you stole it from Yrling's war-chest, and that you would be punished for it! Then I reasoned that perhaps Dobbe had put it there, as she had packed the food bag for me. It is magnificent, Lord Godwulf himself did not own one so fine."

Ælfwyn shook her head. "I knew nothing of this, she never told me of it. How good of her. It was Burginde who

69

stole the spear point from the armourer's shed, but she was never caught."

"That too, was a very great service; the witch-woman's son carved a shaft for it. Gyric used it both as a walking staff and weapon."

"How did you live upon the way? How did you eat? The food Dobbe packed could not have lasted more than a few days."

"Sometimes we went hungry, not often. Fate was with us. We found a few safe places to buy food, and I gathered things I found as we travelled - berries, and greens to add to the night's grain pot."

She said the next more slowly, and while looking down at the tabletop. "Your letter said that you and Gyric found love 'upon the road', I think you wrote..."

"Yes," I said, and touched her hand. "I did not know it, until he kissed me. With that kiss, I knew love, and gave myself to him."

"In...the woods?"

"On the shore of a beautiful lake."

She nodded, but kept her face down. How differently Fate had dealt with us, I thought.

I went on in a light voice, "Then just after we found a monk, Cadmar, who once had been a thegn in Gyric's uncle's hall. Cadmar lives as a solitary now, and by happy chance we made our vows before him." I could not keep the smile from my face, recalling that time. "That night Gyric and I hand-fasted."

Ælfwyn surprised me by saying, "Then you were thrice his, in Nature, in the Church, and by ancient law."

"Yes," I agreed, "I am thrice his. I love him with every part of my body, every part of my soul and mind."

Her eyes were filled with sudden tears. "I fear for tonight...I do not think I can..."

"Look on him?" I asked, as gently as I could.

She nodded her head, swallowing back tears. "I am fearful, fearful of what I might say. O, Ceridwen, how I pity him! Yet you - you do not care...You are a saint!"

"I am no saint. I am a woman in love with a man."

The firmness in my voice made her tears stop, and she smiled at me as she bit her lip.

"Do not wait until tonight to see Gyric," I suggested. "I will send Hrede to you just before we start for the hall. You can come here and speak to him. Will that not be easier?"

"Yes, you are right, it will be. I do not wish Sidroc to sense any strain. Sidroc knows nothing about...Gyric and me. Nor does anyone living, I think, save we three, and Burginde."

"Nor shall anyone ever know, Ælfwyn. It is your story to tell, no one else's."

"How good you are!" she said, but I shrugged in reply. Her eyes travelled to the door. "I have left Sidroc alone a long time, I should go back to the hall and find him."

"Godwin would not neglect his role as host. He is likely taking Sidroc and his men all around the burh."

71

"There is so much to see," said Ælfwyn. "And you recall how Sidroc is - always eager to learn new things, or see new sights."

"He seems so...grave," I offered.

"He is one of eleven Danes in the mighty stronghold of a Saxon lord," reminded Ælfwyn. Then she went on, softly, "But yes, I know he has changed. And so have we all," she ended, rising from her chair.

The afternoon was far gone, but still Gyric and Worr had not returned. Ælfwyn had taken Ashild back to their wagon for a nap, and taken Ceric, too, as the boy howled when they were parted. I was alone in the bower house, re-combing my hair and smoothing my head wrap after laying the fillet of gold upon my brow. I went about this for some little time, trying to drive off my fear of some mishap befalling Gyric.

When I finally heard them I went to the door and looked across the dusky garden. Worr opened the gate and Gyric, spear in hand, stepped through it. He came slowly, and my eyes travelled to Worr's anxious face. He looked over his shoulder at the setting Sun, and with a nod to me, hurried off to prepare for the hall.

"Gyric," I said, so happy to see him unhurt that I forgot my worrisome wait, "you have been gone for hours! Godwin wants you. Is all well? There was no mishap with the horses?"

"All is well," he answered, but his voice was flat.

I sighed, and then regretted it; he tilted his head to me. "Let me help you dress," I said, and tried to make cheerful my voice.

He did not have time to answer, for now Godwin strode across the pathway from the side door of the hall. He was dressed in his finest linen, over which was a leathern tunic cunningly tooled in spiralling designs, and his wrists were heavy with gold. He was dressed thus to welcome a Dane, in enough magnificence to sit at meat with Ælfred, King.

"Godwin is coming," I muttered to Gyric, and he walked inside the bower house. He set down his spear, and stood by the table, waiting.

Godwin walked through the door, his impatience written on his face.

"Have you been to Hell and back?" he demanded of Gyric. "Hurry and ready yourself for the hall. Ceridwen's friend is here, with a new husband. He is the Dane Sidroc, Yrling's nephew. He calls himself Jarl of Lindisse."

Gyric's shoulders contracted as if he had been struck. Godwin went on, "He has a safe-passage from Ælfred; he showed me. A parchment he cannot even read himself!" Gyric answered not, and Godwin went on, "Hurry and ready yourself."

"I am not coming," said Gyric softly.

"What?" asked Godwin.

Gyric turned to face his brother's voice. "I said I am not coming."

Godwin's voice was as cold as steel. "You are coming."

Gyric's answer was quiet, but each word fell like a blow. "I was thrown, like a blind dog, into the cellars of his keep to die. I will not let him gloat over me now."

"That is why you must come!" answered Godwin, in some heat. His eyes darted around the little room. "What will you do, skulk around the bower house the whole time he is here?"

Gyric lifted one hand towards his brother. "Hear me on this, Godwin. That Dane, Sidroc - he loved Ceridwen. I am not going to show myself to him now."

Godwin shook his head in unbelief. "Your wife has nothing to do with this. This is between you and me." He stared at Gyric for a moment, then shook his head again. "Now hurry and get dressed. I need you in the hall," he said, and began to turn to go.

Gyric turned to the table, reached out his hand and found a chair back, sat down. "I am not coming," he said again, and turned his face away from both of us.

Godwin stopped, and stared with burning eyes at his sitting brother. Of a sudden he lunged to the table, and reached across Gyric's chest and grabbed him by the collar of his tunic. The chair fell backward as he whirled Gyric to his feet. He held his brother but a few inches from his face, and spoke through clenched teeth.

"I killed four men and lost six of my own to avenge you." Godwin jerked his head to the hall. "I killed his closest kinsman! I did not do it for a coward! You will come to the hall, and sit at my left side as my brother, and heir."

Now he released his grip, and Gyric rocked back on his heels.

Godwin took a breath and said, "You will back me up on this. I have done enough for you." He looked down at the floorboards, and then back at his silent brother. "You are my pledged man, Damn you!"

At last Gyric spoke, his voice scarce above a whisper. "Do you then order me to come?"

"Yes! I order you!"

"Then I will come. My lord."

These last two words were like a spear thrust into Godwin's side; his face showed it. But he said no more, and strode from the house.

I could not keep my feet and sunk down on the feather cushions of the bed. Gyric stood still, face lowered, in the centre of the room. He shuffled to the small table which always held the basin. He reached for the crockery jar of water there, but overshot, sending the jar tumbling to the floor. It broke at his feet and splashed his wool leggings. He began to bend to the floor, then stopped and leant his arms against the table, head hanging down between them.

"Ceridwen," he called softly, as I rose to my feet. "I need you." His shoulders were shaking and I knew he wept.

I put my arms around his shoulders, pushing the crockery shards away with my foot.

"My love, my love," I murmured, kissing his neck, and trying to get him to lift his face.

He straightened up and turned to me, but his arms hung limply at his sides. "It is true," he whispered. "I am a coward."

"You are no coward!" I answered, crying tears enough for both of us. "You have more courage than any man I know, that I will ever know. Godwin knows this too; he did not mean to injure you with his words." I took his hands in mine. "Godwin was - taken unawares by this; he could never have known Sidroc would be here." I touched his hands to my lips for a moment. "It is hard for Godwin, too. He is host to my dear friend, whose husband he killed. Then unexpectedly she brought Sidroc, who witnessed the slaying. And he is a powerful Jarl now. Godwin is trying to make the best of a bad matter."

He pulled his hands from mine. "I do not want to hear of Godwin. He ordered me to the hall, so I am going." He backed away, pushing against the broken jug. "Is there more water?"

I brought a bucket and poured water into the basin, and went from chest to chest, pulling forth all of Gyric's finest clothes, as he washed his face and hands. He had pulled off his soiled linen wrap from his face, and it lay upon the wash table. I came to him with a fresh one, but he did not turn to me to take it as always, but rather kept his face away and only extended his hand into the space between us.

I placed it in his hand with no remark, but his hiding his wound from me that night hurt me more than blows from his fists would have.

When he was almost ready to go I said, "Ælfwyn would like to greet you before you meet in the hall tonight. Will you let her come so that she may speak to you alone?"

"So she can get over her disgust the quicker?" he taunted.

Now I felt true anger.

76

"Ælfwyn is the best of women. You of all men should know that. You cannot speak of her like that!" I calmed myself and went on, "It is as I said, she wants to greet you before you meet in the hall. Say Yes or No."

"Yes."

I walked out into the garden, glad for the coolness of the gathering dark. I let myself out the gate and went to where Ælfwyn's waggons were pulled up. No one was around, but I could see a flicker of light from one.

"Ælfwyn," I called, and she opened the flap almost at once.

"I am sorry it is so late. Gyric is back, and would like to greet you," I lied.

"I am glad of it," she answered, but her face did not agree. She looked over her shoulder. "Look, Ceridwen," she went on, pulling the open flap wider. "Are you reminded of - ?" I stretched on tip-toe and peered into the dim interior. The waggon was crowded with all manner of baskets, barrels, and trunks. Deer hides lay upon the floor boards, and in the middle upon a slab of thin slate lay a brass brazier for warmth.

"It is so like your waggon, the one we rode in so long on the way to Four Stones!" I agreed, and could not help but smile.

"Yes, save for these little sleepy-heads," she said, pointing to where Ashild and Ceric lay huddled together like puppies.

Burginde came forth from the rear of the waggon, bent at the waist to clear the many baskets hanging from overhead. "Ach!" she complained, her hand on her back. "I be not as nimble as then, and vow never to travel so far again."

77

"You said that last time, Grumpy, and here you are," teased Ælfwyn.

"Aye, Lady, but an order be an order, even tho' I suckled you at the breast I must oblige you."

My smile fell from my face at these words, and I was glad when Burginde went on, "Lady Ceridwen, be you wanting the little lord in his own bed? He's as safe here, I wager, or I will take him to the bower house, as you like."

"We will not disturb them. Hrede will come and take him later." Burginde beamed down in satisfaction.

Ælfwyn and I walked down the gravel path to the bower house. The door was still open, and Gyric stood just within. It was dark in the house as we walked in.

I went up to Gyric and touched his sleeve. "Gyric, here is Ælfwyn," I said, and then turned away to light some cressets.

Gyric's voice was low. "I welcome you," he said, but did not extend his hand.

I went from lamp to lamp, and then returned to stand by Ælfwyn's side.

"Thank you...Gyric," she answered, just as softly.

Neither spoke. Both stood still, facing each other. I made a small gesture with my hand, asking Ælfwyn if I should go. She quickly shook her head, but it prompted her to speak again.

"It gives me great joy, Gyric, to know that you live and are wed to Ceridwen. After what...after what happened..." her words trailed off into the air. The flickering cresset light glimmered off a silver bracelet on Gyric's wrist, and caught

78

her eye. "The bracelet," she said, all in surprise. "You wear it."

Gyric touched the ring of silver with his other hand, and fingered the lapis stones set into it. "Yes. I know it is from you. Ceridwen gave it to me when we set out upon our way South. She told me to wear it as a reminder of you both."

"And so you still do?" she asked.

"I have never taken it from my wrist since the day she placed it on." He paused, and then lifted his face. "I thank you for it, Ælfwyn."

The speaking of her name opened her heart, it showed in her face. "God bless you Gyric! In a better world - we might have -" Her tears stopped her.

"There is no better world, not in our lifetimes," answered Gyric, but into his voice was some tenderness come.

In answer she leant towards him and kissed him upon the brow.

The Welcome Feast that Godwin had ordered was rich as any in Kilton's memory. First wine was poured, and golden mead, gift of the bee; and then followed clear brown ale, sparkling from long-standing in Modwynn's ale house. Milk-calfs and young pig set off with leeks, turnips, skirrits, and late greens followed plate after plate of roast sea fish. Frumenties, rich with milk and thickened with boiled barley and beaten eggs preceded bowls of honeyed dried elderberries and cherries. Fresh pears, so juicy that they spurted at the knife's touch, came last. All this was set off by scores of hot loaves of white bread, crusted and seeded and steaming from the ovens.

Sidroc sat at Godwin's right hand, and Gyric at Godwin's left; and then sat I, and Ælfwyn, and then Modwynn, flanking our honoured guest. The yellow flame of torches glittered on our gold and silver ornaments, and glittered too on the arm-rings binding the brawn of the arms of all of Godwin's thegns crowding that hall. Sidroc sat, adorned too as a great war-chief in leather and gold and silver. He looked out across that hall, and his dark eyes scanned the worth of the treasure he saw, and the mettle of the men who sat before him, and his hand closed around his gold-chased cup.

There was song that night, for the scop, revered keeper of the word-hoard, struck his painted harp with added strength, and sang for these strange North men tales of Saxon prowess. There was gaming, as well, after this, for which Godwin had brought forth ivory dice and gaming bones; and the eyes of the Danes lit with pleasure. Tables were cleared, counting-pieces set out, and men moved around the hall from this game to that, shouting encouragement or whispering advice to the gamers, or stopping to join the sport themselves.

The night went on, and Ælfwyn, carrying a child within her, grew tired, and I slipped out of the hall with her. Modwynn had made ready alcoves in the hall for her and Sidroc, but tonight there was no early rest there, so I walked her to her waggon, where every comfort waited. We kissed each other, and bid each other loving good-night, and I walked to the bower house to check on Ceric. He was fast asleep, and I stroked his soft cheek before I left. The Moon was rising nearly full, and I stood in the garden, breathing in the coolness of the night. Folk came and went from the hall, and when the doors were opened the sound of laughter and jesting grew loud, and then died away.

Now I was out of the hall, I was not eager to return. I stood a long while in the garden, wandering the few paths, and then I heard Hrede's shrill voice.

"Lady," she hissed, and ran up to me from the gate. She thrust a small object into my hand, and said, "From the Dane." Then she scampered away.

The object was rough on one side, smooth on the other: a shaved piece of wood, no longer than my finger. I lifted it to my face. Clouds passed over the Moon, then cleared. Carved onto the shaved side of the stick was a single rune ᛖ , Ehwaz, horse.

Horse. I ran my finger over it. Horse. I crossed the length of the garden, and let myself out the far gate. I walked rapidly across the yard, past shuttered sheds and empty work-stalls, their canvas awnings rolled down against the damp, and past the hawking house, where the fierce birds now slept. Before me was the mare's stable, with its small paddock. Amongst the horses drowsing there was my bay mare, and her yearling daughter.

Waiting before the paddock fence was a tall figure. I walked to him, and stopped just before him.

"I thank you, shield-maiden," Sidroc said.

I did not answer, and he moved slightly. The Moonlight fell upon me; I could see it on my gown. It fell, too on the silver disk bracelet on his wrist. I did not know what to say, but knew I must stay, if only to listen.

"I have never forgotten you, shield-maiden," he began. "I never worked the runes of unbinding to free me of you, never pricked them in my skin or burnt them in fire. I have never had a day without thought of you. This has been my choice. After so long, it is much for me to see you again."

His tone was mild, almost gentle, but I could find no words to answer his.

He lifted his eyes and with a movement of his head captured all of the burh. "He is rich, this Kilton. Richer even than me. One day, one day I will have as much, so fine a hall as his, and as many men to fill it." His eyes returned to me and settled on the heavy bracelet of gold upon my wrist. "But I am glad to see you have your share in this wealth."

I nodded my head, stupidly.

Of a sudden he said, "I could have understood if it was Kilton! If you had run away from me for him, I could accept it. But for that cripple you chose -" He ended with an oath in his own speech.

"He is no cripple," I spat out. "He is my husband. And do not forget your people did this to him!"

He shook his head, and again said something in his own tongue. He took a breath and started again. "You have spoken to Ælfwyn, you know why I wed her."

I did not understand his real meaning, but nodded my head just the same.

He looked into the darkness. "A man cannot keep a hall without a woman to run it."

We stood in silence. I watched him raise his hand to his face and stroke his beard.

"I grew it for Ælfwyn. My scar...troubled her." He touched the dark beard with his fingertips. "Even with it I am not pretty."

He again looked out over the burh yard. "It is strange that I am now here, in the hall of Kilton," he went on.

"When he killed Yrling, he almost fought me too." He spoke easily, without rancour.

"I will not soon forget that battle. It rained all night. We fought at dawn, the mist rising from the wet ground. Warriors came out of the mist like ghosts." He lifted his hands to the remembered fog.

"He is a good warrior, Kilton, one of the best, or he would not have so many men. But that day he fought with berserk fury. He ran through the field of slaughter, screaming Yrling's name, until he found him. Yrling was his match in every way, but that day Kilton fought as a Berserkr. The wild bear had entered him. No man can withstand such a warrior.

"Yrling was dead. Kilton took the trophy he sought and fled. I stayed with the fight, killed many men, gathered booty. Then I saw Toki was gone. I called to my men; those who were Yrling's and still lived rode with me back to Four Stones. I fought Toki. The shield-maidens gave the victory to me." He looked across the dark paddock to the slow moving horses. "I killed him, and then burnt his body in a blaze worthy of a great Jarl. All his weapons I piled upon him, to be taken by the balefire. I kept none for myself."

I thought of this. Sidroc and Toki were boys together, cousins, sharing in every venture; and recalled too that it was Toki's boyish knife which had given Sidroc the great scar he bore upon his cheek. Together they had sailed with Yrling to our lands, to make their fortunes by their able swords. Then I thought of Toki, dead. I saw in my mind's eye his battered body lying upon smouldering heaped wood, saw the curling yellow hair smoke and singe, the wounds burst asunder and bleed afresh at the hungry licking of the flames.

"Ælfwyn was - afraid. She tried to hurt herself; kill Yrling's child within her. I stopped her. She came to me with some tale of being one of your holy women." He shook his head. "She is a good wife, Ælfwyn," he went on. "But she is not...what you would be. We do not have as man and woman what you and I would have."

"She is far more beautiful than me," I mumbled.

He looked back at me. "Hers is the beauty of golden-haired Sif, wife to Thor, or of Idun, silly keeper of the magic apples. You...you are...but like Freyja, goddess of lust and battle." He looked back into the darkness. "And you are...like us." He tapped his chest. "Here, you are one of us. We worship the same Gods, value the same strengths in men and women. No man, Kilton himself or Kilton's brother, can love you as I love you." He turned back to me, finger still resting on his leathern tunic. "I know you. You are like me."

He reached his hand to touch beneath his arm. It came to rest over the scar of the spear wound I had searched and dressed. "You are part of me. Mingled in my blood."

I looked down; I had to. He called out in his own speech a single word, and one of the horses ambled over to us: my bay mare. "She has not forgotten," he said softly, as she lowered her muzzle to be scratched. She gave a little snort and moved away, and Sidroc looked upon the filly who still followed her.

"Why did you do it?" he demanded of a sudden. "Why?" He shook his head, giving me no time to answer. "For nine days I looked for you. Nine days! If I had found you -" he stopped himself, fist clenched in the darkness before him.

"Yes?" I challenged.

"If I had found you I would have made you my woman then and there!"

I swallowed hard, and near whispered my answer to him. "Sidroc, you are wrong. You say that only because you have

84

thought so much on it; lived it over and over in your brain. But I do not believe it. If you had caught me you would not have served me thus. You are a better man than that."

Water was in his eyes. "If you had stayed, you would have wed me."

Tears were in my eyes, too. "Yes. But Fate looked away."

He made a slight gesture towards me. "Only once did I hold you in my arms, and even then did not kiss you." His words were choked and difficult to hear. "I had - too much regard for you. I could have taken you any time!"

All this was true, and could scarce be answered. "Yes," I said, "you could have. But you did not. You are a better man than that."

"In a few days I will ride from here. Only all-seeing Odin knows if we will meet again on this Earth. All things may change. This alone will not: I will love you, shield-maiden."

Then he gestured with his hand, Go. I turned from the dark paddock and walked back to the bower house, still clutching the rune-stick in my hand.

Chapter the Seventh: In This I Am Alone

NEXT day Ælfwyn and I sat together in the bower house, alone save for our two babes who lie asleep upon the dragon bed. The weather had turned cold, and the morning's frost lay silver upon the golden-hearted daises, keeping us from the garden. The day was brilliant with Sun, and the light streaming through the glass casement was strong enough for hand work. We sat at the table, I hemming a linen wrap for Gyric, and Ælfwyn adorning a new sash with coloured threads.

We had spent much of the morning speaking of Modwynn, praising her ways and wisdom, and now had fallen silent.

"Ceridwen," Ælfwyn began, and her voice held the eagerness that bespoke a new topic, "have you yet sent word to your own mother?"

This jolted me so I stuck the needle into my thimble-less finger. Ælfwyn did not notice.

"She is a holy woman of some sort, is she not? A solitary, or contemplative? I recall you said she lived apart from your village." She was still bent over her thread-work. "How happy she would be to hear of your new life. Perchance she could come to Kilton. Your priest would surely welcome such a woman here."

Now she looked up and saw my face, and her needle stopped in the air.

"She is no holy woman," I said. "She is a whore."

Ælfwyn's eyebrows rose so they almost touched, and her mouth opened.

"She lived apart from me my whole life, I think; I have no child-memory of her. She is of the Welsh, dark and small-boned. She lives alone in a long-forsaken mill house. When I was fourteen I began to visit her of times. She knew my name and much about me, but I was stupid of anything about her. I knew her as the Woman who Practices her Art, yet I knew not then what those arts were. The day I left the Priory I stopped to bid her Fare-well. On that morning she told me she was my mother. Then she bid me go. I do not even know her name."

A bead of bright blood had welled up on my fingertip. Ælfwyn reached over and pressed a scrap of linen upon it, and then took my hand. It trembled in hers as my words rushed out.

"No one knows this, Ælfwyn, only you. When I came to Kilton I only told Gyric's people that my mother was not of the village. I think they guessed as you did, that she was a holy woman, and I did not have the courage to speak the truth."

I looked over to our children, sleeping in their innocence. "It troubled me, to keep such knowledge to myself. I have thought often of her since Ceric was born. And I do not know even her name!"

Another thought came to me. "Long ago at Four Stones Sidroc asked me of my mother. I only told him that she was of the Welsh. He answered, 'Your father captured her and did not sell her, because of her beauty.' I think he must have been right. She was a captive, nothing more."

Ælfwyn spoke now, her words gentle and firm. "It matters nothing if they did not wed. There is no shame in

87

being the get of a good man. Your father accepted you as his, and your kinsman also. They raised you in honour; you were their true heir.

"And as for your mother, what woman can stand in judgment? A slave girl, her folk slain, perhaps, and she carried off to a strange land? Then her master is killed. She kept herself alive through it all. The disgrace is not hers, but the men who forced her to such living." She lowered her eyes. "I know how close my own mother and sisters came to such an end."

She laid her sash in her lap and asked, "Would your mother come here, if she could be found? Perhaps she will repent and live an upright life."

"Repent?" I had never before thought of this. "She is heathen, Ælfwyn; she does not fear the things...we fear. To her, Hel is mistress of the underworld, not the fiery place of torment of the Christians. To repent you must first...believe."

I recalled the Woman's sharp, mirthful eyes as she made light of the Priory and all it stood for. I knew too, that she felt no shame at how she earned her silver; but this I could not say, even to Ælfwyn.

She said with real earnestness, "You should tell Modwynn of this; it would ease your heart."

"Modwynn? I would rather tell all of Wessex than Modwynn!"

"Silly! What do you think she is, some saint carved of wood? She has lived long and much, and knows the ways of women and men." Her brow furroughed for a moment. "And the ways of war. Nothing of this sort would make her hold you less dear."

Now she began to laugh. "I cannot believe that I, Ælfwyn, am sitting here counselling you, who used to do all my good thinking for me at Four Stones!"

At this I had to smile too. "There was so much scheming we had to do," I allowed. "Everything was so strange to us then, the Danes, their speech; each day seemed full of new adventures."

"It is much easier now, with some peace in the land, and my mother at my side," smiled Ælfwyn. "But think on what I have said; you should tell Modwynn."

I hung my head. "This one thing is my only secret from Gyric," I confessed.

"That is different. Men can be so ‑ hard about these things, Ceridwen." She shook her head. "Remember in the Holy Book it was the men of the village who wanted to stone the adulteress."

"It was a man who stopped them," I reminded her.

"Yes, yes, but good as he is, Gyric is not our Saviour. If it were me, I would not tell him."

I did not answer this remark, but she went on.

"There is always Dunnere. He is your confessor." She read my face. "I see that he...watches you. Have you quarrelled?"

"No, never. I just do not go to divine service as he would have me. I go only when Gyric does, once only each Sabbath. Edgyth used to go with Modwynn twice each day; I think Modwynn wishes I would, but is too kind to chide me."

"Do they know you were raised ‑?"

"Heathen. Yes; I told Gyric right away, and I am certain that he mentioned it."

"There are still heathen Saxons," she said, trying to make the best of it.

"Not amongst the high-born," I answered. "Gyric was full of amaze when I told him I had been heathen. My father and kinsman must have counted amongst the last."

"Do you still...make Offering?"

I nodded. "In small ways, yes. But in this I am alone here at Kilton. Nor do I feel I can raise up Ceric in the ways of my father and kinsman."

"They are also the ways of the Danes, that is against you now," she agreed.

"It would be easier if I could forget; I know this. I would believe all I learnt at the Priory if I could, but I have thought on it, and it does not make sense." I stopped lest I give her hurt, or made her fear for me.

I searched her face to see if I could read her thoughts. Ælfwyn had never judged me harshly at Four Stones, and she did not do so now. I never loved her more than at that moment, for what she said was, "You are good, and bring good to all around you. I cannot believe that Christ will Damn you for worshipping the Gods and Goddesses of old."

"Dunnere would."

"Priests! Wilgot at Four Stones is just the same, always muttering. Ever since he arrived he has been circling the Place of Offering, throwing holy water at it. If Sidroc and his men did not Offer there, he would order it destroyed, too." She sighed. "Still, he has forbidden me to go there, or even to ride by it, lest I catch a Devil."

"And you accept his order? You have seen what the men do there; there are no Devils. Sidroc does not even believe in such creatures."

"Yes, there is nothing there but the wooden carving of Woden, and the pit at which they sacrifice birds and weapons. But tho' I know this, what can I do? I have my mother and younger sisters in my keeping, Ceridwen. And a hall full of folk, not to mention the whole village. I cannot keep the word of God from my people. Some of the Danish women now listen to Wilgot when he preaches. At least he is a good preacher."

"Yes, of course, you are right," I said, and meant it. Her task was much the greater than mine. I did not have to be an example for anyone at Kilton.

That night I lay awake long after Gyric slept. I was troubled with a sense of unease within me, stirred by Ælfwyn's reassurances and Sidroc's certainty. A thought ran though the core of me, or knowledge, rather, and made me shiver; and this knowledge was: I am not a Christian.

At first I could go no farther with this thought; it was too terrible. The Church was mercy, and good works, and the arts of reading and writing. It was now the faith of nearly all the Angles and Saxons, from the very kings of Wessex and Mercia to the humblest folk who tithed to them one fowl at Martinmas. To be heathen was to forsake all this; or so it seemed. The heathen were such as the Danes, unlettered and unlawed; and such as the fierce folk of Gwynedd, land of my mother. But the baldness of these facts mattered not as I lay there thinking on this. My name was heathen, that of the Abundant Goddess of my mother's people. My own mother was heathen, and lived outside of the laws of the Church. What would those of Kilton think of her, if they knew? What would Gyric think, if he could somehow see me at Four Stones, tying my sash unto the beech tree, and giving it over, with such joy, as an Offering? Could he ever know the wild sweet release I felt in doing so? To worship the woman-Gods of my kinfolk I needed no priest or prayer book, or sacred building; They were everywhere: in all of the sweet Earth which fed us, and the shining Moon that called women to bleed each month. In Their eyes I was no sinner; They knew no sin.

She was Ceridwen to the Welsh, and the sister-Goddesses Frigg and Freyja to my kinsmen and to the Danes. By any name, She was ever the bringer of beauty and pleasure and abundance, and these were all good things. She did not Damn mankind. She was not cursed with original sin. It was She who blest women with rich wombs, and men with good seed to fill them, and made fruitful every field each Summer that both might live and thrive. It was She, dancing with her God, who created first the pleasures that now I knew as woman with my lover-husband; all these lusts and desires and passions were given voice in me by Her.

The Christians had changed all this. Her groves had been burnt, Her wells filled up, those who worshipped Her hunted down and forced to convert; or else ridiculed and scorned. Now She lived on only as a maiden, mute and mild, serving as the vessel for the young Christ. That was her task, to be the Blessed Mother; but now it seemed her only task, and her strength and power was not her own, but only that reflected by Her Son.

The God, in all his forms - wild man of forest and glen, Green Man of High Summer, horned pipe player, All-Father Woden, lusty Thunor - was now the Devil, and wickedness and wantonness was his.

92

And prayer itself was changed. When I was a child my kinsman taught me to speak the names of the Gods and so invite their strengths and natures into my being, and by remembering their qualities, to invoke them within myself. If I was truly part of Her, Her nature was always part of me, and all I need do was to remember it to claim Her strength as mine.

I am no Christian, I thought; and whispered it again into the dark.

For the four days of her visit I had Ælfwyn nearly to myself, and the bond between us, always deep, grew keener by the hour. And now it was not only our bond; watching Ashild and Ceric at play I turned to Ælfwyn and said, "How sad for these two babes to be parted!"

"She cries each night Burginde takes her from him," agreed Ælfwyn, watching the little flaxen and golden heads as they played together with a tuft of uncarded wool.

"Who knows how old they might be when they next meet," I said, speaking not only of the babes, but we two as well. "But they will not forget each other. Perhaps...perhaps one day they will love each other."

"I do not want them to love unless they can wed," answered Ælfwyn quickly, showing that she too had thought on these things. "It is too painful to love and not live as man and wife. And Ceric...he will be powerful and rich. What will Ashild, the daughter of a forgotten war-chief, offer him?"

"I was the daughter of a forgotten war-chief when I wed Gyric," I reminded her. "Ashild is your daughter; that is what matters to me."

Each of these four days Godwin had taken Sidroc and his men off to some new pleasure. They went hawking, and returned with braces of birds slung over their saddles. They hunted boar in the forests one day, coming back with nothing but tales. The third day they rode all about the boundaries of Kilton, past rod after rod of wheat, barley and rye fields; and Godwin showed off countless flocks of fat sheep and many hundred head of glossy spotted cattle.

None of this, I knew, would be lost on Sidroc. Nothing would escape his dark eye, be it the sumptuousness of the feasts, the patterning of the plough work in the fields, or the clean and decently clothed slaves of the yard. I saw him only at night and only in the hall, when he sat on Godwin's right hand. More than once I looked over to see him looking at me, as I chose Gyric's food for him, or paused in my speech with Ælfwyn. Then Sidroc would lift his cup to his face and look at me from over the golden rim, and I would look away.

Gyric spent little time in the bower house and less in the hall. At his brother's bidding he rode out with Godwin and all the Danes the first day hawking, and each night went to the hall and sat at his brother's side. The rest of the time he was off with Worr. Alone with me at night he spoke little; I felt him to be driven out of his own home by our guests and knew the only remedy was their leaving.

On the last morning Godwin took Sidroc to one of the store houses to look at fleece, for he had decided to sell some to the Dane. Ælfwyn and I walked a final time through the garden, and entered the yard near the waiting waggons. One of Sidroc's men held a woven cage carefully in his hands. I knew it to be one of those used for the hawks, and wondered if Godwin had parted with one of those precious trained birds. At the back of one waggon stood Godwin and Sidroc, watching as men heaved bag after bag of shorn fleece onto the floorboards.

"I will be kept busy spinning this Winter," whispered Ælfwyn, and squeezed my hand. And what pleasure I shall have as I touch it, knowing it is from you."

Modwynn was ready, with glittering cups holding the final draught; and now was our formal leave-taking. Godwin came first into the hall, with Sidroc and all his men, two of which hoisted a wicker basket between them.

We took up cups, and drank, and then Sidroc said, "A gift demands a gift. You, Kilton, have accepted me into your hall, sold me good fleece, and made a gift of your fine falcon. Now take this gift from Sidroc."

With his hand Sidroc gestured to the wicker lid of the basket. Godwin took it in both hands, lifted it, pushed it aside. A little gasp of surprise escaped Modwynn's lips, and Godwin's eyes narrowed, then grew large. He reached in and drew forth an animal pelt of tawny colour, marked all about with strange black markings, almost like unto eyes.

All marvelled at it, its great size, odd colour and odder markings; and some pride shown in Sidroc's eyes.

"Magnificent," said Godwin.

"This is from far to the South, from the land of sandalwood and frankincense," answered Sidroc. "More is here," he said, and himself reached into the basket. He pulled forth handfuls of narrow lustrous dark pelts, long-haired and shimmering, and then three pelts of dazzling whiteness set off with trailing white tails as full as foxes'.

"From my country," said Sidroc, as we all goggled.

"Your gifts are rich indeed," answered Godwin. "I thank you."

"I will not forget this visit," returned Sidroc. His eyes roved the length of the hall, rested briefly where I stood with Ælfwyn, then came back to where Godwin stood next Modwynn. "Your hall, your warriors, your women ⁻ these I admire. Sidroc will not forget."

Chapter the Eighth: Stung

The Year 874

IT was Twelfth Night day, and Modwynn and I shook the frost from our hoods as we came in from the kitchen yard. It was a cold day in a strangely snowy Winter, and the huge fire-pit in the centre of the hall was heaped high. We went to it, rubbing our numb fingers together and chafing our wrists by its warmth. We looked up at the carved roof-rafters, feebly lit by a weak Sun, but glorious with drooping tree boughs, their green leaves and garnet berries a brave symbol of rebirth in dead Winter. Lengths of holly, sacred to old Hel, mistress of the underworld and greeter of the dead, had been nailed to the upright posts. Cut slips of pliant ivy threaded through the spiky holly boughs, ever-green. Clustered bunches of mistletoe, waxy with white berries, hung over the two outer doors, reminder to all who walked under that no discord should enter in.

Few folk were about the hall, for it was near time for us to gather, and all were off making ready. We too, should go and dress, but we lingered by the fire's heat.

The coming feast, the last of twelve, put me in mind of all the many tasks which filled Modwynn's day. I thought of how little I did to aid her in running this great hall, and my cheeks grew warm. When Gyric and I arrived at Kilton, Modwynn urged me to spend as much time as possible with Gyric, trying to make happier and easier his life. In those first months I had spent near every afternoon reading to him, but now all the books were read. His wound rendered him unfit for nearly all the tasks of a young lord; he could no longer fight, the first and foremost duty of a pledged man; nor could he inspect fields, grade sheep or cattle, or deal well with

97

merchants. The only hunting he could do was with his hawk, and this was nobleman's sport, rather than real yield for our tables. His restlessness each day was great, and greater still in this cold weather, in which he could not ride out as he was wont to do.

She looked at me, and read my thoughts. "Gyric is...very unhappy, is he not?" Her voice was as gentle as the hand that touched mine.

I nodded my head, afraid for a moment even to speak lest I say the wrong thing. "He is," I agreed quietly. "Sometimes it is like the early days of our journey here; he scarce speaks to me, and broods for hours. He has - no trust in his own abilities; he does not even know what those abilities might be."

She did not speak right away. "Surely being a good husband and father gives him reason enough to trust in himself. And he is still the best of sons."

"These are the things I value, that are dear to me." I did not want to cry, and felt near to tears. "He thinks too much on all that he cannot do, and too little on what he can."

Our speech ended there, for the great door at the end of the hall opened, and in came Godwin and Gyric and Ceric with a deal of stamping, shouting, and laughing. Ceric was in Godwin's arms, and his uncle held him aloft as if he sailed through the sky.

"Goose!" called Godwin, and in answer Ceric lisped, "Goo!"

They came towards us, snow falling from their mantles as they moved. Ceric was wearing a sheep-skin hood, frosted over with snow.

"Here you are, Chirp," said Godwin, setting him down before the fire with us. Ceric raised his arms, wanting to be lifted again, and repeated, "Goo!"

"More like a little lamb, in that cap," laughed Modwynn, pulling it from his head.

I moved to Gyric and touched his arm. "Let me take your mantle," I told him, watching the snow crystals creased in the woollen folds run to water in the fire's glow. "You will get wet."

"I will not melt; I am not made of salt." His voice was low, and there was no mirth in it.

"I am sorry," I said, and moved away. I lifted my eyes and saw Modwynn and Godwin looking at us. Ceric ran to my skirts and threw his arms about my legs, saying, "Me up!"

I reached down and hoisted him. "Chirp, you are getting so heavy," I laughed. I kissed his little round cheek. "Let father hold you, and we will go to the bower house and change your clothes."

Gyric was already moving away from us. "Let Godwin bring him," he said, almost over his shoulder. "I tripped with him in the snow and made him cry." And he walked to the side door, pushed it open against the strong winds, and vanished into the swirling snow.

Godwin took a step forward, but I spoke at once. "O, no," I smiled, and made my voice light. "I was jesting. I will take him now and get dry things on him."

I turned, and Ceric reached over my shoulder to his uncle. "Godwa!" he called, but I only laughed a brittle laugh and carried him away.

Twelfth Night was kept with special merriment, for the day following marked the end of Yule festivity, and signalled the return to work for all about the burh. On Distaff Day women returned to their spinning, men to their work as smiths, cobblers, or coopers; and all who had done little or partial work for the fortnight past were busied once again with Winter's normal activity. Thus the feast given on Twelfth Night took on added meaning for the revellers. Ale flowed with extra freedom against the dawn, and men and women joined hands and danced in circle round the fire-pit, honouring in its red heat the newly reborn Sun.

Modwynn moved about the hall, stopping to speak to this or that man or woman, offering good wishes for a safe Winter, smiling on all. Godwin too roved his hall, golden cup in hand, stood judge as men arm-wrestled, jested with groups of youths, shy and tongue-tied before their lord, bidding all be hearty.

Gyric sat unspeaking by my side. His brooding grew deeper at festivals, but was never so dark as it seemed tonight. He had eaten almost nothing and his ale cup sat untouched. I gazed at the beautiful silver goblet, his name carved into its rim of gold, and recalled its tale. For ten years Gyric had drunk from this silver cup; it had been one of two given him by his parents on reaching his fifteenth year. The second, destined for his wife, sat wrapped away eight years until my first night at Kilton. I drank from it that night in pure joy, and the next morn Gyric had ordered the gold-worker to carve my name upon its golden lip. My fingers traced the lettering now, but the cup that spoke my name remained as silent as Gyric.

Next morning Gyric would not go to the hall; it was bustling with serving men clearing away after the night's revelry. Ceric, tired from the long night, slept late, but I was restless and yearning to be out in the little light. I walked through the yard with the Sun glowing dully through a shifting grey sky. A few snowflakes swirled against my face, and from the tail of my eye I saw the red fox tails of my hood tipped with white.

Much of the burh yard was cobbled, and oxen drew wood snow boards behind them, pushing the snow to one side so that stables and hall were clear. The great entrance gates in the palisade were swung upon, and folk passed in and out, hurrying in the cold about their duties. My boots were short and my skirt hem already crusted with snow; I must keep to the paths made by trampling men or ox-pulled board. The air was sharp cold, and the snow going to ice upon its surface, making it crunch beneath my footfall, but there was little wind. I walked fast, with no goal except to warm myself, and then slowed, trying to take pleasure in the crisp air.

The huts of the villagers looked like white hay stacks, so frosted were they. Smoke rising from outdoor cookfires smudged the sky and blackened the nearby snow, and dunghills steamed their acrid vapour.

I walked on, and near to the core of the village saw a knot of folk, men and boys mostly, gathered in the road outside a croft. Some who leant against a stout paling fence called out direction, their breath smoking, and unseen voices answered them back. I grew nearer, and found within a cattle pen a single cow, lying where she had slipped upon the ice hard against the far edge of the fence. The great size of her swollen belly made it clear that she was heavy with calf, and

101

she lowed mournfully as two men tried with flat boards to prop up her hind quarters.

A young cottar who knelt at her head looked worriedly to the opening of the hut, where his wife gripped the rough wood of the door. Strapped to her hip was a babe in a sling, and a child of three or four clutched her skirt.

Some men now brought lengths of hempen rope, and going to the creature's head, looped it about her short horns. The cottar and another man held the ends of these ropes, and with them pulling and the men behind pushing, tried again to lift the cow to her feet. Her rear hooves thrashed against the straw laid to give her footing, and her boney hips struggled to lift, but she rose no more than a few inches before dropping back to the ice. Her huge brown eyes rolled in her head as she grunted.

They tried again, this time forsaking boards, and four men pressed their weight against her rump as the two at her head pulled. The cow cried out, a sound piteous to hear, and the cottar bid them stop.

Now a group of horsemen appeared, riding from the furthest end of the village towards the burh. It was easy to spot Godwin on his big grey horse, and Wulfstan too, whose mount was black. With them were two snaresmen returning to the hall, for draped over their saddles were hares, white as the ground in their Winter dress, and braces too of ground-running pheasants.

They reined up before us, and Godwin and Wulfstan nodded to me as they looked down from their horses. Godwin leant forward on his saddle bow, and took in the scene before him. He spoke for a moment to the cottar, who nodded silently. Godwin turned his horse into the pen, and tied the ends of the hempen rope to the big gelding's saddle bow. He called out to the men crouched at the cow's hind quarters.

With a sharp kick Godwin urged the gelding forward. The cow's head jolted, horns straight out, and the straining men groaned. Godwin lashed the horse's neck with his rein tips and the animal leapt ahead.

The cow was yanked to her feet, stood a moment, crumpled back to the strawy ice. A groan came forth from all gathered around; they knew now why the cow could not stand, for she had broken her leg when she fell. My eyes went to the face of the woman in the door. Her furroughed brow and drawn mouth said much; the single cow, greater source of their little wealth, was lost; and with her milk and butter for the Spring-time, and the precious calf within her.

The cottar stood by the cow's head, and for a moment plunged his hands through his hair in despair. Godwin, still on his horse, looked back and saw all this, and drew his seax from his belt and sliced through the rope tied to his saddle. The cottar brushed past his wife into the hut, came out with an axe in one hand and a long butchery knife in the other.

"I cannot lose both cow and calf!" he cried, and dropped the knife to the snow. With both hands he took the axe handle and swung the flat of the blade head against the cow's skull. A sharp crack rent the cold air. I turned away, slipping in the churned up snow, and clutching my arms around me, set off almost at a run down the village road.

I went on, and a gust of cold wind blew my hood back, dropping snow against my neck. I pulled it tighter against me, and then heard Godwin's voice call my name. He was astride, walking his horse on the smooth surface, his hand reaching down to me. I stopped and he said, "Will you ride back to the burh? You look half-frozen."

I shook my head, and he swung off the saddle and walked by my side.

"Did he...cut the calf out?" I asked.

Godwin nodded. "It was alive. Some of the other cows have dropped their calves already; if this one can suckle they may be able to foster it."

"I hope for all their sakes it lives."

For answer he only nodded. The wind had begun to pick up, and I clutched myself even tighter.

"Why are you out here?" he asked, pulling his own hood up.

"I wanted air."

He laughed and raised his gloved hand to a few snowflakes. "Well, you have found it." He looked at me and saw I did not laugh. "You are trembling with cold," he said, and put his hand on my arm. "Ride with me back to the hall."

"I am not ready to go back. And Gyric did not want to come out."

"Gyric does not want to do much of anything these days."

"Yes," I said, and lowered my head to blink away the water in my eyes. We had stopped in the road, and were now past the borders of the village. Fields of white lay before us, the mown rye in which we had danced at High Summer blanketed in snow. Beyond the silent field began the grey and green forest edge.

I looked away at the feathery plumes of ice-crusted beeches, and then back to Godwin. Snow dusted the folds of his wool hood, and gave light to his golden-green eyes.

"I used to think you were so much alike," I said. My heart felt pain as if an unseen hand had gripped it.

He jerked his head back, and looked across the snow-still field.

"No," he said in a thin, strained voice. "We are not alike. Gyric does not covet my wife."

He turned away, and my knees near buckled beneath me. I gasped for breath, felt smothered in the cold air. Somehow I kept moving forward, my arms clutching myself against an inner cold.

Snow was falling now, striking my face and blurring my hot tears.

"Ceridwen," Godwin called out, half-order, half-plea.

I stopped but could not turn. He came up beside me, holding his horse by the cheekpiece.

"Come on," he ordered; but would not look at me. "I am taking you back to the hall."

I moved to the gelding, and Godwin stood behind me and held my waist as I put my foot in the iron stirrup. He boosted me up, and swung up behind me.

The rising wind, blowing off the sea, stung, and I buried my face in the cold fox tail fur of my hood as we rode past the bloodied cattle pen.

Chapter the Ninth: End of a King

A week later I sat with Modwynn in the treasure room, sorting bolts of linen. They were all of Kilton's making, but were of differing grades. Those of the finest weave, made of the smoothest flax strands, we set aside for our shifts and head wraps, and special tunics for Godwin and Gyric. Those of a bit sturdier make were marked for linen tunics for the men of the hall. The thickest cloth, those with the widest strands and many tiny lumps, became our bed linens and towels.

Modwynn held one of the bolts to her eye, and then rubbed the fabric between her fingers.

"Who ever spun this will be making horse blankets next season," she muttered. "A waste of good staple to a bad spinner."

"Not me, I hope," I answered, trying to jest.

The treasure room door was open, and I glimpsed a dark figure making its way across the empty hall. It was a bitterly cold day, and the figure stopped and turned to the fire-pit, sinking down on the hearth-stones to rest. I thought nothing of it until the figure rose and began making its way to our door.

It was an old woman, swaddled in layers of cloaks. She drew closer to the stone step on which the high table was set each night, and I rose and said to Modwynn, "A cottar."

I walked out to see what she wanted. Folk often came to Modwynn, asking her to intercede for them in some case in a coming hall-moot, or bidding her aid for a sick child. The woman stopped before she reached the step, and I looked at her pinched and whitened face, mazed as an old pottery crock.

"Yes?" I asked, and smiled at her. I did not recall her face.

In answer she dipped her head to me, and with a movement of her eyes indicated Modwynn.

Something about the woman made me turn without asking her again.

"There is an old woman here, who wants you," I told Modwynn, and felt foolish not to be able to tell her the nature of the request.

Modwynn raised her eyes from her work and paused. She nodded and rose wordlessly and went out the door. She looked at the woman, who bowed her head.

"Yes," Modwynn said quietly, and at once came back into the treasure room. She went to a chest where I knew she kept a small store of silver, and counted out a few coins. She turned and went to the waiting woman. The woman reached out her withered hand, and Modwynn dropped the coins into her palm. The woman bowed again, and without another word from either one of them, began shuffling to the door of the hall.

It was unlike any alms-giving I had seen her do, not only the large size of the gift, but the wordless exchange between her and the beggar. I said nothing, and busied myself stacking folded lengths of cloth.

She sat down, and bent her head over a bolt, examining the weave. After a moment she spoke in a low tone. "Do you know who that is?"

"No," I answered in truth. "I have never before seen her."

She set down the cloth. "She is the mother of a girl, now dead, on whom Godwin fathered a child."

"O," I said stupidly. "Gyric told me, on the journey here, that a village girl -"

"Yes," she said. "It was years ago; Godwin was but seventeen. Godwulf and I did not even know. One day the girl's mother came to me, after the girl and the babe had died. The girl was the mother's sole surviving child, and she had expected to live with her when she wed. Instead the girl had lain with Godwin, and got his child; and then within a week or two of birth both babe and girl caught fever and died. The mother made moan to me, seeking redress for her loss. Each year on the day marking her daughter's death, she comes to the hall, and I give her three pieces of silver."

I nodded my head rapidly, not knowing what to say.

"I tell you this so that the payment will continue should I die."

"You will not die, Modwynn," I said, flustered. "And the woman is old; far older than you." Another thought came to me. "Why did Godwin not settle a fixed sum on the mother when the daughter died?"

"He had but seventeen Summers," answered his mother.

I said the first thing that came to mind.

"When you were seventeen you had been wed, and running this hall, for two years."

She nodded, and a faint smile lit on her lips. "It was hard enough for Godwin. He was in over his head. He was shamed; I do not know if he could have faced the mother." She took a breath, let it out slowly. "Not that we punished him in any way; he reaped punishment enough. The girl was willing; no force was used. I do not know what happened when she told him she was with child. I think he panicked and avoided her; my piety may have frightened him. At any rate, the girl died, and Godwin lost his son.

"Sad as it was, we did not grieve over-long. Young men are unthinking; their blood is hot. When Godwin married we had great hopes for him and Edgyth. But year after year she lost her babes in the womb, and year after year this old mother would creep to the hall and take silver for the death of her daughter, and her, and my, grand-son."

She sighed, and folded her white hands upon the cloth.

"Why...why does not Edgyth return?" I asked, and hoped my cheek did not flame.

She shook her head before she answered. "I do not know. I think she is waiting. Waiting for Godwin to call her back."

"Godwulf returned to her the equal of her dowry," I began, remembering his will.

"Yes; there is a mixed meaning there. Such a rich bequest frees Godwin from having to redeem the dowry should she renounce her marriage vows. It also provides amply for Edgyth as endowment to the convent. Most of all I think she read it as Godwulf's affection for her; for he did value her as daughter. Still, it did not prompt her to action. Godwin insists that the choice be hers, and I think she demands the same of him."

"Godwin would never tell Edgyth to forsake her vows of marriage," I thought aloud, "nor even ask such a thing."

She nodded her head, and then ended quietly, "And Godwin now has twenty-nine Winters."

Outside upon the parapet a brass horn began to sound. Three short blasts, repeated twice. "A messenger," said Modwynn, but she did not rise, nor did I.

We heard the hall door swing open, and the sound of men hurrying towards us across the stone floor. Godwin appeared in our doorway, wild-eyed, followed by a heavily wrapped rider with a young but weary face.

Godwin opened his mouth and said, "Burgred has fled. The Kingdom of Mercia has fallen to the Danes."

Godwin prepared to leave the following day, in search of Ælfred and news; and with him would take a third of Kilton's thegns, should he find war. They would ride off, heavily armed, in the grip of a bitter Winter, destined to camp in frost and ice along the road.

The hours were worrisome and rushed. Later that day I came out of the treasure room, where I had been helping Modwynn prepare Godwin's clothing, to find him sitting alone with Wulfstan, eldest amongst the thegns, at the high table. Wulfstan's head, with its drooping brown moustaches, was bent close to Godwin, and he held his bad leg rigidly straight in front of him. They spoke in low tones, but with urgency; Wulfstan arguing that he should accompany his lord.

"And if the Danes land by sea at our backs?" demanded Godwin. "No, Wulfstan. Gyric is no good to me here, and you are no good to me in the field. You will stay and command the burh."

At this point my shadow, cast by the torch light of the treasure room, fell across the two men, and they turned their heads to see me. I nodded to them and hurried off.

Once in the bower house I went to Gyric, sitting motionless by the brazier. I put my hands on his shoulders, but he moved not. I sat down next to him and asked, "Why is there war now? It is hard Winter; no warrior chooses Winter to fight in."

"Yes," he answered. I sat with him in silence a long moment. At last he said, "The days of Summer fighting are over for the Danes. In years past they sailed across the North Sea only in Summer, raided, and then left. Then they began to stay, Summer and Winter, as their numbers grew. Now they have halls and men and horses, just as we. They attack when we least expect it. That is their strength."

"Burgred had ruled a long time, and in peace," I thought aloud.

Gyric's voice was flat. "Twenty-two years or twenty-two days matters not; what matters is who rules now."

The Danes now ruled my home country of Mercia, and overran, perhaps, all of the land, even onto the shire fast by the marshy River Dee which my own father and kinsman had ruled. Burgred, honourable King and famed warrior, was put to flight. His wife, sister to King Ælfred - what thread had Fate spun for her? I recalled my journey with Ælfwyn through the wasted lands of Lindisse, burnt and trampled by the Danes, the Angles and Saxons put to the sword or enslaved, the good Earth laying fallow and untilled. Was Mercia suffering thus? In my own shire lay the Priory, where the kind, sad-faced Prior who had taken me after my kinsman's

111

death dwelt; he who had baptized me, taught me sums, and most of all given me the arts of quill and ink. The Priory was a poor one, with little treasure; but I thought of the silver cup of the sacrament ripped from the altar, and the silver and crystal book casing stripped from the Scripture. And there too, along the banks of the silted Dee, lay a tumbled-down mill building, home to my wild Welsh mother...

I closed my eyes against this; it was all I could do. I was of Mercia, and no one in the burh of Kilton could share this sorrow or fear with me. In truth it seemed my fear was doubled, for I feared both for what my home land was suffering now, and what might soon befall Kilton and all Wessex.

"What will happen now?" I asked Gyric.

"Godwin will look for Ælfred. He will soon learn if the borders will hold, or if the Danes will even try them."

"And King Burgred?"

Gyric shrugged. "Most likely he is seeking Ælfred too. Perchance he will stay with the King, or sail across to Frankland."

I said nothing, and he lowered his voice and asked, "Do you fear for your mother?"

I placed my hand over his for answer.

"Mercia is a big country. Your shire is not a rich one, and it lies far to the West. It will attract little attention from the Danes. They seek the strongholds where wealth in the way of arms and silver is kept."

I kissed him for these words. Just to hear him speak to me was so important, and he spoke now with calmness and reason.

There was a knock at the door; not the light rap of Hrede, but that of a man. I rose and went to it, and pulled it open to find Godwin, muffled against the cold. He tossed back his hood as he stepped into the centre of the little house, and spoke at once.

"Gyric, I leave behind Wulfstan, Warenoth, and Aldgisl with you; my three best men. I ride with twenty men, so over sixty remain. I am taking two waggons, a total of twenty-eight horses. Every week I will send one rider back to Kilton so you might have word."

Gyric stood up. "I will not need word; I will be with you," he said.

My mouth opened but it was Godwin who spoke our joint surprise.

"What?"

"I said I will ride with you. I am of no use here; Wulfstan commands the burh in your absence."

Godwin said nothing, just stared at his brother.

"Worr will ride with me," said Gyric, and ended, "I will not be in the way."

Finally I found words. "Gyric," I said and touched his hand, "you cannot go into such danger; you must not."

"There is no real danger," he said. "The Danes cannot have amassed warriors enough to take all of Mercia and try Wessex, too. Burgred has fled, not been slain on the battle field. He has been driven out by fear, or show of force; but not, I think, by war itself."

Neither Godwin nor I answered this, and Gyric went on, in a low voice, "I can ride as hard as you, Godwin, you know that is true. Worr will ride with me." His voice fell even more. "You will be unfettered."

Godwin did not answer this, but asked a question instead. "You say you do not think Burgred was driven out by war...What do you think the Danes are about?"

Gyric's answer was slow and thoughtful. "We cannot know for sure, but they are seeking more than gold. Think on Lindisse, and the other conquered Kingdoms. They wish to settle here, and live like us; this we now know. If I wished that, I would destroy as little as possible, for it would be my new crops and folk I would be destroying." He lifted his head and his words grew more certain. "Think on it: a Winter attack, swift and unexpected. Burgred was wholly unprepared and fled. Few men may have been lost on either side, just as the Danes hoped."

"And now -?" asked Godwin.

"The Danes might set up a Saxon of their choosing to rule in name only, as they did in Northumbria. That would offer some constancy and order to the rulership, while the jarls share out the Kingdom."

Godwin nodded his head, then spoke in answer. "Get ready to ride," he told his brother, and turned and left us.

I could not speak. The door closed behind Godwin, and I stood mute looking after it, clutching Gyric's hand. He took the measure of my silence. "I have some things together," he told me, and raised our clasped hands to a jumble of clothes on the bed. Two hours I had spent in the hall with Modwynn, gathering clothes and kit for Godwin, while unhelped by me my own husband did the same in our bower house. I fought to swallow my rising tears.

In answer I lifted his hand to my lips and kissed it. He reached his arm about my shoulders, and pressed his face close to mine.

"You must not fear for me, my love," he whispered. "There is no especial danger. And it is only my duty. If I were - whole I would go with a few men while Godwin commanded the burh." His voice dropped even lower. "But since he himself must go, I will ride with him."

Much tenderness was in his voice. I nodded my head, and tried to make steady my voice. "We have never been apart, even one night..." I began, and resolved not to speak of my many fears for him.

He exhaled a long breath, and said, "And if I were whole our nights together would have been few. I would be off with Ælfred even now." He turned away from me, but still kept my hand in his. "You do not think what my life should have been like."

I shook my head. "I cannot think of what should have been; I can only think of what is." I bit my lip against my coming tears, and the heartache forcing its way up through my narrowed throat.

I asked the question all women ask. "When will you return?"

"I cannot know. If Ælfred is at Witanceaster and we find him soon, and all is well with the borders, a month at least. If there is trouble -" his shoulders moved slightly, and he finished in a lowered voice. "Longer."

I was in the village at the croft of Berhtgit the herb woman, refreshing the supply of dried wort in the Simples chest. She was a cottar widow in mid-life, possessed of true wort-cunning, and her browned face and lined eyes betrayed the hours she had spent hunting favoured herbs by burning Sun and power-giving Moon. With her darkened skin and wisps of yellow hair she looked herself like some wind-blown wild plant. Of those who gathered herbs for healing, it was Berhtgit who had won Modwynn's respect, and she was skilled too as a birthing-woman, so that the village women revered her. Her drying shed was hung about with every sort of wild green that grew to give strength to the weak or ease to the pained.

A rider had come to us at the hall saying the men would return this day. Five weeks had passed, and the fields they had left in frost were now flecked with green shoots. I took small crocks of comfrey, and bone-seal, and talked with the woman of the warming Spring and the lambing sheep, and all the while hoped we would not need these herbs to treat any wound or illness amongst the returning men.

Ceric was with me, and as Berhtgit packed my basket he ran ahead to the croft gate. "Be ye ready for another?" she asked me as our eyes followed him. He was rising three, talking freely and running about everywhere.

"Another...?"

"Child, Lady; another babe." She turned to her work bench, unstoppered a clay pot. "Tis flower of henep, I had a fine crop. Take this in hot wine or honeyed ale, three nights running, at the half-Moon. You'll be got with babe again in two months, I warrant."

The dried blossoms in her hand fell to dust beneath her testing fingers. In truth I did not know why I was not with child again; Ceric had been weaned fully a year. But even the

116

sweet burden of a coming babe would be just that - another burden in an uncertain time. I had no answer for her, but Berhtgit was already folding the herb into a packet, so I took the herb just the same.

Ceric scampered down the road toward the burh walls, and I followed thinking of the welcome feast tonight. Perhaps their riding together had narrowed the breech between the brothers. Godwin had shown great patience to Gyric, I knew, and indulged him in ways which sometimes had troubled me. I knew the sea-swims and galloping of horses were one way in which Gyric felt less maimed. Yet I wondered if the sheer recklessness of his acts was what Gyric sought, as if he now held his life less dear. And Godwin was still young himself, hot-blooded, and denied the pleasures of wife and children; he had in him the thirst for daring which his innate judgement and new duties had not yet fully tempered.

I recalled again my first meeting with Godwin, how he had run boldly to where Gyric stood upon our return to Kilton, and how looking upon his face for the first time I felt my heart turn inside my breast, and a voice within tell me, This is Gyric, whole.

It was not just their faces; there was from the start the knowledge that Godwin was a link between Gyric and me, that we three were bound together. I had brought Gyric home to Kilton. Godwin had ridden to avenge his maiming, and told me when he left: I will finish what you began. I felt that Gyric knew me partly through Godwin's eyes, and knew that I had cherished Godwin's regard of me.

Before the setting of the Sun I stood on the broad oak threshold of the hall with Ceric and Modwynn awaiting the coming of the men. They had left in orderly file. Now they rode back with joyous cries and answered the welcoming calls of their families with grinning faces. Though Worr was nearby, it made me glad to see Godwin himself holding the reins of Gyric's horse. The two swung down as I ran to Gyric, Modwynn holding Ceric up out of harm's way. Gyric was flushed from Sun and the new colour in his face gave him a glow of health I had never seen. He kissed me, and I hung about his neck. Then Godwin slipped his arm about my waist and kissed me upon the cheek. His arm slid down my own and he held my wrist around the gold bracelet he had given me. He took hold of my hand, and the warmth of his palm and the strength in his grasp made me grateful that Ceric broke and ran to us. Godwin freed me, and I turned from him to my son and husband.

At table we drank mead with our meal, and gave thanks that no man nor horse was hurt upon the journey.

"Burgred lives," Godwin told us, "tho' he escaped Mercia with little save his life. He sheltered briefly with Ælfred and then rode for the shore, there to take ship to Frankland. He told Ælfred that Rome is his goal, and his sole hope to end his days as a monk."

"And of Æthelswith, his wife?" Modwynn asked.

"Safe, and with her brother Ælfred."

I feared to ask my question. "And what of Mercia? Be it fully overrun with Danes?"

Godwin shook his head. "A Saxon, Ceowulf, rules in name. The Danes have not gone far into the country. Having chased such a king as Burgred away, they have seized some of the large shires without much spilling of blood."

Gyric lifted his head and spoke. "Now they will turn their attention to richer lands. Burgred was old; his fighting days behind him. He acted for the best interests of his land in abandoning Mercia quietly and so sparing it. But Mercia's loss is a further blow to Wessex."

The news that Mercia had not been served as Lindisse and Anglia and Northumbria gave me quick comfort; but the fact that its fall would only fatten the war-chests of the Danes quelled any joy I could take.

We feasted on roast pig that night, and sweet mead swirled in our drinking cups. The scop plucked his painted harp and sang for us of valour; but we knew no bard sang such in Burgred's forsaken hall.

Chapter the Tenth: A Challenge, and A Promise

The Year 875

THE bounteous land of Kilton yielded much, from the first picking of the peas and cresses of early Spring to the robbing of the bee hives in the last days of Fall. Cottars worked rows where turnips and onions showed green leaves and rising shoulders from the Earth. Fields of wheat, barley and rye bent under the weight of their yellowing heads, and in the milking pens greedy lambs cried loudly for what was taken from their mothers for our cheeses. Sea and forest offered up their plenty, as gasping fish were dipped from weirs in the swift channel, and deer and boar and hare speared and snared from woodland and meadow. Life in village and burh went on as it had for half a hundred years, save for Godwin who with his thegns rode three months of each year to serve with the King in his fight against the Danes.

Each day was full and for me, mostly happy. I missed Ælfwyn in a way that only two women who have shared much together can, and I could not write to her. The bearing of a letter was too great a task and so I had no way to lessen this want of her. I wrote instead to Edgyth, a two days' ride away in Glastunburh, and in this way kept up the arts of quill and ink, for to craft a letter to her was a test of skill. Her letters far exceeded mine in style and grace but she welcomed them, and though she never wrote of matters of her heart I felt a friendship beyond our kinship through them.

Compared to Edgyth I had little learning and less wisdom, and this I knew. Amongst her tasks at Glastunburh was the rendering of letters from the Latin tongue into our own speech, and thinking of this labour made me recall how little of that Holy Tongue of the Prior's I had ever been able to write, and how much less remained to me. Beyond this certain of the women at Glastunburh were famed for their leech-craft, and Edgyth with a gift for healing others had proved a ready initiate. Under their guidance she mixed philtres of powerful herbs and sent them as gift to Ælfred that they might keep him from bleeding within from the distress he suffered.

I knew that Modwynn greatly missed Edgyth, and tho' I knew she valued me, felt that I was never the companion to her that Edgyth had been. Since her visit to Kilton, Godwin had ridden twice to see her, short visits of which he did not speak. Riding home without her said enough. I wondered if during his visits to her they were man and wife; and then forced myself away from this thought in shame.

Ceric was grown into a sturdy, active, laughing boy. He had learnt to be careful of his father and seemed at last to understand that when Gyric caused him some hurt it was because he could not see him. Once when Ceric was coming three and standing upon his father's lap he in play pulled at the linen wrap covering Gyric's wound. It came away, but I do not know if the howls of the boy were greater at what he saw or at the way his father pushed him from him.

At no given interval the horn upon the palisade ramparts would sound and we would know a rider, not of Kilton, was come. These messengers, usually haggard young men on spent horses, brought word from Ælfred or from other ealdormen about the movement of the Danes. The war lord Healfdene now ruled all of the Northumbrian kingdom, and in proof of his desire to make this land their home, shared out the land amongst his men. The war lord Guthrum, who was now called by his men a King, ranged with some lesser jarls throughout Anglia, casting out the Danes who had earlier conquered it, and built a mighty fortress there. The steady knowledge that the Danes were here for good grew, as did the fear that the troops of Wessex would not withstand a determined onslaught.

One Summer afternoon the horn again sounded, but this time instead of a solitary rider came four horsemen to the gate, one of whom bore a banner emblazoned with the golden dragon of the King. Ceric ran ahead of his father and me from the pleasure garden, and we joined the small group who stood with Godwin. The visitors were thegns, well armed and well horsed, and from their clean tunics and unlathered horses I saw they had ridden easily and well. Two of them were of high estate, and I recalled from being in Ælfred's very train. One of these was young, as young as Gyric or the King himself, and the other old, in his fourth decade to judge from his battle-creased face.

Godwin welcomed the men as I went ahead to the hall. Modwynn was already there and serving men were setting up the high table on its trestles. Basins were brought that the men might bathe their hands, and as it was not the King or an ealdorman amongst us, I instead of Modwynn took up the silver ewer and poured out ale into their cups. The first cup was drunk when the eldest thegn, Ulric, delivered his news.

"Ælfred sends you God's greeting and his own, and asks Godwin of Kilton if he will stand the cost of one of a fleet of ships the King is building to pursue the enemy at sea."

This was news indeed. Godwin and Wulfstan leant forward at hearing it, and even Gyric's lips parted slightly in surprise.

Ulric scanned the faces before him and went on. "The King has sent to you, Godwin, for he needs men reared on the coast and who can sail. Danes are ranging up and down the southern shore. The ships the King are building number ten, one to be yours."

I recalled all that Sidroc had told me without boast about his people, that the Danes could summon ships almost without number, and were seamen without peer. With their swift ships and greater numbers, ten ships of Wessex seemed to me like madness.

But Godwin's eyes glinted. "And the terms?"

"Forty men to row, twenty at a side. Armed with your own men, the cost is three thousand pieces of silver."

Three thousand silver pieces, more than half my entire fortune, not counting my jewels. But then Godwin must have many times this amount in the treasure room.

"Booty from any Danish ships you take will be wholly yours. And of those the King takes, he will grant you a tenth share."

Godwin looked about the table at the faces of the men who listened with him. The way he gripped the hilt of his seax told me his mind was made up, but what he asked was, "Gyric, what say you?"

Gyric was quick with his answer. "I say Yes."

"And you, Wulfstan?"

"I am for any way, by land or water, that brings their heathen necks within range of our steel."

Modwynn spoke now. She turned her gaze at Ulric and tho' her voice was calm it was firm. "And what is our good King's plan for this small fleet?"

"To harry in and out of the coves off the southern coast after the heathens."

"It is a dangerous shore, even for seamen who know its shoals. Which men of Kilton do not."

"Each ship will have a steersman from the port of Swanawic to guide her." Ulric turned to look at Godwin. "This is ready booty, and a chance to strike the Danes at sea, off-guard and unawares."

"You will ride back with the silver on the morrow," Godwin answered.

Within a week Godwin was gone too, tho' Modwynn was not happy with this. It was not the haste in which he had agreed, nor the great cost in men and silver of such a pledge. Godwin was the sworn man of the King, and must answer such a call. What troubled Modwynn, and me as well, was the venture itself, at sea, in untried ships.

The morning they rode off Godwin clasped me about the waist in farewell, and circled his hand around the gold upon my wrist. "I will bring you a necklet to match," he laughed, but in reply I said, "Only come back to us."

We did not know how long Godwin might be gone, as none could guess how soon the King's ships would find favourable winds, nor when or if they might encounter Danish raiders coasting the shore. High Summer and its fire passed by us, and threshing had begun when a rider came to warn us that Godwin and his men were near. This thegn said little, save all was well, and that but four men had been lost.

124

Wulfstan and Gyric questioned him more, but Modwynn and I were too busy in the kitchen yard ordering the welcome feast for the morrow to learn much.

The Sun was casting long shadows by the time they rode in the next day, Godwin alone at the head of his thegns. In his battle gear he filled one with awe; his ring tunic blackened so no light shone from it, his baldric and belt from which sword and seax hung studded with iron bosses. But it was easy to see that Godwin's hope of ready booty had not been met. The men were glad to be home, and glad too for the fine feast awaiting them, but there were no hooting cries of joy as men showed off the treasure they had won, for they had won none. Godwin told us in words simple and few that they had sighted a score of Danish ships, to no avail.

"We could not catch them let alone force a fight. They would spot us and flee in their long-boats so fast it seemed they had their own wind. At last Fate turned and we surprised a few as a fog was dropping. We tried to beat them into shore but could not; they slipped through us tho' our archers fired a sleet of arrows through the mist. One only we caught, surrounded it, and when it found itself trapped they rowed full bore and rammed one of the King's ships. I came up alongside and we fought before Ælfred called for their surrender. Our ships were high-sided, our fighting platform well above theirs, and in this alone we had the advantage. The King spared their lives and shared out to me my share of the plunder, but save their arms there was little aboard."

So there were no prideful tales nor boasting talk, and the men drank the deeper for it, tho' four of their places now sat empty.

The next day I saw Godwin walk alone into the great stable. I followed him in, and found him checking on his grey horse which had been slightly lamed on the ride home. I did not like to be alone with Godwin in this way, but would ask that which I could not in front of Gyric.

He had his hands upon the front fetlock of his gelding as I walked up to him.

"He is better, is he not?" I asked.

He nodded. "To lose such a one as he is for so little gain would be hard indeed."

I nodded, and then nerved myself and spoke. "What manner of Danes were they?"

He shrugged. "Those we captured spoke no tongue save their own. I think their camp was in Frankland." Now he stood up and looked at me closely. "Why? Do you fear that Sidroc was amongst their number?"

I closed my eyes a moment in silent protest. I had been foolish to think he would not read my thought, and more foolish still to think he would not be vexed by it.

"I know he is a friend to you," he said, and could not hide the edge in his voice. I looked up at him, and he went on. "I wondered what more he had been. When Sidroc came here, that Harvest, I saw how his eye hungered for you. I knew, before Gyric ever told me, that he wanted you. His boldness in so looking at you in my own hall angered me, and angered me the more that my own brother, due to Danish treachery, could not see it." I was staring at him now, my eyes burning, wondering if he found me guilty, but he himself looked away as he spoke again. "I could have killed him for the way he looked at you."

Now he faced me, his words hard and cold. "Why do you care for him?"

I cast about for an answer. "He is wed to a woman whom I am pledged to as a sister."

His eyes held fast to my face. "Yes. He wed her - wanting you."

"Why do you taunt me?"

"Because I want you too."

I turned from him as two stablemen came through the open doors.

I was wakeful in the dragon bed, and felt that dawn must be near. Gyric was asleep at my side, one arm thrown over his head. I heard from the pleasure garden a thud, and a cracking sound, such as is made by rent wood. There was a scraping on the gravel path. I glanced at the door. It was too early for Hrede to come, but I slipped from bed and pulled on a shift.

I opened our unbolted door. Standing outside in the dimness was one of the serving men from the hall. His eyes were starting in his head, and a trickle of blood dripped from his mouth. I do not think he saw me tho' he stood inches from me. Protruding from his breast-bone was the tip of a spear head. He reached for the open door, grasped it with one hand. Still speechless, he crumpled into the room at my feet, an issue of blood vomiting from his mouth over my shift. The spear in his back shuddered forward as he fell. I watched him not knowing if the scream I heard came from my own throat.

Gyric was yelling, screaming my name. I turned to see him hurtle from bed, only to knock his spear away from his reaching hand. He dropped to the floor, sweeping his arms before him, and caught it up. He whirled towards me.

"Ceridwen! Where, where?" he yelled, unwilling to move lest he hurt me.

"A kitchen man is dead in our doorway, with a spear in him," I choked out.

He crossed to me, pressed his spear in my hands, knelt down. He heaved the body fully into the room, shut and bolted the door.

Ceric had begun crying from his alcove and now ran out to me. His terror grew as he saw my blood-spattered shift, and he shrieked wildly.

"Ceric! Is he all right?" cried Gyric.

"He sees the blood on my shift."

Gyric reached out to me, open-mouthed.

"Blood from the man," I told him. "I am not hurt."

We clung together, Ceric between us, clutching my loosened hair and naked arms.

"Get my seax," Gyric ordered.

With the sobbing Ceric clinging to my neck I fumbled in the chest where it lay. Mine was next it, and I pulled it out too.

Gyric stood, barefoot in a pool of blood, his ear pressed to our door. He buckled on the seax belt.

"Get into the alcove with Ceric. Cover yourself well with blankets. Do not make any sound."

"No," I said. "We are staying here, with you. I have my seax."

"Do as I say."

"I will die fighting, like you."

"Shhh." He head was to the door again. "There are men running, not ours or they would be yelling." He turned to me. "If I sound the alarm, they will likely come here to kill me. If you are hiding with Ceric they might not discover you."

Gyric willingly offered his life to alert the rest of the keep. I knew this, knew the justice in it, that the life of one pledged man, be he even the brother of the lord, was a small price to pay in the attempt to preserve the lives of many more. I stood light-headed and trembling, the sickly warm smell of blood from the slain man all about us, my shift wet through from it, legs sticky.

I did not move. From outside we heard a man yell out in awesome war-cry, then whistles and shouts.

"They are roused," said Gyric.

Now we heard many men running through the pleasure garden. From somewhere a horn sounded. There were more whistles, and the sound of things being hurtled down the cliff side. There were yells and curses, and I heard the oaths sworn by the Danes. Now for the first time was heard metal upon metal as swords and axes struck.

Something heavy shuddered against the bower house. Now we could hear the thegns of Kilton calling out encouragement, one to the other, and hurling taunts at their foes.

129

Gyric slid back the bolt. "I am going out," he told me. "Hide in the alcove."

I flung myself against the door. "You will be killed! Battle is joined, there is nothing you can do!"

Outside a man called Godwin's name, whether in tribute or distress I could not tell, but hearing it, Godwin's name too escaped my lips.

Gyric's shoulders' slumped. He pushed me and the bawling Ceric away, and with face turned from us reached for the door. He did not open it tho', but stood again listening.

The clash of metal had ended. All the voices were those of Kilton.

Someone ran to our door and stopped outside it. "Open up," Godwin yelled.

The door swung back at Gyric's pull. Godwin stood before us in the grey light, clad in leggings and tunic, barefoot, his helmet pulled over his sleep-tousled hair. In one hand he bore his spear, in the other his lowered shield. Our threshold was slick with blood.

Godwin looked at my blood-streaked shift.

"You have not been - hurt," he asked. He did not take his eyes from my bloodied shift.

"The blood is a serving man's. He came to the door," I stammered. There was a spear stuck in our wall at an angle.

Gyric still gripped his seax in his hand. "We are none of us hurt," he said. "Who was it?"

"Small band of Danes, seeking food. They came by boat and climbed the cliff in the dark They raided the kitchen yard, killed three" - he looked at our blood-slicked floor - "four. They had no hunger for fighting tho', and are gone."

The pleasure garden was now full of thegns, clothes askew, but all with weapons in hand. From the hall door a few women peered out, clutching themselves.

"We killed two," Godwin went on. "The rest got off."

On the gravel path outside our door was a broken sack from which grain spilled.

"They did not get much," Godwin said, but in truth it felt a great deal had been lost.

By the time the Sun was high all Kilton knew of the raiding party. The dead from the kitchen were buried, but not the Danes. Godwin had their bodies stripped and thrown down the cliff face to the sea rocks below. Those thegns who had fought now laughed about it, and complained that no booty had been won. Godwin jested with his men, but no swaggering words could conceal his regret at this attack.

He had the landing stage hauled up at once, and later scolded me, loudly and in front of Gyric and Modwynn, for not bolting our door and for opening it to a strange sound.

"Anything could have happened. They could have carried you off."

Gyric spoke for me, impatience in his words. "Leave her alone. She has been through enough. And they would have had to kill me to get to her, or Ceric. As slight a feat as you hold that to be."

Godwin snapped. "Do not push me, Gyric," he answered, but swallowed his rising anger. "You did right to stay in the bower house and listen."

"I did nothing, just what I always do," said Gyric.

"You wanted to go out and fight, and I stopped you," I protested.

Godwin regarded his brother standing before him, gripping his spear with white knuckles. "You are no good to Kilton dead, Gyric."

"I am not much good to anyone live, either," he answered.

"Enough, both of you," said Modwynn. "Four of our staff are dead. Gyric, may God forgive you for slighting His gift of life." She turned to Godwin, saying naught save with her eyes, searching and angry.

The next morn I carried our two small jewel caskets from the bower house to the treasure room. There they were lowered into the hiding places beneath the floor stones, where lay my five thousand pieces of silver, amongst all the other coins and jewels of the family of Kilton. I kept in the bower house only a few brooches, including the silver and emerald one Ælfwyn had given me on the long-ago morning of her hand-fasting to Yrling. Circling my wrist was the heavy bracelet of braided gold which Godwin had placed there, and which I never took off. About my finger was the carved gold ring set with the emerald stone that Gyric had given me as my morning-present. These jewels I wore each day were large and bright and ready targets for a raider's eye, but if they were to be wrenched off of me I was soon to die anyway, and so chose to die wearing them.

Over the next few weeks the whole burh was in a tumult of building. A long house was raised near the great stable, such as might shelter the bulk of the village at night in simple cots. Rails were split and readied to form new pens for additional beasts. We brewed as much ale as we could, carrying cask after cask into the new store houses, laying it deep in the cool Earth so it would not sour. The kitchen yard was enlarged, and its new fence was fast by that of the pleasure garden. But as no more Danes appeared, the folk of the village stayed on in their own crofts.

The shouts of workman and the sounds of sawing and hammering took hold of the yard from daybreak to dusk. The approach of each rider to the keep walls was regarded with an eagerness bordering on fear. The air of watchfulness made us all, I think, tense and wary.

One noontide I wove alone at my small linen loom in the treasure room. A series of blasts from the sentry horn had earlier told me of a coming messenger, but I had not left my work to see who it was. Now Godwin walked in. He carried a hide travel pack and his sword-baldric, and spoke to me as he opened a chest near my loom.

"I am going to Ælfred. He has gathered the Witan around him for counsel." He stuffed a handful of cloth into his pack.

"Leaving Kilton? But it is not your time to go."

"The Dane Sidroc has come to Ælfred," he told me. "I will go to Witanceaster to bargain with him."

I hoped my voice did not show my startle. "He is seeking peace?"

He gave a snort. "He is seeking silver. Thousands of pounds of it, to leave Wessex alone. But paying Sidroc does nothing but increase our risk from Healfdene or Guthrum or some other marauding Dane."

"And because you...know Sidroc, you might be useful in bargaining with him?"

"Know him? No man can know a Dane. There is no truth in them, nothing to be known but their own heathen treachery." I must have flinched at this, for his eyes latched onto me. "They are all one to me," he tried. "I should have turned on the field at Cirenceaster and killed him then."

"What if you yourself had fallen?" I tried back. "Godwulf was already old. You would have left Kilton lord-less."

"You are wrong, Ceridwen." My name fell like an oath from his lips. "No man could have killed me on that day."

There was no answer to this truth; Sidroc had told me Godwin had fought with berserk fury. I wished he would go and turned back to my loom.

He would not relent. "He has some claim on you. What is it?"

I could scarce breathe. "I have not loved any man, none but Gyric..."

He looked straight at me and then nodded. "This I believe." His green-gold eyes were bright as metal, and they did not move from my face. "But there is something in you, Ceridwen, - a challenge. There is a challenge in you, and...a promise." His eyes were fixed upon me, and I could scarce stand under their glare. He shook his head, and his voice dropped low. "I am no better than a renegade Dane, far worse, for you are under my protection in my own hall."

"I am wed to your own brother," I managed to choke out.

Now he turned on me, almost with violence. "Why did Gyric get you?" he demanded. "Is God just making good on his blindness? Are you his great reward for his suffering? Does he even know what he has in you? Or in the son you gave to him your first year together?"

"Godwin, stop it," I begged, tears flooding from my eyes. "He loves me, truly, he does. But..."

I could not finish; I did not know the end of my thought, nor what words could explain or excuse what I could not wholly understand. I forced myself to speak, tho' my voice be but a whisper. "I am blameless, I think, in every dealing with Sidroc, save for that which I did to escape Four Stones. I could not help his love for me. If I have been less than blameless in my dealings with you, I ask your pardon. But do not blame me for your own desire."

He drew back an instant, as if struck; then reached out and grasped my gold-encircled wrist. "It is I who should be asking your pardon. But I do not. I do not wish to be forgiven my desire, for I will not give it up. At times it is all I have to live for."

With this he picked up his baldric and pack and left.

The following day a wardman who had ridden hard from a forest tower came to the hall.

"There is a whole column of folk, coming with waggons and on foot, heading our way. They are from Mercia."

"Any armed?" asked Gyric.

"Those who have spears carry them, but there are no thegns amongst them save those sent by Ælfred to escort them."

"Then we are to give them shelter, by the King's wishes," said Gyric. "Wulfstan, send men to go and meet them."

"Begging your pardon sir, a few waggons might be sent as well. Some of the folk are all done in, and can scarce walk."

So it had begun. Those who had fled Mercia were now reaching Wessex, seeking refuge, and Ælfred had parcelled them out to each burh to shelter.

Modwynn spoke next, and was already rising. "They will be hungry, and need rest. We will feed them here; they can shelter in the long house."

I knew I should go with her to alert the kitchen, to help with the gathering of linens, and all the other needful tasks before us, but instead I said, "Gyric, I would like to ride out to meet these folk."

I caught Modwynn's eye as I spoke thus, and she paused. "Of course," she said, all understanding my desire, "they are from Mercia."

Gyric sat quietly. I could not think that he would like to join me, but I asked him just the same.

"No," he said, "go on. Worr will ride with you."

The Sun was high in the sky when the wardman had come to us. By the time Worr and I could see the coming folk, the Sun was well along its westward travels. I was not good company for Worr, and answered his few remarks with short phrases and with less thought. The knowledge that I could be riding towards one who had word of my mother, or even the woman herself, kept circling my mind. Would I be glad to see her, I wondered, and she glad to once again regard me? I wanted her to be well, to be safe, but to be here at Kilton...? I began to fear I would be told our shire had been overrun, and she dead or taken captive; and then feared almost as much that she might be at the tail of this ragged column of fleeing folk, kept apart by her strange ways and whore's repute. I recalled her flashing eye and proud manner, the feyness of her dress and speech, the rich trophies of jewels she owned. How could I welcome her as my mother into such a hall as Kilton, where such a woman as Modwynn ruled?

The two thegns who rode at the head of the column reined in as we approached them, and Worr spoke to them as I rode on, walking my mare on the edge of the road and looking down upon those who had fled. There were four score at least, a huge number to provide for, and many of them were old or very young. Most looked from a cottar's estate, save the few men who bore spears. These were ceorls and their families, left lordless by the deaths of their chiefs. All were dust covered, weary with long walking, and dull with the sorrow of having left their homes and the bulk of their few possessions behind.

"Any from the River Dee?" I called as I passed the first group. They looked up at me, wonderingly, and a man answered, "None here, Lady," as he dipped his head.

I went on, pity moving in my breast at the sight and sound of crying children and young mothers with no rest to give them. "Any from the River Dee?" I asked as I moved, and was met with shaken heads. All had stopped moving now, Worr must have told them to wait whilst the waggons from Kilton came to meet them.

"Any from the River Dee?" I asked, fearing and hoping at the same time. I had reached the end of the ragged row. "You will have rest soon, and food too, at the hall," I said to those I was passing. Some reached their hands up to salute me, but I turned from their thanks. I returned to Worr and the thegns, and one of them said to me, "You seek news of Mercia, Lady?"

"Yes, of the shire of Dee. My home shire," I added as if recalling this myself.

The man was older, battle wise, and as he looked upon me his creased eyes squinted against the lowering Sun. "We have some news. I fear it is not good."

"Then it has been destroyed by the Danes," I said for him.

"No, Lady. Overrun by the Welsh."

I turned my mare away. By the Welsh, I thought. And my mother is herself of the Welsh. Perchance she was not slain; perchance it was even her own tribe who were the victors. I uttered a prayer to my namesake that she who named me as hers still lived, and in peace.

Before the month had turned the folk from Mercia had been more or less settled on new-made crofts beyond the village. Modwynn and Wulfstan were careful not to impinge on any lands that the folk of Kilton had from long usage considered as their own, but instead to settle the newcomers upon pasture lands owned by Modwynn. I had seen myself the faces of our Kilton folk as they lined the road to watch the Mercians file by. It was easy to read the seeds of resentment against these strangers now to be thrust amongst them.

"In time of coming need it is hard to be open-handed, if you fear lack yourself," Modwynn told me as we rode back from visiting the new settlement. It was not a simple task for the Mercians to be accepted into the life of Kilton, and to confound things they were themselves from various shires and differing backgrounds and ways. Modwynn had tried to ease this by setting all to needful tasks, "For idleness grows isolate."

Isolate. I nodded my head. This was what Gyric had become, truly; alone and unto himself, entering less and less into the life of the burh or even of the hall. With Godwin gone he had scarce been part of the daily actions or decisions to be made, leaving more and more to Wulfstan and Modwynn. He had not ridden out to address the Mercians in those first few days, and left to me to make the welcome that he ought to, and to receive from them the thanks and homage that should be his.

"I want Godwin back," I said suddenly.

Modwynn turned to me, and some little surprise was in her face at the energy of my words. "So do we all, Ceridwen." She considered a moment. "Before he left I asked him to stop at Glastunburh and see Edgyth on his way home."

"Then she will return with him, perchance."

"Perchance. Her coming home would be a boon. To all of us, I think."

I nodded my head, but said no more.

Chapter the Eleventh: Like Coinage, Spent

The Year 877

BUT Godwin came from Witanceaster alone. I saw Modwynn's face fall as he rode in one morning, alone save the men he had taken with him. When he was unpacked we gathered in the quiet of the treasure room. He called Wulfstan in as well, and Godwin stood before us, walking back and forth and turning often to scan our faces.

"Sidroc has grown rich, both in silver and in men. He says he commands 400 warriors. Half that is a fearsome force." We were all silent, but I felt my eyes grow large at hearing how quickly Sidroc's boast of an army had come to pass.

"He came before Ælfred, and the whole of the Witan, with the boldness that surety gives. He asked for 10,000 pounds of silver, and hostages of twenty of Ælfred's best men."

This last demand was hard indeed to hear, and Gyric lowered his head for a moment.

"Would I could be one," Wulfstan said, his lamed leg before him, "and repay him double for what he wreaked upon me."

I did not dare to speak, for fear of further angering Godwin or sorrowing Gyric. Wulfstan mastered himself and asked, "And what does the filthy heathen offer in return? Naught but his turning tail and fleeing back to his stolen keep?"

"He does offer more. Protection."

"The Danes to protect Saxons!? I would sooner send my hawks to guard the chicks in the fowl house!"

"He claims he will not attack Wessex, and will actively fight with Ælfred's men to keep other Danes from attacking."

"You mean, fight as a mercenary army against the other heathen hordes?" Wulfstan would not believe it.

Words escaped my lips. "So he would...join with us?"

All looked at me, and Godwin answered, "Join with us? He would take our treasure all right, and anything else he laid his eyes upon he wanted, and he may or may not keep his pledge, but he would never be 'joined with' we Saxons."

His words were very hot, and Modwynn spoke with calmness to temper them.

"Godwin," she said quietly. "And how did Ælfred and the Witan decide this matter?"

"It is not decided. Nor do I think it will be. Firstly, there is not 10,000 pounds of silver left in all the kingdom."

This quantity of treasure was beyond my ken. I had seen caskets of coins and hack-silver weighing perhaps forty or fifty pounds, but could not imagine 10,000.

"Do you mean that once there was that much?" I hazarded to ask.

"Far more," he told me. "Ælfred, his brothers, and their father before them have paid over 25,000 pounds to the Danes already."

Wulfstan spoke from his long memory, and spoke in heat. "And what have we to show for it? Wessex now stands

141

alone against the heathens, all six Kingdoms have fallen, save us."

Gyric stood up, gripping his spear shaft. "Sidroc came before the Witan alone, and made his offer?"

Godwin turned to face him. "Alone. He rode with a heavily armed band, but left them beyond the city gate. He stood before us alone."

"You could have seized him then and there," said Gyric.

"We could have. But we did not. You know there is to be no violence in the Witan hall. Not only would we not break the avowed Peace of the Witan in doing so, but Ælfred now thinks Sidroc may be the best of a bad lot. Killing him serves no purpose."

"Ælfred knows nothing of Sidroc; that is why he sent for you," answered Gyric. "You were the one to counsel him thus."

Gyric did not wait for his brother's answer. He groped his way to the door and was gone.

The next afternoon I was crossing the pleasure garden to the bower house to lay Ceric down for his nap. Tho' he had been nodding in the hall he did not want to go, and once into the garden pulled from my hand and called out, "Godwin!" His uncle was standing near the edge of the sea cliff, looking across the uneasy waters as they foamed and tossed. The wind was rising and a few large rain drops spattered upon the gravel walks.

Godwin picked him up and swung him through the air as Ceric loved. As I watched Gyric came to the door of the bower house and stood there, listening to his son's whooping cries of joy. He could not play thus with his own boy for fear of hurt, and knew full well the affection that Ceric bore for his uncle.

I said, "Enough now, Ceric. You must lie down now." The boy protested, and I saw Gyric turn and withdraw inside the bower house.

"Now, Ceric. Stop it, Godwin," I said, more sternly than I meant. Godwin put him down at once, and Ceric, dizzy, wobbled his way with me to the bower house door. When I came out Godwin was gone. I crossed to the open hall door and shut it behind me against the damp. Godwin was just inside, and stopped me in the dim hall passage.

"You should not play thus with Ceric," I blurted out.

"Why?" he asked, surprised. A moment passed. "Because of Gyric? He does not play with Chirp himself. If he cannot enjoy him, I will."

"He does play with Ceric, you know he does. It is just he cannot play as you do." I did not want to be angry at Godwin, and slowed my words. "It is not fair to say that about Gyric."

"Fair," he repeated, trying the word. I turned to leave, but he spoke again. "A few days past High Summer I will go. Ælfred has called up the fyrd. The massed armies of Guthrum are heading for Exanceaster. We will fight them there."

I could not keep my alarm from my words. "Then it is starting?"

He nodded his head once. "Or it is ending. I do not expect to come back."

I had never heard a warrior speak this way. I had heard them full of ale, boasting to their fellows of the prowess they would show upon the nearing field of battle; I had heard them, with clasped hands and heated eyes, swear oaths of fealty to their lords; I had heard them say nothing and only laugh the night before they faced death. Never had I heard an omen so evil as the words which Godwin had just quietly uttered.

"You must not say that. You must never say that," I urged, and could just stop myself from grasping his arm. He did not reply, and looked at me as if he had not heard my words. I did not know what to say and began to go.

"Wait. I have wanted to see you. I have said things to you..." His voice trailed to nothing. "Words once spoken can never be reclaimed. They are like coinage, spent."

It was too dim to read his eyes clearly. I knew I should speak, and yet did not.

He lifted his hand slightly. His voice was low, and even tender. "I meant no insult, in telling you of my desire for you."

Insult. To be desired by Godwin, by such a man as he...Insult was no part of all the things I felt. Shock, fear, honour, disbelief - all of these I had lived with since he had revealed his desire to me, and all grew steadily in my breast as I grappled with my own feelings for him. I knew I was sister to him no longer, nor perhaps had ever been. Yet he was kin to me, and treachery unspeakable it was to covet your brother's wife...and a soul-death to Christians to act on it.

A few rain drops had wetted my skin. Now I felt bone-cold, and shivered where I stood.

"You do not know what you are saying," I whispered. I gathered my skirt in my hands so I would not trip in the darkness about us. "I will not listen..."

He caught at my hand. "You will, Ceridwen, if it is the only thing you give me. You will listen."

I had only words to defend me. "Why did you not bring Edgyth back with you?" I demanded.

"Edgyth cannot give me what I want," he answered, and said this so quietly that I could scarce make out his words. He pressed me to him, but so gently that the arms that lay across my back were like wings. His lips were by my ear as he murmured.

"I do not want you to say anything, just hear me. I am a cursed man, Ceridwen. I had a son once, on a girl from Kilton. I was too stupid to look after her, to bring her to the hall. The boy died, and the girl too. A few years later my father brought me Edgyth. She was rich and clever, could make me laugh. Some day I would be Ealdorman here. I thought she would be a worthy successor to Modwynn. And she was, in all ways but one. She bled away her youth, and nearly her life, attempting to bear our child."

Pity moved within me as he murmured this, and the arms about me tightened. "I am cursed, and this curse extends to Edgyth. She lost so many babes...I could not bear to share a bed with her anymore, for fear she would surely die with the next one. But she would beg me, beg me, wanting so much to have what once I had thrown away."

He pulled his face from mine, and raised it to the blackness of the ceiling. "I did not want to be the death of two women."

I knew these things of Godwin, each one of them, and yet hearing them afresh from his lips I felt how green was this wound within him. Nothing had healed it, his sorrow had bred only despair.

There were noises now in the hall beyond us, the sounds of serving men dragging the trestles from along the walls. At any moment one of them might enter the passageway where we stood, and find the Ealdorman of Kilton with his arms about his brother's wife. I forced myself to think of these things, and to think of myself in this way.

I must speak; I had borne witness as Godwin had asked, but now the danger of being in his arms was surpassed by the greater danger of discovery.

"Godwin," I breathed. "You must let me go."

"I cannot let you go," he answered, but he let fall his arms around me just the same.

I groped my way outside and nearly ran into Gyric, heading to the hall in the gathering rain.

No night had it been so hard to sit at table as it was that night. I sat thigh to thigh with Gyric, sharing food from the same silver plate, when a few feet away Godwin ate from his solitary salver. I could not look his way, and feared even raising my face lest my cheek flame. None of us had much to say. Even Modwynn between us was more thoughtful than usual. Ceric sat next her at nearly every meal, but tonight I had Hrede feed him in the bower house. I did not want to see Godwin and Ceric together just then.

The quiet at our own table made the noise of the hall seem the greater. All of Godwin's men, their wives, and older children were gathered, much as any night. Their tables rang with talk and laughter, and with the endless clatter of copper and bronze, and thud of pottery and wood.

Dunnere the priest sat with us, as did Wulfstan and a handful of favoured thegns. Since Godwulf's death Dunnere was not so high regarded as he once was, for he had been Modwynn's choice, and as she was not truly Lady of Kilton, but served such only until Edgyth might return, there was some little fall in his rank. Then too Godwin was not as patient with him as Godwulf had been, and went to the little stone church even less than Gyric and I.

The lull tonight prompted him to speak. "My lord, with the growth of the village there is a pressing need for a church to serve it. My gathering the faithful at the preaching cross on the Sabbath sufficed when I first came to Kilton, but with births and the keeping of festivals, it would be more seemly to have a church built there."

"We cannot spare the seasoned timber," answered Godwin, scarcely looking up.

"Spare the timber? With the quantity lying, sawn and ready to use, all about the yard?" I could not tell if Dunnere truly knew surprise, or feigned it.

Wulfstan, hearing this, spoke himself. "Each board is marked for its purpose. There is not one too many for all that will be needed."

"There can be nothing more needful than a church," replied Dunnere. "And the new Mercians, their faith is perhaps...not as strong as we would have it. A church is made more needful by their waverings."

I did not look to see if Dunnere's dark eyes darted to me as he said this. Godwin's next words ended such talk, both by the flatness of his voice and the finality of his words.

"Any church built in the village will likely soon be burnt by Danes, along with every hut and corn-fold."

Chapter the Twelfth: Kindled Fire

HIGH Summer's Day was now upon us, and with it the burning of the need-fire kindled by all the folk of Kilton. I again, as in years past, sewed a pennon for the withy-work man to bear in the flames, but now as I stitched the red rays of the Sun they looked like rivulets of blood dripping down upon our good fields. On High Summer morn Modwynn told me that she too would ride out to the fire with Ceric so that he might for the first time see the festival. He now slept with Modwynn and Hrede each night in the treasure room, for this was the strongest room within the hall, the fortress within the fortress, and as sole issue of the sons of the mighty Godwulf it was meet that the boy's slumber be guarded with the gold and silver won in the old warrior's life.

I knew Gyric would not ride out with us; not since our first High Summer at Kilton had he done so. This year I did not wish to go myself, to watch something of beauty be burnt, tho' it be its Fate. Yet in late morning I left a silent Gyric with a kiss and walked to the stable yard. Ceric and Modwynn sat together in a low waggon drawn by a yoke of oxen, my boy crowing with eagerness so that I smiled despite my mood. Godwin stood holding the reins of my bay mare. He barely greeted me, just took the pennon from my hands and helped me mount my mare. A stableman brought his horse, a prancing and quarrelsome chestnut stallion, not the steady grey gelding he usually rode with me. As soon as he was mounted the chestnut reached forward and tried to nip my mare on the neck, the first of the forays a rutting stallion tries. Godwin slapped his horse's poll with the rein ends, and we turned and filed out of the emptying yard.

149

The day was warm and close, the Sun all obscured in a haze of bluish-yellow. No rain had fallen for a fortnight, and the pounded clay road rose in clouds of ruddy dust around our horses' hooves. The fields of wheat were yellowing, and the bearded barley hung heavy on its thickened stalks. We rode in silence broken only by Godwin as he curbed the tossing head of his horse with harsh words.

The mown field which held the fire pile was already crawling with folk. We left Ceric and Modwynn in their waggon at the field's edge by the ale-carts. Two village men offered to hold our horses, and we slipped into the gathering crowd. I followed Godwin through the throngs, and wordlessly watched as he spiked the pennon pole fast through the body of the withy-work man. The figure was hoisted upon the fire pile, the whole set alit by flaming torches made puny in the daylight. The dance begun, one youth choosing a maid, and her a youth, and then another, a whole coil of the young men and girls of Kilton weaving and spiralling about the base of the crackling fire. I stood still near Godwin. A slight breeze fanned the fire's breath away from us, nor were we beaten back by the growing line of dancers. We found ourselves encircled by them, cut off from the rest of the crowd, the faces of the dancing youths eager and shining. One boy swooped near me, his empty hand the last link in a growing chain, and I let myself be carried off by his grasping fingers. I caught up the hand of a girl, and she took the hand of an older man, and each link was forged one upon the other. We turned outward, circled the whole base of the now crackling fire. I did not see Godwin, nor did I wish to; I wanted only to be pulled along by this hundred legged serpent.

We circled, dipped, wove in endless spiral, the fire's glow hot upon my cheek. I raised my eyes to see my Sun pennon crimple, then burst into devouring flame. Water ran from my eyes, my gown stuck to my back, I could not breathe, I could not stop. Cries of victory went up, the withy-man toppled and died. We would once again live. We dancers stopped, our slipping hands slick with sweat. I stood barely on my feet on the far side of the fire pile, with the halls of Kilton beyond shimmering through the waves of rising heat.

Then Godwin was before me, panting and with glowing eyes. All around us young people, giddy with heat and dancing, lay sprawled in the trampled barley. Godwin walked a few paces away. There was no clump of trees, no shelter of any kind, but we were out of earshot. He stood a full arms-length from me, and did not extend his hand, just stared at me with his golden-green eyes.

"Say that you want me," he whispered.

I stood still, spoke not, and he too moved not. "I will not touch you," he assured me.

"You have already touched me," I told him, and let him see my eyes wet with tears. "You have touched my heart, so that it will never be the same."

He took a small step towards me, but did not close the space. His voice was low and urgent. "I am cursed, and now cursed again to so want you. I have fought against it, Ceridwen, all these years, from the first time you stood outside our walls. Almost from the first hour I beheld your face. I have never known longing like this. God knows I have fought it." He shook his head. "Now I do not care. About the law, about the judgement of God against me. I would gladly burn in Hell for eternity if you could bear my babe."

Now he had said it, but paired it with the terrible suffering such desire had brought him.

"Hush," I told him. "Do not say that. You would never deserve such punishment, nor is there any such place. Hel is the Lady of the Underworld, a place of shades, not fire."

151

"I would believe that if I could."

"I do believe it. This desire is unlawful, but it is not unnatural."

His words were low, insistent. "Say that you want me. Say it."

I could not lie. I closed my eyes, then opened them to a greater darkness. "I want you, Godwin."

He breathed out. Something like a smile flickered in his face and was gone.

"I will die soon, Ceridwen, I know it. I feel it. And die without issue. Ceridwen...I do not want to die without this hope..."

I fought the rising lump in my throat. "What good is a child you can never acknowledge?"

He near whispered his answer. "I will die knowing this part of me lives on. And that I had you, for a short time."

A blue cloud of smoke curled near us, bringing with it the scent of destruction. I thought of the dark stain on my threshold, unmoved by scrubbing with water or sand. My words sounded hollow in the chary haze. "The war will be here soon. Like as much, all of us will die."

"Not you! You will live, you must live."

These were the same words I had once uttered to him, the eve of his riding to avenge Gyric. More than all I wished him life; now more than all he wished new life for me. I looked into the haze of the hot sky. I knew the Moon was rising half.

I spoke the awe-full word.

"Yes," I said, and trembled as I spoke it. His hand bridged the distance to mine, but my next words stopped him. "But we must go to Gyric, now, this moment, and tell him."

Nothing I could have said would have stunned him more; his face showed it. "We must go to Gyric now," I demanded, "and tell him."

A man with a hand-cart came bumping across the field to us, the ale within sloshing over the rim of the barrel. He took a crockery bowl from a pile of them, dipped it brimful, handed it to his lord with a grin. Godwin took it up, drank deep, passed it to me. I too drank deep, and then Godwin, as does a bridegroom, drank again, draining it. Without taking his eyes from me he smote the bowl over his raised knee, and threw the broken pieces to the ground. We turned and walked through the field to our horses.

I did not see Modwynn's waggon, perchance she had already taken Ceric back to the hall. We rode on at a canter, against the stream of laughing folk drinking upon the road. Once inside the walls we made straight to the pleasure garden. It was empty, but the door to our bower house was open. We walked in and found Gyric sitting at the table. He took his spear in hand and rose. "Ceridwen?" he asked.

"Yes, it is me, and Godwin is with me."

He turned a little away from us in response. The closest I had ever seen to fear was now on Godwin's face. He stared at me, wonderingly, but I looked at Gyric's lowered face. My words tumbled out, I could not stay them.

"Godwin wishes to bed me in hopes I might bear his child. I told him I would do so only if you knew."

Gyric jolted; looked as if he had been slapped. He was silent, but his mouth moved, and then his shoulders began to shake. He turned his back to us. "You mean - you are not already lovers?" was what he asked us.

"Lovers?" I almost choked on the word. My eyes swam. So great was grown the gulf between us that Gyric found us guilty before the fact.

At last Godwin spoke, and with resolve. "I have never even kissed her, I give you my oath." He glanced at me. "And she has in no wise wronged you."

A long moment passed before Gyric turned back to us. "I could in law slay you this moment," he told us in truth. His voice caught as he spoke. "But I cannot. I love you both. Tho' it be damnation for all of us, I will not say no."

He let fall his spear behind him. He put his hands out to us, a gesture not so much of welcome as of supplication. Then I was in his arms, and I felt the stronger arms of Godwin behind me, and heard him murmur over our heads.

"Tonight, I will come tonight. After the hall sleeps."

Chapter the Thirteenth: Kilton

THE cresset I had kept lit had burnt very low. I lay silent and naked by Gyric in the dragon bed, wakeful and waiting. I heard a rustle from the pleasure garden, then the two taps on the lock iron that told me Godwin was outside. I threw back the linens and stood before the door. Gyric lay still upon the bed, sitting up, his hand closed about the gold cross on his chest. I drew breath and pulled open the door. A figure swathed in a dark cloak moved in, shut and bolted the door. Godwin pulled off his mantle and stood before me.

The wind from the opened door had made the cresset flame leap high. Now by its flickering light I saw for the first time a man's eyes fall upon my naked body. A lock of my hair, fully loosened, lay over my breast, and I pulled it back behind my shoulder. Godwin stood soundless before me, his eyes travelling slowly from my face down the curve of my neck to my breasts, across my waist and belly to the roundness of my hips, then to the felted brown fur where my thighs met, and down my legs to my feet. Each moment that his gaze lingered upon me felt precious, and I stood boldly before him. To watch his eyes, the set of his mouth as he thus saw me, moved my heart within me, and kindled my desire.

I yearned for him to speak to me, to say one word to match what was in his eyes. Without lifting his gaze from me he drew his seax from his scabbard. He took one step and laid the bare blade upon the bed, then turned his back upon it. He reached his arm around me, pulled me to him with strength. His seax belt dug into my waist with the force of his embrace. At last he spoke, but his words were meant for Gyric, and were terrible to hear.

"Gyric, your wife is naked in my arms. My seax is by your hand. My back is turned to you. Kill me now if you do not consent."

I would have cried out in horror had Godwin not grasped me so tight. I watched over his shoulder as Gyric reached forward, found the seax with his fingers, took the hilt in his hand. He rose in the bed, but not at his brother's back. Instead he grasped at the rising dragon bed post behind him and with violence drove the quivering blade deep into the wood above his head.

This was his answer. In response Godwin placed his hands on my face and lifted it to his. His lips brushed across my cheek, found my mouth, and his tongue forced open my lips and filled me with his wet savour. He held me fast so I could not move nor even breathe. Then he dropped his arms from me and was pulling at his seax belt, tearing at his leggings, stripping off his tunic. He was like one starved who comes upon a feast, or the drowning man desperate to stay afloat. He lifted me in one motion unto the bed, his fingers sinking into my flesh, and gave a little strangled moan as his mouth swept over my face and breasts. His hands were everywhere upon me, plying the length of my body, almost hurting me with the strength of his touch. Such was his need that I was fearful for him. I tried to slow his hands with caresses of my own but could scarce move. Gyric lay inches from me, on his side, his face turned to us, his linen wrap ghostly in the dim light.

Godwin could stay himself no longer. He reared back from me, lifted my hips in his hands, then fell upon me. His arms came up beneath my own, across my back and pressed me to him. He buried himself in me so that a cry escaped my lips. I gasped under him at the power of his stroke and the weight of his body upon mine. Tears were running from my eyes from his hunger and the violence with which he used me. His fingers were tangled in my hair; I tried to turn my head to see Gyric and could not. Then he shuddered, and almost soundlessly grew still.

He gave a slow exhalation of breath, and raised himself a little from where I lay, crushed beneath him. He looked down at my face, wet with tears, and slowly pulled his hands from my hair. He touched my cheek with his fingertips, and lightly brushed the salt tears away. Then he pulled himself off me and lay on his back, his hand upon my belly.

Gyric, so still beside me, reached his fingers to me until they lay over my heart. I clutched at his hand, thankful for his willingness to touch me.

We lay unmoving for some time. Godwin's hand never left my body, and Gyric too did not let his hand fall from me. The shadows of the carved dragons' heads were made huge upon the wall by the guttering cresset, their painted tongues gaping dull red. They stared down at us, one bearing the blade thrust deep into its wooden throat.

Still Godwin spoke not, and Gyric had said not one word. I longed to hear them speak to me, but was mute myself, all unknowing what to say. Godwin's hand slid from my belly up to my breast, and he raised himself on one arm and bent over and kissed me. I wrapped my arm about his neck. Now his lips were soft upon mine. With tenderness he probed my mouth with his tongue, tasting me gently.

He pulled back, looked down the length of my body.

"I never beheld such beauty," he murmured. "No woman is so fine as she, Gyric."

Now Gyric spoke, as of an old memory. "Like the painted statue of St Ninnoc in the chapel," he answered slowly.

157

"Yes, you recall the beauty of that statue. But no saint has flesh like Ceridwen's."

I could scarce believe it, and would have closed my ears if I could. I lay here between the brothers, and they spoke of me as of a costly sword, or a fine horse. I turned my face away from Godwin, shut my eyes. I had wanted the gaze of Godwin upon me, wanted his praise, wished to delight him. Of all this I was guilty. But I had wanted too the greater treachery of his love, and not just lust. Tho' my eyes be closed tight I could not shut out my shame.

"There are four days before I must leave," Godwin said softly. "Having this pleasure now will make my death the easier to bear." His lips again brushed over my throat and breast, his breath hot against my skin. "You are well worth Hell torment."

I pushed myself up. My lips were trembling, and my words flew from them. "There is no such punishment! There are only the halls of the Gods, where those who have fought well, loved well, lived well, go to dwell in peace and plenty. And their hall is finer than yours, Kilton!"

He lay staring at me, open-mouthed for an instant. I did not give him time to speak, for I swung astride over him and bent my mouth down over his. Now I kissed him, slowly, letting my lips linger, flicking just the tip of my tongue against his, withdrawing it when I felt his own, then plunging my tongue fully into his mouth. I kissed too every inch of his face, his chin and jawbone and nose, my mouth resting on his perfect eyelids and brow, feeling the strength of his man's beauty through my lips. His face and form were faultless; there was no mark upon him, nothing save the small scar upon his hand he had received in winning vengeance for Gyric's maiming. Freed from his weight I moved my hands upon his chest and arms, swept my tongue over each inch of

158

his neck and chest, breathing in his smell. With my hands I pinned his above his head so he could not touch me as my tongue explored him. He sighed and moved beneath me, shifting his hips. The breadth of his shoulders and brawn of his arms lay open to the sweep of my nipples as I bent over him. Then I felt another hand upon my flank, and turned my face to see the hand that Gyric had laid upon me. He was on one arm, and with the other hand traced my body as I knelt astride his brother.

Godwin arched his back, raised his hips in answer. I felt Gyric's hand run along my face and throat, seeing all through his touch. Godwin groaned; his passion could not wait. I eased myself lower over him, making him gasp with the slowness in which I took his prick within me. Once within me, he let me ride him freely, at my own pace, looking up at me with glistening eyes.

When at last he came off he cried out, his body quaking beneath me. I leant forward and kissed the single tear that escaped his eye.

Chapter the Fourteenth: What We Have Lost

I sat alone in the bower house, the Sun now lowering in the sky. Godwin had left us in the dark, and I had not seen him all day. Gyric had ridden out with Worr. I was grateful to leave the hall, noisy with women weaving, and turn to the solitary work of hemming linen at my table. Of a sudden the door shut behind me, and I rose and saw Godwin. He was dressed as if for hunting, with leathern leg-wrappings and short gloves, and leant his back against the closed door.

"Godwin! Are you mad? Open the door. It is broad day outside."

He moved not, just looked at me with a hard smile. "Last night you called me 'Kilton'. Tell me if you did so because you felt compelled to give your body to me."

I blinked at him, not understanding, knowing only my own fear. "Open the door, Godwin," I breathed. "Any one could have seen you enter."

"Tell me. Is it because I am your lord? Because Gyric is my pledged man?" His eyes were burning from lack of sleep and some inner fire. I crossed to him. At arm's length he snatched at the hem of my gown, and pulled me near him. "Did I force you?" he demanded. He gathered fistfuls of the wool in his hand, and now pressed the mass of cloth up against my breast so that I stood revealed to him from the waist down.

"I came to you willingly," I told him. He had one hand between my naked thighs, was pushing me to the bed. "And willingly I will be yours again tonight. But I will not bring disaster down upon all of us." I did not fight him, tho' I was

160

truly afright. I felt the bed clothes against the back of my bare legs; in another moment he would push me down upon them. His fingers were cupped tight between my legs, hurting me so that my fear turned to anger. I braced myself and spoke again.

"Last night you used me roughly, then named me as the tool of your damnation. Now you steal into my house to ravish me as if I were your battle-gain. I called you 'Kilton' because you were not Godwin to me last night. Yes, you are the law here, and my lord, and now you are acting it. You think only of yourself, of your own need and desire. It is the truth that you may die next week or next month; all warriors run this risk. And so may we all die soon, by the flame or spear."

He dropped his hand, let go my gown which he held bunched at my breast. I smoothed my skirt, and would not look at him for fear my eyes fill with tears. "You blame me for your desire, so that my fault is doubled," I told him. "I could not know you would be thus to me...A gift I meant to give you joy has brought you torment."

He shook his head as if roused from a dream. "You did give me joy. Pleasure like I had never known."

"Is it your pleasure then, that drives you to treat me thus?" Now I was warmed I could not stay my words. "Even Sidroc, whom you love to hate, never dealt with me thus, nor did he lay one rough hand upon me - and he be a heathen and a Dane!"

He closed his eyes. "No, it is not pleasure."

He would not name that anguish that drove him, but shame spoke loudly by his silence.

He stepped to the door, opened it to the bright day, then came to my side. "I told you I would never ask your

161

forgiveness for desiring you, for it was all I had left. Nor am I worthy of your pardon. But do not withdraw your great gift from me, Ceridwen."

Fear and anger both were spent in me; tender truth remained. "How can I withdraw it, when it was my desire, too?"

Now the gloved hands which had hurt me took up my own, and lifted them a moment to his lips.

At table that night I forced myself to speak, to smile, to raise my eyes to Dunnere, and far worse, Modwynn. I pushed my food about, barely tasting it, with Gyric by my side; and tried to look composedly upon Godwin while my stomach lurched beneath my gown. By day I had hastened to Berhtgit's croft and begged of her her wort-cunning. In the back of my throat I tasted still the bitterness of the crushed henepflower she had given me to open my womb, and drank many cupfuls of ale to quell its flavour. I felt certain guilt was on my cheek, and when I went to the kitchen yard to fetch mead for our use in the night thought the steward noted my every move.

Dark was fully come, and the night many hours old as Gyric and I lay in the dragon bed, waiting. Again there came the faint two taps on the lock iron, and again I pulled open the door in answer. Godwin came in, bolted our door behind him, and turned to me as he had the night before. He did not stand and stare this night, but took me in his arms at once, the linen of his tunic smooth against my naked skin. I felt the power in his arms and the hardness of his body as he pressed me to him, but his lips as they found mine were gentle. Together we took off his clothing, and he followed me to the bed.

Full pleasure was ours that night. The urgency which had driven Godwin the first night was gone, and he took his

162

time with me, stroking me slowly and tenderly with his hands, and kissing me deeply. I grew wet under his gently probing fingers, and he parted my thighs and with his fingertips teased me until I panted.

I lay between the two brothers, and now Gyric reached out his hand and found me. He touched my face and throat, and began stroking my breast and armpit. Then he swept his mouth across the breadth of my belly and hips. Warmth rose within me from their teasing mouths and fingers and flooded every part of my body, till I cried out under their joint caresses.

We slept, the three of us, the fitful sleep of those too aware of the passing of the night hours. The skies were still pitch when I urged Godwin to leave. He kissed me a final time as he dressed, and I spoke my fears by saying, "How can you come again tomorrow? Surely some one of your thegns have seen you slip from the hall. What if you be seen coming here?"

"I leave through the main door, as if going through the yard and through the gates to the village. None of them would begrudge me a night with a village girl."

But I am not a village girl, my heart cried out. What my lips asked was, "But if you are seen coming to the bower house? Any of them could challenge you, call Dunnere, anything."

He shook this away. "In three days I will be gone. Give me these nights, Ceridwen."

I took his hand and placed it upon my heart. "I will play my part, I have said I will. But I am fearful for us all." I did not name this fear, but it was quite apart of my fear of discovery.

Godwin saw only the risk at hand. He looked me steadily in the eye and said, "You have said it yourself: I am the law here. Gyric has given his consent, and you, yours. If I am challenged I will take what comes in life, and after death, too."

He pulled me to him. "Nothing can keep me away now, any price I would be willing to pay to have this." He turned to the bed upon which Gyric still lie. "Gyric, I would let no blame fall on you, nor Ceridwen. You know that."

Gyric nodded, then said slowly, "And I am your man, Godwin. You know that."

Three days came and went, days of little sleep and no rest. To spend the daylight hours in the needsome tasks of the hall was torture to me, so eager was I for the falling of dusk. The paleness of my cheek was such that Modwynn asked if I were ill. I drank the powdered herb in wine, praying fervently to Frigg that my womb be opened, and filled my silver goblet with ale each night in the hall, and in bed with Godwin and Gyric shared sweet mead from a single cup. Each night we gave ourselves to fleshly joys, and each dawn found me more unsatisfied and restless. Godwin spoke boldly to me in the dragon bed, openly praising the beauty of my face and delights of my body, exclaiming over the pleasures I brought him. But never did he speak one word of what was in his heart about me.

There was a feast in the hall on the final night, for tomorrow Godwin would ride out with fully half the thegns of Kilton for their largest battle yet. The food was rich, but the mood was sombre. All knew that Guthrum's army awaited them at Exanceaster, and that it was a force never before gathered by the Danes. Some of those who rode forth on the morrow rode to their deaths, and all who rode forth left Kilton to its Fate.

When the hall was quieting for the night I returned to fill our ewer with mead. Entering the dim kitchen passageway I heard a giggle and saw a flash of light linen. There against the wall was our serving maid Hrede with a young son of one of the thegns, her gown pulled up about her waist. She had now thirteen or fourteen Summers, and was still in my care. The boy ran off when he glimpsed me. I opened my mouth to rebuke her but her crimson cheek and fearful eyes kept me silent. I could find nothing to say to her, and with a bob of her head she scampered away.

It was late when Godwin finally tapped upon our door, and I knew he could not stay long; the men would be up before dawn to make their start. The light of the single cresset showed me Godwin's eyes, fevered and burning as they were the first night he came to us. He held me hard against him and whispered, "This is the last night, the last of these pleasures I shall know."

"You speak as if you wished to die," I told him, blinking back my tears. He would not answer me, only bent back my head and kissed me. As it had so many times before, his hand closed about the gold bracelet on my wrist. He opened his eyes and said, "I have no gift to bring you for all you have given me."

"I want no gift," I stammered out, barely able to keep control of my words. Gifts were for bridal mornings, from new husband to his wife; or for nights spent in secret with whores. "I want only for you to live and return to us."

For answer he led me to the waiting dragon bed.

In the morning when the men rode off I could not weep, as did Modwynn and all the many wives and daughters of those who left. I raised my hand in salute to Godwin as he rode by, and smiled so that I thought my face might crack from the strain. I put my arms about Modwynn, when I myself could scarce keep my feet. Gyric stood by my side, and later went with me to the hall. This day he did not ride off with Worr, but stayed with me as he had of old, and he and I and Ceric sat in the pleasure garden in the Summer Sun.

Alone at night with Gyric in the bower house I wept at last.

"Who do you cry for?" he asked in a quiet voice. "For Godwin, or for yourself?"

I did not answer. He came up to me, found me with his hands, turned me to him. Anguish was in his words. "I am the one who loves you, Ceridwen."

Now I began sobbing.

"You are my whole world, Ceridwen. Everything to me. You are my wife, the mother of my son. In one beat of my heart I would die for you. I am the one who loves you. If you cry at all, cry for all of us, for what we have all lost. But I am the one who loves you."

If the ground beneath my feet had been able to swallow me whole, I would have leapt into the abyss, and welcome.

He would not stop, would not relent, tho' his words were choked with his own grief. "You saved my life, and then gave your body to me. I could not help but love you, and had nothing to offer you but my hand. Even whole I was not the man Godwin is. Blind as I am, I know I am far less. But I am the one who loves you."

166

I could no longer stand; his words rained down on me and I sunk to the floor at his feet. I was sobbing so I could not catch my breath, and the hot tears that lashed my cheek were made bitter by the truths falling from Gyric's lips. I could not defend myself from my own wrongdoing, my shame was too great.

I wept at his unmoving feet until some spark of pride spurred me to speak. I knelt and looked up at him. "On the road coming to Kilton I thought I could never know such joy as I first knew with you, Gyric, tho' we be in danger every day. I knew you loved me, and wanted to live, and I loved you with my whole heart. When we reached here at last, alive and together, then I saw your happiness in me, in everything, begin to slip away. I thought Ceric's birth would bring you joy, but it only deepened your sorrow. I no longer knew what to do to make you happy."

His voice was steady now as he answered me. "I have not made it easy for you, I know. I could not know how hard living was to be for me. No one can count the times I have wished I had died that night they took my eyes." He stopped my tearful protest with his hand. "When Godwin pursued you, you could not say No. None but Heaven itself has ever said No to Godwin. This is what he could not endure, your returning with me, redeeming the life he rode to redeem, and then giving me the child he so longed for."

I recalled Godwin's words to me: There is in you a challenge, and a promise. This was what I had been to him, no more. My tears of a sudden stopped. "Why did you consent, then?"

His voice dropped low. "I cannot say No to him either. Next to you I love him best." He reached down, helped me to my feet. "Just as you saved me, you have kept me alive."

I still held his hands, and I knew he felt me tremble. "Gyric, I love you," I whispered. I was about to beg forgiveness, when his fingers touched my lips to silence them.

"That is all I need to hear," he told me, and enfolded me in his arms.

As the Summer nights passed I watched the Moon wax full, then wane, dwindling to a dark face. I did not bleed. The Moon grew large again. One warm afternoon while I sat with Gyric and Modwynn and Ceric in the pleasure garden I felt my gorge rise as I lifted an ale cup to my lips. I stood up of a sudden to clear the smell of ale from my nostrils, and as I took gulps of fresh air began to laugh. Modwynn and Gyric turned to me in wonderment, and tears formed in my eyes as I told them, "I think I am with child."

Modwynn's arms were around me at once. "A babe! O, Ceridwen, Gyric, how happy I am for you, for us all! Little Chirp, a brother or sister is to come," she sang out to Ceric's puzzled upturned smile. Gyric had risen to his feet, and I buried my face in his hair. I was laughing and crying at once, and could not stop either one. We said nothing to each other, just clung together.

Modwynn's next words were, "Now I know why you have been not yourself, dear daughter; you have been with child these many weeks. How glad Godwin will be for you!"

And in this month I reached also my twenty-first Summer.

Chapter the Fifteenth: Another Arm to Fight

"THE well is fouled again." The quietness of Modwynn's words could not mask her weariness. She raised her head from the bucket she had just sniffed, and beckoned across the kitchen yard to Wulfstan. Without a word she extended the battered bucket to him, watched him wince as he glanced into its oily waters.

"The latrine must be moved. Again," she told him.

He nodded, but not without a short release of breath, which smoked in the drizzle. "Third time in as many months, Lady. With the whole village crowded into the yard, and all their sheep and kine, and now these rains..." He shook his head, seeing that Modwynn had closed her eyes against his protests.

He left us, and Modwynn turned to face the baker. The rains had spilled in through a weakened roof in one of the storerooms, leaving kegs of flour and meal floating in muddy waters, their precious contents mostly spoilt. We had tried to dry what we could in the ovens, but much was now fit only for swine. "Mix what is muddied with the soured ale, and bake it in loaves," she ordered. "We will share it about the yard so that each family's pig gets a loaf."

We turned away from the baker so that only I heard her next words. "With the way we are losing food God knows we will have to slaughter the remaining pigs long before Martinmas, so they might as well be as fat as this little flour can make them."

I watched her eyes sweep past the wattle fence that surrounded the kitchen pens and out across the reeking burh yard. The inner part of the great oak palisade wall now formed the back of scores of hastily constructed huts, wherein now sheltered the greater number of the village of Kilton. Beyond the palisade wall, awash in a sea of mud, stood their deserted crofts, and the sodden fields spiked with mouldy, ungathered grain. Near the silent orchards lay the huts which had been trampled and laid waste during the two further raids we had suffered. Buried not far from where they had been speared were the bodies of those cottars the Danes had overrun. But nothing remained of those few the raiding parties had ridden off with. Six young women, two of them mere girls, had been carried off, and two young men as well; and what fate they had met at the hands of their captors could only be imagined. A few of the war-driven Mercians conjectured that the Danes were far more short-rationed than we and would eat their captives after taking their sport of them. Tales such as these went round the burh yard and neither the sternness of Wulfstan nor the ministrations of Dunnere could quell the fear that clutched at the hearts of all of us penned within.

The cries of the villagers had alerted the night wardmen at the hall within moments of the first attack. By the time Wulfstan and the thegns had armed themselves and poured out through the palisade gate the raiders were gone. It was then nearing dawn, and after the men returned and told of what had happened Modwynn and I readied ourselves to go out with them and visit the village. I did not want to go. All of Kilton was in an uproar; Ceric was pestering me with endless pleas to be allowed to join us; Gyric was downcast and silent; Wulfstan furious with anger. The danger was passed in the village, nothing but misery would await us, and that I did not want to see. I could not but think of Edgyth and wish some of her quiet strength was mine.

The crofts which had been attacked were those nearest one edge of the orchards. Modwynn and I rolled along towards them in a small waggon down the dull red ribband of pounded clay. Gyric had surprised me in the hall by ordering his horse saddled, and now his reins were held by Wulfstan as they rode alongside us. It was meet and right that Gyric should be here, and I was grateful for it. A few thegns had already gone ahead with Dunnere on his task of blessing the bodies where they fell.

The whole of the village of Kilton was gathered about the tumbled huts, so that they must part to allow our waggon through. Save for a few still wailing, the folk stood unmoving and speechless. Out the tail of my eye I saw Dunnere, kneeling over one of eight or ten bodies now lying upon benches under the brightening sky. The soft ground all about was churned up by the hooves of horses. Worr was wandering the grounds, looking at tracks of booted men. A fowl coop had been upturned and a few ruffled hens clucked and dragged their spotted wings in the mud. The raiders had used no fire, simply smashed the doors of the huts in, trampled the low withy fences, grabbed what food stores they could.

Wulfstan had already dismounted and was talking to Dunnere. I helped Modwynn down and we crossed slowly before the line of cottars. They nodded their heads to her. She said little, and I said nothing at all, as we bore witness to what her folk had suffered.

Wulfstan limped towards us with something in his hands. He crossed to where Gyric still sat upon his horse, then pressed the iron points of two throwing spears into his hand. "Feel the notch just before the socket," he said.

Gyric took one of the points in his hands and ran his finger along the edge. "Cornish. These are of Cornish make."

"Yes. And the folk say they heard amongst the Danish yells Cornish voices too."

171

I knew not what all of this meant, but the older man's eyes opened wider. "They are in league."

"Yes," answered Gyric. "The Cornish have thrown in their lots with the Danes."

We rolled back to the hall too numbed to speak. The Danes were ranging almost at will through Wessex, and had struck many places to the East of us. Far North the wild Welsh had joined with them, and now, here from the West came a mixed band of Cornish and Danes, ravening at our doors.

That morning I took out my father's old seax, and had the weapon-smith grind the chipped blade. Henceforth each morning I tied its worn leathern sheath onto my sash by my keys.

Later I followed Modwynn back through the kitchen passage into the tumult of the hall. Most of the women and children of Kilton were crowded within, for the packed huts which sheltered them at night afforded no room for spinning or weaving by day. Relentless rains had forced them all inside, and the smell of wet wool and bodies long unwashed rose sharply over the smouldering tang of the dampened fire pit. Women stood in pairs working at their drop spindles, girls sat on benches teaselling wool. Little ones crouched on their haunches, blinking in warm delight at the edge of the fire pit. Boys were everywhere, shouting and calling out as they raced around and under tables or barricaded themselves with trestles in mock battle. Modwynn and I both paused, our eyes searching out the darting form of Ceric. With his bright head of coppery curls and vivid tunics he was easy to spot. Just now he stood in the opened sleeping alcove of one of the thegns, a place strictly forbidden. His hands were on his hips and his play wooden sword on his back was askew as he laughed at a cottar boy who lay sprawled upon the stone floor. His peals of

172

laughter made it hard to be harsh with him, but I caught his eye and with a gesture made it be known he was not to enter the alcoves again. He jumped down and scampered away with the other boy as we crossed to the door of the treasure room.

I thought Modwynn pressed the heavy iron key into the lock with an effort, but with the noise of the hall she would never be able to rest until nightfall. At least within the treasure room we were alone, and its comforts were mostly unchanged. The massive carved bed in which she had lain with Godwulf for so many Summers and now alone for five stood at one end. Wooden chests and kegs strapped with iron bands ringed the room, holding within them everything of value from linens to weapons to silver pieces new-minted. Her loom stood braced against one wall, bearing a length of linen of the finest weave in the making. She had been at this piece for many months, and though I had feared to ask I felt it was the burial shroud she now wove for herself.

I looked at the plain creamy linen, and my thoughts went to my little son in his bright blue tunic laughing beyond the door. Modwynn had spent much time cutting and embellishing clothes for him, lavishing her finest thread work to enrich the neck and cuffs and hem of everything Ceric wore. About his little belly was a fine leathern belt with a chape and buckle of pure silver chased with gold, also a gift from her loving hands. He stood out amongst the thegns' and cottars' boys like a pheasant amongst starlings.

"Modwynn," I began. "I want to - to make Ceric another tunic." I faltered as her face creased in a gentle smile.

"Another? The boy has more and finer clothes than ever Godwulf and all his thegns did!"

"Yes, of course, I know. But I thought - something less - they are all so rich..." I did not know how to say it, the thought beyond it was so terrible, but it was the thought that made my words tumble out. "He dresses like the son of the house he is, making him an easy mark for Danes. He would be snatched away for ransom, or killed first to end the line, if - if -"

Now she understood. Tears welled in her faded eyes but her voice was steady. "If the Danes should breach Kilton."

"Yes," I nodded, tho' my throat seemed near to strangling me. "If that happens, would it not be better for Ceric to look as any other child? Sometimes I think yes, but other times I think he might be spared for ransom if they realise he is the son of the house. As a cottar boy they might hack him down just as they did to those village children at Hlafmesse..." I hid my face in my hands a moment to steady myself. "Tell me what to do, Modwynn. Is he safer dressed as he is, or shall I make him a plain tunic? I cannot ask Gyric about it."

Modwynn's voice was very soft. "Make him a plain tunic, Ceridwen. It will ease your mind to have it at the ready."

A messenger came from the convent at Glastunburh, a serving man who had walked without rest to reach us. In his meagre pack was a letter for Godwin, Lord of Kilton, but he gave it up readily enough to Modwynn. She opened the scroll before Gyric and I, and her eye scanned the contents before she read aloud.

TO MY LORD HUSBAND GODWIN OF KILTON,

And Lady Modwynn of that place, and to my brother Gyric and sister Ceridwen. Know that in her wisdom our dear Abbess has determined we should seek safer ground. Most lay-women amongst us have returned to their homes, yet fearing that I would be but a burden at Kilton and desiring to be of service to the elder and infirm sisters here, I have with our dear Abbess' blessing, chosen to abide with them and share in the Fate God in his Mercy has in store for us. We move now and in haste to a rock cave, well-hidden and wholesome, in the East of our donor's holdings. We are well provided with grain and have kept with us the staff we can support. I beg you to shelter the bearer of this letter, to look to your own safety and to not fear for your loving

EDGYTH

Modwynn lowered the letter with moist eyes. We all of us were silent. I had sent no letter to Edgyth since before High Summer, and now even if I could find words to write, none could reach her. In her desire to serve those weaker than she, she chose the danger and discomfort of a forest hideaway over the safety of her rightful home. I had taken much of the place and honour that was hers, and now her husband's child grew in my womb.

The next Sabbath I stood as I always did in the front of the little stone chapel as Dunnere offered the Mass. Beside me stood Gyric, his face lowered in thought, and on the other side Ceric wriggling between me and Modwynn. Behind us were the thegns and their families, and as many as could crowd in from the yard stood beyond them. The incense with its odd cold smell smoked from its censor, and I felt breathless and stifled. A dull ache was forming in the small of my back, and to keep from shifting my weight I let my eyes travel. Modwynn stood as she always did, with her feet just pressing upon the polished stone which covered Godwulf's resting place before the altar. I raised my eyes and saw the back of Dunnere as he moved across the tiny chancel. For one moment my eye flicked across the wooden statue of St Ninnoc. I could no longer gaze at her face, so much like my own, and the hardness of her painted eyes forced my head down once more.

After the final benedictus we filed out into the watery Fall Sun. A young thegn approached us from the yard, his eyes shifting from Wulfstan to Modwynn. He stopped before us and announced, "Lady, a group of folk are at the gate, petitioning."

Gyric's mouth twisted at this unwelcome news, and Wulfstan gave a snort but said nothing. Modwynn's white hand flew to her brow, but it was Gyric who spoke first.

"Mother, we can take no more in. We can scarce feed ourselves and our own folk. They could be renegades or thieves."

Modwynn had made her decision. "Let us look at them. If they can give a right accounting of themselves, we cannot turn them away. There may be room yet in the barns for them to sleep."

I clutched at Gyric's hand, for I too wished no more haggard strangers to share out what remained of our stores. Wulfstan could not hide his impatience, but chose well his words.

"Lady, you have ever been open-handed with all, but Lord Gyric speaks truth. There is no hayloft left to shelter them, and no bread to spare to feed them. Soon we will have nothing but browis to eat, and little enough of that. We are strained to breaking."

"Let us look at them," Modwynn repeated.

And so we went.

A knot of Kilton folk had gathered already, their faces filled with distrust, waiting to glimpse the new arrivals. Atop the ramparts of the palisade two thegns scowlingly looked down at those standing on the other side. The young thegn who had fetched us called out, and the oak door was swung open.

It was a small group, a half-score, men mostly, ragged and filthy. They stood without any animals of any kind; no pig, sheep or even fowl to bring with them. A few clutched hide packs, but some had nothing in their hands nor on their backs. In their faces were fear and hunger and silent supplication.

Wulfstan went forward to question them, and I saw amongst them a man who stood apart and a little to one side. He was massively built, above middle age, with a dense curling dark beard just showing strands of grey. His hands hung down at his sides, and I saw that the tips of two of his fingers were missing.

"Can it be? Gyric," I whispered to him, "one of these men - I think it is Cadmar."

Almost at this moment the man's eye caught mine, and in it I saw the same twinkle I recalled from our night at his forest retreat. Other than this slight acknowledgement, he stood still and steady.

Gyric stepped forward with a lifted hand, and called out in a clear voice, "Cadmar of Sceaftesburh!"

177

The monk raised his arm in return, and answered in a lusty voice, "Lord Gyric of Kilton."

All stopped as Cadmar came forward and took the hands that Gyric extended to him. In a moment Gyric was enfolded in his strong arms. "You are come," was what Gyric said, and Cadmar echoed in a low voice, "I am come."

Modwynn stood, hands clasped to her breast, watching. Cadmar stood back now from Gyric and bowed his head to her. As he did the iron cross swung freely from his neck.

"Daughter of Maerwine, best of lords, I, Cadmar, salute you."

"Nay, holy brother, it is I who salute you," she answered. "You who were my father's beloved warrior, and now the beloved of God - and he who blest the union of my son and daughter," she finished, with a smile at us.

I had come forward to stand by Gyric, and as the monk's bright eye rested upon me I could not help the warmth from mounting to my cheek. In that one moment I recalled all of what had befallen me on the forest path to his fastness, and recalled too the gentle way he had looked upon me when Gyric proclaimed I was his wife and sought his blessing. That night I knew a happiness so supreme that even in my innocence I knew that no later moment would surpass it.

Now I closed my eyes against the years that had passed, and knew my face bore my pain.

Cadmar spoke again to Gyric. "These few are all that is left from the trevs North of me. I was on my way to you myself when I joined with them. There is no settlement left from there to Caeginesham." He paused a moment. "I am another stomach to fill, but another arm to fight."

Gyric's answer was swift. "I myself will arm you, and name you my man," he said, and the two once again embraced.

Modwynn gestured the whole of the group in, and she and Cadmar and Gyric and I went straightway to the hall.

Cadmar washed his hands in a basin I held for him, and Modwynn herself poured out his ale. He would take no flesh other than fish with his bread, and showed in all his actions and speech the mild and gentle manner of the monk I recalled. He and Gyric sat side by side and spoke at length about the movement of the Danes, Godwin's long absence with Ælfred, and finally life at Kilton after Godwulf's death.

"There will not be his equal," Cadmar murmured. "No warrior so great, nor lord so wise." Then he seemed to recollect himself and added, "Your brother Godwin is a great fighter, and one day will equal his father in wisdom."

Gyric said nothing at first, then only muttered, "He is a good warrior."

Now Cadmar looked over to me and addressed me directly for the first time. "And you, Lady, are as fair as ever you were."

Modwynn smiled at him and said, "Ceridwen is the flower of the hall. You will soon meet Ceric, the fine son she has given Gyric. And in the Spring she will give him another babe as well."

The pride in her voice forced my head down, and I simply said, "How grateful I am to have you join us." I turned away from them with a few feeble words about looking in on Ceric, certain the cloak of shame lay upon my cheek.

Much later I returned to the hall. The torches were being lit for the night, but the high table was empty. Upon it

179

sat a costly ewer of carved silver and I went to it and took it in my hands. The door to the treasure room was ajar, and I glimpsed Gyric and Cadmar alone within. They still held their drinking cups and their voices were low and earnest. On top of one chest lay a baldric and sword, and on the top of another a seax.

"I give you also my good black gelding, should we engage the Danes outside our walls."

Cadmar's answer was heartfelt. "Pray God I never ride to fight again; that Ælfred will drive them from Wessex before the main host reaches here."

"Pray God," echoed Gyric, and was silent a moment. "Cadmar," he began again, with a new gravity, "your coming answers a prayer. Kilton is a strong fortress, but with determined effort even the greatest stronghold can be breached. If that happens -"

He paused so long that my knuckles grew white gripping the ewer. Their backs were to me; I could not see their faces, and though I edged a little away from the door I could not make myself go.

Finally he said it. "My wife and boy. Modwynn. If we are overrun, I will likely be killed at once. I do not want them to be taken by the Danes. If Kilton falls, there will be likely none other alive to meet a ransom." Here he lifted his hand towards the wrap that hid his empty eyes. "And I know myself the treachery of Danish ransom calls!" He steadied his voice. "I want you to swear that if all is lost, you will kill them by your own hand before they are butchered by the Danes, or are fallen into Danish slavery."

I heard Cadmar's rapid intake of breath, followed by his urgent answer. "I cannot, cannot do such a thing. I have come into the world once again, have been driven from my hermit's hut. You reproached me years ago for wasting my warrior's arm when Danes ravaged the land. Now I am come, and pledge my arm and my life to you. But I cannot slay your wife and child and mother, no matter what their Fate may be. It lies, as all of ours do, with God."

"You know too well what they will do to her! To my boy. Cadmar, you must pledge me this one thing. Be the man I cannot be. Say you will spare them that torment!"

Here the ewer dropped from my bloodless hands. They both whirled around, Gyric with his mouth open. My eyes locked with the monk's for a moment that felt a year. Then with great gentleness he nodded at me. "It is only a serving man, who dropped a ewer," he told Gyric, as I hurried away.

I was in the pleasure garden a few days later savouring a rare afternoon of Sun. It was no longer the refuge it had once been; the din of the packed yard be all around it, but still I welcomed the chance to sit at the little pavilion table and finish the tunic I was sewing. Today the yard was noisier than usual, for Cadmar had begun to train the village men in the use of arms, and ranks of cottars more used to ploughbats now wielded spears as they thrusted at shapes of baled hay. The warrior-monk's voice boomed over the massed men as he himself took up a spear and thrust left, right, and down through the crude man-form, urging the disabling cut to the foot or knee rather than a riskier try at an upper body target. Worr was with him, and the older man used the younger to parry with. The sharp rap of wood against wood was followed by shouts and yells of encouragement and mirthful laughter as the cottars paired off to practise. My back was to this as I sat there facing the sea, but my ears heard it all.

At length the lesson came to an end, and Ceric, always underfoot when it came to weapons, came running back into the garden swinging a sapling stick through the air in play. After some little coaxing he stood still long enough for me to hold my work up to his quickly sprouting frame. As I did so Cadmar came to the garden gate, his undyed woollen surplice stained with sweat at chest and underarms. He mopped his brow with a long sleeve, and his dark eyes twinkled at me.

"Lady, I would have a word with you," he asked, and I nodded him in. He came to my side and stood a moment looking down at the jagged red rock face and the foaming waters below. A breeze cool with coming Winter wetness blew against us. Then he cleared this throat, and mindful perhaps of Ceric playing nearby, spoke to me in a low tone.

"What your lord Gyric said to me was said out of love."

"I know that; of course I do." My voice caught a little, and I tried to draw calmness from Cadmar's own easy presence at my side.

He nodded his head as if he understood the fear within me. "It is just the fact that men must speak such words at all."

Now I nodded, and looked down. "Godwin rode off with no hope for himself," I told him. "Now I know Gyric feels the same for us."

He answered with a force that startled me. "You are wrong, Lady. Kilton will not fall unless all of Wessex falls. I have almost twice your lord's years, have seen many battles, and nothing will make me believe we will be driven from this land." He drew a breath, and exhaled slowly. "Gyric is more thoughtful than other men; he has need of it, and he has suffered cruelly at the hands of this current enemy. I cannot

182

condemn him for asking me that I spare those he loves from their clutches."

I heard the whish of Ceric's stick as he whirled it about him, and his peals of laughter.

I could not speak more, fearful of what I might ask. Each night I fought to keep from riding the night-mare in which I saw Kilton overrun, Gyric and Ceric slain before me, and me taken into slavery with every woman who lived.

"Your father's seax?" Cadmar asked. His voice was light and low again as he looked down at the blade tied on my sash.

"Yes," I answered and drew it from its sheath for him to look at. The polished blade shone, the large chip grown small under honing.

"A fine piece," he said, fingering the silver wire inlay. He smiled at me. "Worthy of the fierceness of the Mercian ealdormen. Gyric has told me of how well you used it during your long journey to Kilton."

I smiled back, and gestured to the yard. "How lucky we are to have you with us now. Our folk could not learn from a better master at arms."

Here he laughed, but I went on. "O, yes. Gyric told me upon that same journey of your skill, that you were the warrior of greatest renown in his uncle's hall. All men respected your prowess."

He shook his head but smiled. "Modwynn's brother kept a fine hall, with good warriors, all. For me, it was my size. I am big and can fight without tiring a long time. Men would strip off their ring-shirts and even their helmets after fighting went on, too burdened by their weight to stand beneath them, but tho' I move slow I can move a long time without

183

rest." A smile spread across his face. "The last man standing is the man who wins."

He paused now and looked down at his sword hand. "It was a faster man who got my fingers," he said, wiggling the two stumps with a laugh. "All warriors form their own style if they live long enough.

"Gyric, now. He had quickness. He moved with decision and speed. He had a sword, light in weight and a little shorter than most, a piece ordered for him by Godwulf when Gyric reached his fifteenth Summer. It had a good deal of spring, that sword. Gold-wrapped pommel. A beautiful piece. He was lightning fast with it."

I had never heard about this sword, the one I knew must have been wrenched from his hand when Gyric had been captured by the Danes. I closed my eyes for a moment thinking on it, grateful to hear of its beauty and Gyric's lost skill.

"Godwin has cunning. He will size up a group of fighters at once and know their weaknesses, and their strengths. In a moment he will pair his best men with the best of the enemies, always singling out the finest spearman or swordsman for himself. In battle he is a boar, furious and fierce." He paused a moment. "I recollect when Godwin was not yet twenty, the families joined in a dispute against another chief about land-theft. It was his first real battle. Godwin knew like a hardened veteran where to gain the advantage. He took and took ground without fear and without yielding quarter. When he has set his mind he is unstoppable. He will find the weakness in every opponent and drive until he wins."

There was nothing I could say to this, and only gazed down at the tossing of the waves below. Cadmar recalled himself and with a shake returned to the day.

"Do not fear, Lady. There are many good arms here at Kilton. Mine is one, and your own is another. And the grace of God be above us all."

I dipped my head, grateful that he held me in such esteem. "I thank you, Cadmar. And I thank you too for being what you have been these past days to Gyric. It has been hard for all of us to be shut up within walls for these many weeks, but harder still for Gyric, who was used to ride out each day with Worr to gallop or to hawk. He has borne his restlessness well, never complaining, but I know it has chafed him. Since you have come, and spend much of your time with him in converse and in jest, his heart is lighter."

"Tho' he was not much more than a boy when I left the world, I always held Gyric in high regard. He grew in Godwin's shadow, but the two loved each other and were as one in everything. Gyric was always quick with a jest but quick as well to see deeper into the minds of men. Tho' his brother bested him in everything Gyric was never selfish about winning praise for himself. If he had not suffered the Fate he has, he might have grown into a better man than Godwin."

"He already is," is what I murmured back.

Chapter the Sixteenth: Shattered

PEACE can come more sudden than war, and it was word of peace that came to us. A rider came first from Ælfred, telling of our King's siege at the fortress Guthrum had taken at Exanceaster, and telling too that Ælfred had the victory. We waited then from day to day for word from Godwin or for he himself, but a full month passed before one of Godwin's own men rode into Kilton, with news that Godwin and his thegns would return in two day's time. But this was not his only news, and after he had told us that Ælfred and his ealdormen had had possession of the field of battle he looked with furrowed brow upon us. Nineteen of Godwin's men had been lost, perished on the field at Exanceaster or in the many skirmishes before. The thegn stood encircled by us of the hall, and with a single word or gesture signified which woman was now widowed or which aged father bereft of a son. Silence and gasps turned to wailing. One of the slain warriors sat at the high table with us each night as one of Godwin's closest companions. Since he would have always fought close at Godwin's hand in battle, this told us the fighting had been very hot around him. Modwynn went from each sorrowing woman or man to the next and placed her hand upon theirs in comfort.

At the first message we were gladdened, but one man riding fast from burh to burh bearing such news did not loosen our resolve nor soften our defences, tho' he bore the King's signet mark and was known to Wulfstan. It took the thegn of Godwin's, known to us all and part of our everyday life, bearing Godwin's own message, for us to believe that peace had finally been won. And this was a true peace, for instead of our King paying much silver to the Danes to

186

withdraw, it was Guthrum who had willingly offered up hostages to Ælfred so that he and his men might depart.

So Godwin lived, and was coming back to us. In the four months he had been gone I had never allowed myself to think otherwise. He must live to rule and guide Kilton, and all its riches of field and pasture and woodland. Gyric was not fit to be ealdorman, and Modwynn was growing old. Without Godwin the fate of Kilton was in Ælfred's hands, and the King, wise and just as he was, must use such a burh to reward one he knew faithful to him, or take it, with proper recompense, for himself.

But Godwin lived. Despite his doubt, and the Fate that shadowed him as he rode away, he lived. Modwynn rejoiced to know she would soon see his face again, but as much as I had prayed to the Gods to direct his hand and shield him from hurt I dreaded his return.

It was Modwynn who spoke to the village folk, still massed within our walls, and told them the great good news, and told them too they might with safety return to their crofts. The palisade gates were swung open and they streamed out with gladsome cries to their deserted plots and common fields. Some began gleaning what grain was left from the furtive gathering that had been made from the spoiled crop. Sheep and goats long confined in too-small pens within the burh now kicked and ran over the furrows in eagerness for fresher fodder.

The burh yard, awrack with cattle pens, long houses and sheds thrown up to house the village and their beasts, stood nearly empty of any save the hall's own people by mid-day. We turned to the task of providing a fitting welcome feast. This time we had no great stores of smoked meat, scores of geese, fowl and eggs, sweet cheeses, or fattened milk-calf ready to be slaughtered to welcome Kilton's lord. Indeed there was little of anything with which to make a fitting feast. But now the sea could be used, and Modwynn sent at once men to repair the steps down the rocky cliff face and landing stage so that the weir could again be reached and fish dipped up. Of fine drink, there was some wine left, but too little to share out amongst the hall. Only our mead remained untouched, but so strong a stuff must not be quaffed, but only tasted. The remaining grain was sorted and from this must be baked both fine loaves and better ale, for that which we had been brewing was poor in flavour. Dividing up the grain Modwynn choose the best for brewing, "For Godwin will want most my good ale over a good loaf."

She smiled at her jest, and tho' I smiled too my heart clenched at the thought of the coming meeting.

After the Sun passed its highest point on the second day we heard the horn sound, telling of Godwin's coming. I went from the hall hurriedly to the bower house. Gyric sat at the table, dressed in a fine tunic and leggings, waiting.

"The horn has sounded; Godwin is here," I told him.

He was silent. I went to the little carved chest and drew out the gold fillet for my brow. I moved to his own and pulled his out as well.

"I have your brow-band, are you ready?" I scarce knew what to say and wished he would speak. He rose and stretched out his hand and when I placed the slender fillet into it he grasped my fingers.

"What will happen now?" he questioned, his voice a whisper.

I did not speak and he went on. "Now that he is come. Will you be my wife, or his woman, or both?"

188

I steadied my voice for my answer. "I will be Ceridwen, and your wife," I told him. He nodded his head and then lifted my fingertips to his lips.

All of Kilton was lining the clay road as we gathered outside the opened gates to greet Godwin and his thegns. They came slowly, at a walk, without cantering their horses as was their wont on other returns. Modwynn squeezed my hand and I knew she was of a sudden fearful Godwin had in some wise been injured. We saw them stop at the very fringe of the village and look over the handful of destroyed crofts, and saw too them questioning those who worked there. As they rode closer to the gates they picked up their pace, and we saw that Godwin looked whole. His ring tunic with its blackened rings bore no rent, and from his iron-studded baldric hung his sword. The men behind him grinned and shouted and the folk shouted back in greeting, but Godwin's face tho' it wore a smile was strangely still.

He swung off his horse as Modwynn came forward and enfolded him in her arms. He kissed her and then embraced his brother, nodding at Cadmar who stood nearby. Now I stepped forward and Godwin took me briefly in his arms. Our faces touched and his hand stopped against my thickening waist. His eye pierced me and I lowered my head, Yes.

He was pulled away now and in a swirl of jingling horses and noisy men we moved through the gates and into the yard. He stopped at what he found there, the remains of the settlement of the whole of the village within. He looked to Cadmar, walking at his side in his simple robe but with a seax strapped to his belt.

"Now I have seen what befell Kilton I am glad to have such a man as you join me."

"My arm is pledged to Gyric and to God, but it has not yet been tried against the invader," he demurred.

189

While the men were bathing their hands and faces Modwynn called Gyric and me to her side. She had a leathern scroll carrier in her hand, and closed the treasure room door behind us.

"From Edgyth," she said with true pleasure. "Godwin stopped at Glastunburh and found her well." She unrolled the short piece of parchment and squinted at it near a taper's glow.

TO MY DEAR LADY MOTHER MODWYNN,

And my brother Gyric and my sister Ceridwen. I rejoice to tell you that our dear sisters are again safe here at Glastunburh. No harm came to buildings or land and with the Great Peace wrought by our dear King we praise the Mercy of a good God. Know I pray for you all each day and ask I be remembered thus in yours. And that Ceridwen take up again her quill as her letters are missed by your loving

EDGYTH

Modwynn smiled over at me. "She does not even know about your new babe to come. Write her, and give her the pleasure it will bring to hear your happy news."

I could find no word to answer this and was grateful the noise of the hall summoned us away. The tables were now set upon their trestles, and the men filling the hall. Godwin let no seat be empty at the high table, and had already picked another thegn, young and eager to win fame, to take the seat of the dead man. Modwynn and I went from place to place with silver ewers and poured out yellow mead. She filled the golden cup from which Godwin drank, and I the silver cup with the golden rim that was Gyric's. She filled the cup of Dunnere, and I of Wulfstan, until every cup at the high table was filled. Serving men moved about the many tables with bronze ewers of mead, so that each cup in the hall was filled with the strong stuff.

Godwin took his cup in his hand and stood. "I salute Ælfred, King, and the men who rode with me and helped win the field. By God's grace I return to you, and honour those men who fell at my side. I salute too the men and folk of Kilton who stayed to protect our home, and those who met their Fate at our enemy's hands. To our living and dead, I drink."

We all raised our cups and tasted of the honeyed mead, but Godwin drained his cup.

"There is peace now over the land. Ælfred by God's grace has driven the Danes from Wessex. This peace was won not with our silver but by show of arms on the field of battle at Exanceaster. Guthrum could not withstand our siege of his fortress and begged to settle. I myself witnessed the terms, and that Guthrum and all his chief men swore with their own blood upon their sacred arm-ring that they would forever leave us in peace. This act the heathens had never before done."

All within the hall cheered at this, but Godwin himself seemed void of gladness. He spoke to us as if he had thought long of what he would say, and spoke well. But he himself seemed apart from his words. I wondered who had been amongst Guthrum's men, and why Godwin had tarried so long in returning home. Tho' the fighting at Exanceaster had been fierce the battle-gain was small; few of the returned thegns brandished weapons or jewellery torn from the bodies of the dead. I wondered if he had taken his men and gone in search of another fight, in the hope of catching other Danes or Welsh or marauding Cornish-men in the chance of winning booty, and losing his life.

"To seal this victory God has granted us an even greater boon: A whole fleet of Danish ships were lost at Swanawic, run onto the reefs in heavy fog, with six score ships or more sunk."

The hall cheered anew to hear what toll those danger-filled waters had demanded, but I shook my head to free the awe-ful vision of so many men drowned.

"Therefore let us thank God for our deliverance. And for the damnation of the heathen."

Dunnere was raising his arms and slicing the cross through the air. I hung my head as if to receive his blessing.

Godwin glanced into his empty cup. It was not the custom of the hall to drink more than one cup of mead, and I could only recall one night at which the yellow liquid had flowed like ale, the night of Godwin's return after avenging Gyric's maiming.

A serving man moved forward with a ewer of ale and began to fill Godwin's cup. But Godwin stopped him by jerking the cup away and flinging the contents over his shoulder against the wall. He uttered a single word, "Mead."

The men in the hall roared out their approval. Modwynn's lips parted in her startle. Never before had I seen Godwin act thus. I rose in haste and took up the silver-carved ewer and went to where he extended his cup. I would not meet his eyes and kept my gaze upon the stream which I swirled into his golden cup.

The splashed ale behind us dripped in streaks down the treasure room wall. I saw Cadmar watching Godwin with narrowed eyes. I went from place to place, filled every cup at our table. Cadmar held his cup close before him and his dark eyes met mine and lent me calmness.

192

After we had supped the scop set his harp on his knee and sang a curious song of his devising, about a sword that once drawn could never be re-sheathed without tasting blood. Godwin listened with closed eyes, his gold cup clenched in his hand, and when the saga ended pulled a new silver necklet from his own throat and tossed it to the man. By now the mead had gone around many times, and thegns, wearied from the journey and filled with strong drink, lay sprawled across the benches and atop tables. I slipped from the hall unmissed. When Gyric finally came to the bower house the Moon had already set, but my wakeful ears told me he bolted our door behind him.

We all met next day in the stone chapel for a service of deliverance. Godwin made offering to the poor of fully half the battle-gain he had taken on the field at Exanceaster; a portion so huge that even buying costly grain from Frankland none should go hungry. Dunnere made much of this, but Godwin seemed as careless of this gift of wealth as he was of his ways in the hall.

I wanted to be joyful, to feel deeply in my heart what Modwynn and the thegns felt, but I could not. They had lived in fear as long as I had, and those thegns who had gone out to fight with Godwin these many years faced great danger as well, and now it all dropped from them at once, like a fleece shorn from a lamb. Neither the coming Winter nor the diminished stores of the burh could dampen their spirits, and it seemed that I alone with Gyric and Godwin shared no part of their joy. Relief was in my breast, and thankfulness, but under that breast grew the child of the man who thought himself dead.

As dusk fell I was alone in the bower house readying myself for the hall. The door was shut against the sharpness of the Fall night, and two taps on the lock made me nearly drop the brooch I was fastening. I moved to the door as it opened and Godwin slipped in. He came upon me so quickly that his mouth was over mine before I could speak. His arms, full of power and urgency, wrapped my back and pressed me into his body. When he drew his mouth away his hand slipped down my gown over my belly, and he spoke in my ear as he held me.

"It is true, then. This is my child."

I pushed myself a little away. I could scarce breathe, he held me so fast.

"Yes. And my child."

He pulled me to him once more but I stopped him with both hands against his chest. "I am not your woman," I told him.

"You are," he breathed to me. "It was the thought of you, there in my dragon-bed, that kept me alive."

"I am glad you live, glad for all our sakes. But what I gave to you was wrong. I do not fear Lady Hel, but I will pay for the rest of my life for those few nights."

"And if I burn for eternity for what I did with you it will be a small price for the pleasure you gave me."

"I do not want to hear of your pleasure, or of your damnation. I only tell you this: This child is ours, but I am not your woman."

He lowered his arms and looked at me. "I mean nothing to you then?"

"You mean much to me," I answered, fighting back the lump that rose unbidden in my throat. "More than I do to you. You have ever been the brightest side of Gyric, the one who made him feel more whole. From birth you have been

194

the pride of Kilton, ever strong and daring, a warrior without peer. I had but a few years with my kinsman before he died, and then I lived in the Priory. I then went amongst the Danes, and saw their ways, closer to my kinsman's than they are to yours. When I came to Kilton, saw what it was and what its folk were made of, I knew I had seen the best that this land can yield. But you, who have so much, want everything. And you are used to getting it. You desired me, and in my pride of this desire I allowed myself to think you also loved me, and thus we might break our vows to Gyric, me as wife and you as brother. This madness and selfishness was mine, but it is over. You are the law here; you can cast me from your hall or cast me over the cliff. But I will not help you betray Gyric, and I am not your woman."

He blinked his eyes. "Did I truly injure Gyric?"

"How can you ask? You think because he followed you in everything you can wrong him not. Ever since you were boys together you had the advantage. You were older than he, taller, and stronger, and it was you who would one day rule here. Yet he did not envy you in anything. It was you, you who envied him, and you would not rest until you had won me from him. Yes, you wronged him gravely, but not so cruelly as I. I too wanted everything; I desired you and him too, and nearly cast away his great love to reach it. In my madness I wounded his love for us both more than that flaming poker wounded his eyes."

Godwin stood as if stunned before me, then with a sharp intake of breath spoke. "You are too harsh on yourself," he said, and closed his eyes a moment as he shook his head. "I felt I could not help my lust for you, and cursed God for giving you to Gyric. Yet I could not stop, and cursed myself a hundred times more for being a renegade in my own hall." He lifted his hand to me. "But do not be harsh on yourself. The blame should be mine."

My anger at last gave way to my tears. "I deserve my own harshness, and the ill regard of everyone, should they learn the truth! On top of all the grief I have brought Gyric I have had to bear the false regard of your own dear mother, and of all else here in the hall, who think me good and true."

Now he answered with strength of his own. He put his arms around me and spoke over my head. "And so you are, Ceridwen; you are good and true. The fault is mine, and I ask your pardon for all you have suffered."

Yule came, and with it much wet and hoary weather, but little snow. The fields stood brown and lifeless outside our walls, the shocks of sodden stubble thrusting up from the ruddy soil. Now a tracery rime of frost lay upon them. For many weeks the thegns of the hall had ranged out over the forests fronting the burh, and the deer they had speared formed the bulk of our Winter's feasting. Few fish could be dipped from the weirs in the cold Winter water, for they had all fled to warmer climes, and it would take many months before our fowl and geese regained their prior numbers. But with careful management of the remaining wheat and rye and the ceaseless hunting of the men, we would have enough to see us through.

On the ninth day of Yule, a morning dismal with damp and with a light fog rising from the grey sea, Gyric and I were walking from the bower house to the hall. The Sun was nearly overhead in its low crossing and shed but feeble light upon the Winter-blasted rose bushes and blackened clumps of flowers. Gyric walked ahead of me across the wet gravel path, me looking down at the remnants of blossom. A strange scraping sound, such as metal upon rock, made me lift my head and turn towards the sea.

I saw a man's head and shoulders, and then another, and another, and within a moment or two a score of men, warriors all, appeared from out the abyss of the cliff face. They were shoulder to shoulder in a line, all helmeted, and all silent. Naught but a strangled cry rose from my throat, but six-months swollen as I was, I rushed forward into Gyric and grabbed his hand and pulled him along towards the hall door. A spear flew through the air and landed just in front of us, and I found my voice and screamed with all of my might, expecting every moment to be felled by a spear through my back. Gyric had held fast to his own spear and was yelling at me but I could not answer him. My only thought as I pulled him along was to make it to the hall door, and to safety.

We reached the door and as Gyric opened it I turned and glimpsed the men now running behind us. Another line had taken their place and were swarming over the cliff face. No battle yells escaped their throats; they were as soundless as their ring shirts and steel weapons would let them be.

"Danes," I screamed, once inside. "Many of them - two score!"

Gyric had dropped his spear to bolt the door, and now reached for the wooden chest that always stood close in the passageway. Together we heaved it in front of the door. I plucked his spear from the floor and pressed it into his hands.

"Gyric, where is Ceric? He was with Modwynn." I could not think and my hands went to my head. "He must be with Modwynn, here in the hall," I answered myself. We were still in the dim passageway, and the hall itself was alive with noise. I had no seax but Gyric wore his own as well as carried his spear. I looked around in the darkness for anything that might serve as a weapon, and took up an iron toasting rod about the length of an arrow.

Gyric drew his seax from the sheath at his waist. He spoke me to very low. "Take this. Use it at the thigh or wrist as I have taught you. Do not try to pierce a ring-shirt."

"No, my love," I hissed back. "You need it more. I have a poker, I will do better with this." I was trembling and tears ran down my face. My heart was pounding so that I thought it would burst in my chest.

"Whatever happens, recall I loved you always," he whispered.

My tears blinded me for a moment and my throat closed. "And I you, Gyric," was all I could say.

The door shuddered behind us and made us leap forward. We heard the sharp crack as the wood was rent by the blade of a broad-axe, and a splinter of oak sailed into Gyric's hair. From the hall itself we heard the scream of a woman, but it did not sound like Modwynn. We heard the yells of thegns, and a clatter of metal. Few folk would be in the hall at this hour, but I could only hope that Modwynn and Ceric were within the treasure room and that at the first alarm she had bolted herself in.

From far way it seemed we heard the horn upon the palisade rampart sound. In the middle of a long note it stopped short, telling us he who blew it had been silenced by the flight of spear or arrow.

Another axe had joined the first upon the door at our backs, and Gyric clutched at my hand and whispered into my ear. "We must move into the hall if we can. Keep to the wall and tell me what you see."

We slid forward, our backs to the wall. The fire-pit glowed in the centre of the hall as always, the fire banked low. The great upright timbers which held the roof of the hall were festooned with the holly boughs and ivy vines that were nailed there a fortnight ago. The high table was set up upon its raised step, and was empty. A woman was still screaming, a sort of low wail. I could not see her. From outside the hall now we heard the cries and yells of the folk of the yard, and joined with them, the battle-yells of Kilton's thegns. I crept forward to gain a view of the lower part of the hall.

"There are four thegns, one is Wulfstan and I think one is Worr, pulling on their battle-gear. Eight or ten others are within the locked doors. They have no helmets nor ring-shirts yet. Now the first group is going out."

"Anyone else in the hall?"

I swept my eyes up and down its length. "Some women, standing by the trestles. And some I think hiding in the alcoves." I looked opposite, to the other side of the treasure room. "Serving men and slaves are crouched in the kitchen-yard passageway." I wracked my brain. There were less than a score of thegns in the hall when the attack began. "Was Godwin riding out to hunt this morning?" I asked in despair.

Gyric shook his head. "I think not. If so, he is dead already. The Danes have come both from the landing-stage and through the village."

Repeated blows from axe-blades fell upon the passageway door. Gyric jerked his head back and took a breath. "I want you to go to the treasure room door. Call out to Modwynn and go within when she opens."

Within my heart I said: I want to die with you, fighting; but the thought that Ceric was alone and frightened with Modwynn made those words impossible to speak. Within that

199

room we three should have nothing to do but listen and wait until the fighting was over, and all our men were slain. Then the door would be forced and -

"Is Cadmar there?" demanded Gyric. "Is he amongst those by the door?"

I swallowed the cry that rose in my throat. How grateful I would be for Cadmar near us, but one glance at the men shouldering against the door told me his massive strength was missing.

"They are through the main door!" I said, and watched as those who crowded against it were flung back. Danes tumbled into the hall and amidst yells and oaths fell into sword play with the thegns.

Gyric pulled me to him and his lips just brushed my cheek. "Go, go," he ordered, and flung me from him. As I rushed to the treasure room wall one of the serving men from the other passageway ran to Gyric. May Thunor shield him, I thought, seeing that this man would stand unarmed by his master and be slain by his side.

I had just reached the raised step where sat the high table when the passageway behind Gyric was flooded with day light. Wood groaned and snapped and the Danes surged in, pushing and tripping over each other. Gyric whirled around with his spear braced before him. He had pressed his fine seax into the hands of the serving man who had chosen to stand with him, and the man stood wide-eyed gripping the weapon. Two of the Danes had spied me and one hooted loudly and raised his spear overhead. There was no time now to reach the treasure room door and I would not by my actions give away that this was where I was headed. I stood frozen waiting for the moment of Gyric's death.

They were upon him now. The serving man leapt to one side and brandished his short blade in the empty space before his master. A Dane with a sword and round shield came up from beside him and thrust the sword while swinging his shield arm with violence. The serving man screamed and crumpled as the sword vanished beneath the shield into his body. Gyric fell as well, his spear striking another shield and sticking harmlessly for a moment before dropping to the floor. Gyric rolled to the wall, a seam of skin opening through his hair and reddening his linen eye-wrap. One arm was flung over his head and for that instant I recalled the first time I had seen him, in the foul cellar of Four Stones, and thought him dead.

I stood upon the raised stone step and lifted the poker in my hand. At the end of the hall the main doors were thrown open and bodies clogged the threshold. Framed in the opening I saw both thegns and invaders leap through, turn and fight, and be cut down. The woman who was screaming now whimpered by an alcove, and another knelt upon the floor stones and was mouthing silent prayers.

The Dane with the spear leapt after me upon the step. He laughed at the poker in my hand, showing sharp white teeth. He was beyond youth, with long pale hair that trailed from beneath his iron helmet. His ring-shirt was mashed in places and even torn, stripped from the body of one who had died in it. He spoke something in his own tongue, and gestured with his spear to drop my poker. Instead I thrust it quickly at his thigh, but he jumped easily beyond reach. He grinned at me, and holding the spear in one hand leapt forward and snatched at the trailing hem of my head dress. He yanked it from my head and hooted again at the sight of my hair. I edged back against the table, and in a swift gesture he swung his spear against the short poker I held, sending it skittering across the floor. I threw my weight against him to try to catch him off balance. His arm swung around and caught me against the ear and I staggered beneath the blow. He grabbed me, and dropping his spear, pulled a short knife from his belt. He slipped the blade under my sash and my keys fell clattering to the floor. He pulled me to the upright timber nearest him and seized my wrists with such force I thought they must break. Once, twice, thrice he wrapped the sash about them and tied the free end about the timber, fixing me with a short tether. I lashed out with my feet and he again struck me. Then he picked up his spear and held the point just under my throat. He moved to the edge of the fire-pit and took up a cold piece of charcoal. With two rapid strokes he drew the blackened point across my cheek, marking me as his own.

The Danes who had entered the passageway were ranging about the hall. Some were slicing back the curtains to alcoves while others joined in the fight at the main door. Down the length of the hall I saw one man free himself from the battle and come running towards us. The Dane who had tied me was now bending to pick up his spear. From over his head I saw the warrior who ran to us: Cadmar, come to kill me.

"You will not take me alive," I said to the Dane, and laughed in spite of myself. I had not spoken before and he looked at me with interest. I pulled hard at my wrists where I was bound, and my long gown sleeve flew up. For the first time he saw the circle of braided gold upon my wrist. His eyes bulged at the sight of this treasure, and he placed his hand upon it, but saw he could not pull it off without untying me. I smiled at him, seeing over his shoulder that Cadmar was now just behind. The Dane's hand went to his knife again, and as he was looking down, Cadmar, sword drawn, ran him through.

The Dane's eyes popped open in surprise, and his knees buckled. Cadmar flung him from me and stepping on the body wrested his sword from out the leathern ring-shirt. Blood was running from my nose and I think my ear too. Water flooded my mouth and I vomited.

"Where is my lord Gyric?" asked Cadmar.

I could not answer and only nodded my head to where he lay in the passage opening. Cadmar turned to him and kicked away the body of the serving man, but before he could reach Gyric was forced to turn back to the body of the hall. The fighting had moved into the very heart of it, and there on the far side of the fire-pit three thegns were facing five Danes. They hacked at each other with sword and thrust with spear, but the Danes were steadily gaining ground, edging the thegns back toward the stone rim of the fire-pit. Cadmar joined them, rushing at the Danes with a fierceness so great they fell back a few paces. One of the Danes staggered into a hanging cresset and the lamp fell to the floor, shattering against the stone. The oil was sprayed across the fire-pit and the banked coals flared fire up into the air, sending both groups flying. One of the Danes grabbed at a long piece of charcoal and flung it upon the stone floor. At once brown acrid smoke billowed from the pool of spilled oil. The flaming brand lay at the base of one of the timber uprights, and the holly boughs, dry from hanging, caught fire upon it. One of the thegns yelled and grabbed at a bench and flung it upon the smouldering oil to smother it, but the smoke filled my nostrils so that I choked from it. The holly crackled and the flames shot up the timber as it raced toward the thatching of the roof.

More men came pouring in, and with them the serving men and slaves from the passageway. These latter warriors, new minted in their lord's service, carried spears from fallen warriors and kitchen axes. I saw a woman with a butchery knife and knew her to be the thegn's wife who had been on her knees in prayer. My heart swelled to see this courage of

203

the folk of Kilton, and tho' most of these were readily cut down by the enemy, they took a bloody toll of their own.

The fighting was moving back down the hall toward the main door, as all attempted to flee the smoke and the licking flames that now crowned the timber upright. I saw one thegn hack away at the fire, and a ball of flame fall at his knees.

My wrists were raw from chafe, but the knots only grew tighter and the hold firmer as I struggled against them. I tried to use my teeth but could not grasp the edge of the knot. As I looked down I saw some movement upon the floor, and my heart leapt. Gyric was alive, and crawling away from the passageway and into the hall. I could not tell how badly he was hurt. His tunic was soaked with blood but I prayed it was not his. If I yelled to him a Dane might leave where he fought and come and kill him with a single stroke. I judged they would not leave the fray for a man already injured.

I opened my mouth but before I could yell two men came hurtling through the passageway, leaping over the body of the dead serving man. Gyric stopped and collapsed. The first of the men whirled around with his back to me. It was Godwin.

He wore a leathern tunic and leg wrappings of leather, dressed for hunting. He had neither helmet nor shield but grasped in his left hand his jewelled hilted seax and in the other a sword not his own. He was panting and his teeth were clenched, but tho' it was clear he had been fighting some time, no blood stain was upon him.

The Dane he led was of high estate, for he wore a ring tunic of perfect make, and an iron helmet chased with silver. Godwin glanced at me and then around his hall, now filled with smoke and with the oaths of thegns fighting to preserve it. The flames were crawling up the length of the timber upright. Serving men and kitchen women threw buckets of water at the fire, unmindful of the spears of the invaders. I saw Gyric rise up again, and now called with all my might.

"Gyric! Godwin is here, he is here!" Even should we all die I wanted Gyric to know his brother had lived to defend his hall, and had not been slain in the forest.

The Dane bore a sword and shield so that Godwin by quick leaps and rapid thrusts must keep his ground without defences. Their swords crossed and rang out together, and Godwin's struck dully against the linden shield of the Dane.

They fought so close to me that my eyes closed, certain a sword tip would drive home in me. As I stood there my womb turned and I felt for the first time the babe within me move. I drew breath and opened my eyes to see Gyric pulling himself steadily along the floor.

Godwin had leapt upon the stone step, and for a moment had the advantage of it, but without a shield was now driven fast against the table. The Dane grunted and took a mighty swing. The sword sliced through the space where Godwin stood but he had flung himself back upon the table and flipped upright on the other side. From the back of the hall a voice bellowed, "For Kilton! For Kilton!" and Cadmar, followed by a thegn, rushed to the front. But the Dane was not alone, for now his men had seen him as well, and the thegn just behind Cadmar was cut down. Cadmar reached the stone platform and the Danish chieftain whirled at him. His skill was great, and he was well-armed, and much the younger of the warrior-monk. But Cadmar, bellowing at the top of his lungs swung his sword through the air and stood unmoving against the faster man's onslaught. With shield he parried and pushed. Then the Dane dropped back and in an instant lowered his sword and caught Cadmar across the thigh.

Cadmar dropped to one knee as a river of blood streamed from the gash. The Dane turned back to where

Godwin stood against the treasure room wall. Cadmar dropped his sword and reached forward to my headwrap lying trampled on the floor. With face gone white he bound it tightly against his thigh. He pulled himself near me and tried to take hold of me and so to stand, but the strength was fled from his leg, the creamy linen newly red.

The Dane now joined Godwin and they fought along the wall. The space was narrow and Godwin used it to advantage, as the Dane could not fully extend his shield-arm. Gyric had told me his brother was the smartest fighter he had ever seen, and Cadmar too had spoken of his cunning. Now as I twisted against my bonds I saw how true their praises were.

But then a throwing spear whistled through the air across the table. It caught Godwin in the left shoulder and pinned him through the flesh to the wall beyond. He screamed and dropped the seax that he held in his left hand, and drew the sword in his right across his body to shield himself. The Dane who had thrown the spear stood laughing by the fire-pit, his helmet under his arm. The Danish chieftain turned to him and nodded and laughed back.

Cadmar, on his knees near my feet, pulled his seax from his belt and with a yell hurled it at the spear-thrower. It caught the man full in the face as he turned to look at us, the blade driven deep through the nose into the skull. The man fell backward with a grin still upon his face, his helmet rolling to my feet.

The chieftain looked in fury to Cadmar, but the monk collapsed in a pool of his own blood before me. I saw Gyric shouldering his way along the floor stones now slick with the mixed blood of many men. Tho' his hair was clotted with blood his face looked resolute and set, and he moved as if no limb were broken. With every pull he extended his hands to left and right, seeking a spear or sword with groping fingers. I felt his movement was hidden from the Dane by the length of the high table, but dared not look at him just the same. I stared down the hall for a moment and spoke as loud as I could.

"Gyric, if you go on, you will soon reach the table platform. A little to your left is a spear. Its point is to you. Godwin is alive against the treasure room wall, but cannot move. His enemy is before him, his back to you."

I looked back now at the treasure room wall. Godwin's face was white with anguish, and his green hunting tunic red from blood. He could not drop his sword to try and pull the spear from his shoulder, and held it extended in front of him. The chieftain had resumed his good humour and seemed to give thought to the best way to dispatch his opponent. He grinned and spoke something to Godwin while waving his sword just out of reach. A spear would be safer, and I wondered if he might turn to look for one and so discover Gyric now underneath the table behind him. I could just see Gyric's lower legs and feet and saw too that he trailed the spear in his hand.

Of a sudden there was a noise like the sizzling of a hundred braziers. I turned to look and saw that the thatch far above the burning upright timber had crackled into fire. Men and women about the hall began to yell with renewed frenzy as the flames shot out in growing circle about the timber support. Tufts of flaming thatch fell onto the stone floor and onto the heads and shoulders of those beneath.

The Danish chieftain looked at this too, and gestured to the flames as if he might leave Godwin pinned to roast. Then he glanced quickly along the wall behind him and saw the treasure room door. He waved his sword at it, mindful perhaps that this was where the real booty lay, and turned to face the door. He drew back and with his shield and sword

207

before him lifted a booted foot and rammed it against the stout planks of the door. He tried again, but it did not yield.

The air was filled with smoke and screams. More serving folk had braved the hall and were hurling buckets of water about at everything near the rapidly growing circle of flame. They could not reach the fire itself, but wetted what they could. Some died doing this, cut down by Danes as they fought what seemed to be a growing number of thegns within.

The Danish chieftain turned from the door, spitting at it in disgust. He glanced down the hall and saw the battle that raged, and looked too at the fire above. Godwin's strength was spent; he could no longer hold his sword upright as the Dane wheeled on him, sword drawn. I saw Godwin close his eyes to accept the death-blow, and saw too Gyric rise up on his knees behind the Dane. With the spear in both hands he drove it low into the back of the chieftain's thigh. The Dane staggered back, howling. He fell backwards upon Gyric and the sword dropped from his hand. Gyric rolled over on the Dane's chest and in one movement slid a hand up the front of the ring shirt until he found the man's throat. I saw the helmeted head forced back, the cords of the neck revealed before Gyric ripped a seax blade through the flesh and hacked away.

Even in the clamour of that hall I heard the sucking gurgle of the chieftain's last breath.

Gyric sat still upon the man's chest for the few moments it took for life to flee. Then he reached out a hand, found the edge of the table, and raised himself to his feet.

"Gyric, Godwin is pinned to the wall to your right," I called.

He reached backward until he found the wall, and slid forward against it. Godwin's eyes were glazed but open. The groping hand of Gyric found his brother's arm and then the spear head driven through the shoulder-joint. He grasped it in both hands just behind the iron and pulled with a loud cry. Godwin grunted as the point left his shoulder and Gyric dropped it clattering to the floor. He staggered forward into Gyric's arms and the two fell upon the table before them.

They lay there a moment, blood-soaked and sweat-stained, and I saw Godwin speak into the ear of his brother, but those words were theirs alone.

Then they stood upon their feet. Godwin bent to the floor and picked up his sword, and with his foot freed from under the dead chieftain's body the spear Gyric had used. He pressed the spear into Gyric's hand and looked over to me. They began moving towards me, Godwin wincing as he clutched his left arm with his right.

Godwin was before me now, Gyric at his elbow. Gyric put out his hand and touched me. "Thank God you live," he said. I could not speak to answer him, my sobs were so great. With the seax bloody from the Dane's throat Gyric cut away the sash binding my wrists. When free I lifted my hands to Gyric's face for a moment.

Cadmar had moved at my feet. "He lives still," I found voice to say. "Gyric, Cadmar is wounded at my feet."

First I plucked a cloak from a fallen Dane from the floor and bunched it up over Godwin's wound. I then knelt upon the wet stones and together Gyric and I rolled Cadmar unto his back. His loss of blood had been great. I pulled a bench alongside us and lifted the leg up upon it, and re-tied the dripping linen head dress over the wound. I saw a length of woollen cloth, a woman's cloak or shawl, and wrapped it as tightly as I could over all. My whole body was trembling as with cold but my fingers felt feverish and I had a hard time controlling them. For the few moments I worked I spoke.

"Gyric, shall I look for Ceric? I am fearful to go to the treasure room door should more Danes come." He was slow in answering, and I went on, "Are you hurt, my love? You are soaked in blood."

"I am not hurt," he answered. "A rib or two is cracked from my fall, nothing more. Stay here with me a while more. If Kilton is to fall it will make no difference, and I would rather die near to you."

I fought back my tears and squeezed his hand. I looked up from where we knelt at Cadmar's side. Godwin was moving slowly, sword in hand, away from us. The fire had stopped its spread, and I became aware that it was raining outside. The hall had quieted and few were left save serving folk and slaves, and the bodies of the dead and dying. The place was filled with the smell of sweat and blood, the smell of death. The stone floor was slick with water and gore. I saw Godwin stop and look down where a Dane groaned, and saw his sword come down and be driven with all his weight behind it into the lower part of the man's body. But he himself could barely walk, and I rose from Cadmar's side to go after him. Someone lying upon the floor, thegn or enemy or poor serving man, tried to pluck at my skirt but I kept going without looking back. I could see no thegn within the hall; perhaps all were slain and we awaited but the second onslaught of the Danes.

I had nearly reached Godwin's side when the forms of two men darkened the open doorway. Against the drizzling day light which framed them I could not tell if they were friend or foe. I only knew that soon we should be dead, or saved. Godwin kept walking towards them, sword drawn before him, his left arm hanging uselessly at his side. The men stood for a moment behind the bodies at the threshold before calling out, "My lord! The victory is ours!"

210

Chapter the Seventeenth: As From the Dead

KILTON was spared, but at a cost so great that it defied reckoning. But in the hours that followed what I most recall was the treasure room door opening at Godwin's bidding, and Modwynn and Ceric coming safe and whole from out that storehouse. Ceric shrieked when he saw the blood that stained his father's tunic, but ran to us and was gathered up into our arms. Modwynn was straight and tall as ever; only the seax she still clutched in her white fingers gave proof of the suffering she had endured.

"We stood the whole time behind my loom, another bolt of linen covering our feet. Ceric stood before me without moving and without fear," she smiled at him, tho' his round cheeks were streaked with tears.

Godwin now lay upon the high table, with Cadmar, still alive, head to head. The Simples chest was brought and Modwynn with a pair of shears cut through the leathern tunic that Godwin wore and stripped off his linen shirt. She looked down into the wound, gaping wide at the front and narrowing at the back. His chest and face was very white.

"Warm some wine with honey, a whole ewer full, and bring it," she ordered. She laid her hand upon Godwin's brow, and spoke gently to him. "The shoulder joint is shattered, my boy. The bones may not be able to mend, but I will do my best."

Meanwhile I had unwrapped the shawl and my head dress from around Cadmar's thigh, and cut open his legging. My hands were red with blood and I did not know how he still lived. His breath came very shallow, and Gyric stood at his head and spoke to him as I worked. The gash, mid-way up

211

his thigh, cut straight across the mass of his muscled leg. I gestured helplessly to it, and Modwynn looked over.

"Pour in the wine when it comes, and with a steel needle and linen thread sew it up."

Someone had brought basins of water and I doused my hands and took a needle from the Simples chest and began to thread it. From the tail of my eye I saw two thegns approach the table, carrying between them another man. One of the thegns was Worr and I rejoiced to see he lived.

"My lord," he called out. "It is Wulfstan, dead."

Godwin raised his head. It took him a moment to speak. "Lay him on a table by the fire. A sword by his side."

Wulfstan, Godwin's most trusted companion, who had had the ear of Godwulf before him, dead. I recalled my last glimpse of him, strapping on his sword-belt and heading out the great oak doors. Lamed long ago by Sidroc's spear, he could not hope to live long in joined foot-battle. I had dressed that wound, just as I now worked over another good man wounded by another Dane.

"Where is Dunnere?" asked Godwin. His voice was hoarse and did not carry. "Is he dead?"

Someone went to look for the priest, but the honeyed wine came and we poured it into the wounds until they overflowed, and then I set to my thread-work, pulling at the skin and piecing the edges of it with the sharp point of the steel needle.

Thegns and serving folk moved around us, pulling apart bodies where they had fallen, stripping the Danes naked and dragging them from the hall, strewing straw upon the wet and slippery floors. Modwynn made her son drink much broth and ale, and I too tried to get some into Cadmar without his choking. Gyric took a little broth into his own mouth and holding the monk's head in his arm pressed his mouth to his and dribbled the liquid in. At first Cadmar sputtered and choked, but then began to take small swallows. I knew this was good and I had Gyric give him as much as he would take.

Worr was standing by Godwin's head, giving him an accounting of all who lived. Kilton had lost half its thegns, and of these remaining a third had suffered some hurt. They came within the hall now, supported or carried by their brethren, and tables were set up to hold them. I saw the wizened scop move amongst them, and again rejoiced in his life, for he was a jewel of the hall. Now he went to work upon the injured thegns, and proved his skill in more than his sagas. I saw too dark Dunnere range about the hall, coming first to the high table and then going to bless the dead. I knew he had some skill at leech craft, all Christian priests did; and wished instead of praying over good Wulfstan, gone already to his God, he would go to those men who groaned in pain and whose blood dripped upon the tables.

"Those Danes that lived fled through the village and back into the forest," said Worr. "No more than two score. The ships that carried those who came up the cliff are long gone. It was most of these that lay dead around us."

"Horses?" asked Godwin. He spoke with his eyes closed and I knew his pain was very great.

"We have gained in that. Those of ours they loosed from the stable stayed mostly in the yard. All the Danes from the forest were mounted, and many of their horses remain."

So Kilton had horses, but no thegns to ride them.

"They used no fire, save what the rain put out here," Worr went on. "The stable and all outbuildings are intact."

"They wanted the yard whole, to make it their own," Godwin murmured. "And our village folk?"

"Few were killed. The Danes rode fast and hard through the village, and the folk fled into the trees."

Godwin paused before his next question. "And of the yard folk?"

Worr raised his head for a moment before looking down at Godwin. "The losses are heavy, my lord. Stablemen, joiners, the cooper, kitchen men and woman, a few thegn's wives and young sons. Many slaves."

"Godwulf would be proud, as I am, to know they died for Kilton."

Worr's answer was swift. "They died for you, my lord. You are Kilton. I saw you gallop down the road, driving your horse so hard he foundered beneath you. I had not killed one man before you had killed five. Wulfstan and I fought shield to shield, and crippled as he was he gained steady ground to try to reach your side and take his place next you. His last word was your name."

All of us raised our heads at this tale, and I saw the scop where he bent over a thegn cock his ear to Worr's words.

"And I live only because of Gyric, who saved my life when it was lost." At this Godwin raised his right hand into the air, and spoke his brother's name again, and Gyric rose and went to him and grasped the hand of Kilton.

The next day Godwin sent two heavily armed thegns to Glastunburh, with orders that they ride as fast as they could

214

to bring Edgyth back. He mounted the men on two of his own horses, and had them lead a third. Unspoken in his orders was that they should return without fail with the lady, be it only her body they carried. They thundered away down the deserted village road at mid-day, with promises they should return before dusk on the next.

Early the following day a strange rider dared to approach the gate and declare he was come from Ælfred. He was brought inside the hall where Godwin and Cadmar still lay upon the high table and told us in breathless speech that Ælfred himself had been attacked, keeping his Yule-tide at his hall in Cippenham. He and his household had fled in time but the Danes took possession of his hall. Not only this, but it now seemed that they had in one accord stuck at every burh in the kingdom, and that few if any other than Kilton were still held by their lords. Only one other ealdorman was known to be alive. Families of high estate took ship for Frankland, thegns were left lord-less, and folk cast from their homes wandered the Winter wilderness.

We were struck dumb at this news, worn out as we were from fight and weariness. So much for Danish oaths, sworn upon the mighty silver arm-ring wet with the blood of Guthrum and his jarls. My legs went numb and I sunk down upon a bench against the treasure room wall.

"Where is Ælfred now?" asked Godwin after he had absorbed all this.

"He and his picked companions are in the marshes at Æthelinga," came the answer.

"Æthelinga? A wasteland of rushes and wet," said Godwin. He shook his head. "I have neither men nor stores to send him, but if he has want of horses I can give him sixty head."

"Sixty head?" The messenger's voice spoke his disbelief in this good fortune.

"Yes, but most of my thegns are dead or unfit to ride. At least the men who gather with the king now can be horsed, and should it come to it, none of them will starve." Godwin shifted and closed his eyes a moment. "I will give you five slaves to ride with you and take the horses, and will free them and arm them before you leave. With all my heart I want to ride with you myself to the King, but I cannot, and no more can I spare a single warrior. May God preserve Ælfred."

So Ælfred's man rode away with the great treasure of sixty horses, but the two thegns Godwin had sent to the foundation at Glastunburh did not come back that day. All night ward-men upon the ramparts strained into the dark looking for them, but dawn came without them, and another dawn. I caught Modwynn weeping in the treasure room, but none of us gave voice to the dread we felt. A hall full of women was an easy target, and there was no reason to hope warning had come in time for the nuns to seek the shelter of their hidden cave. Yet we could not speak our fears with so much grief about us.

Godwin gained steadily in strength, and in another day was standing. His wound had not grown hot, and no fever was upon him. Modwynn bound his arm close across his chest with a linen wrap, but still his pain when he moved could be read in his face. It was Cadmar we feared for now, for he seemed to hang between life and death without choosing either. He still lay upon the high table, and could take now many spoonfuls of broth, but he never opened his eyes nor deepened his shallow breath. Gyric and I spent hours at his side, Gyric at his head speaking to him, and I soundlessly at his feet.

"Was I like this?" asked Gyric in a small voice. He had been sitting by Cadmar as I washed the monk's wound with betony-water.

"You were very quiet, yes," I told him, thinking back to the long days and dark nights we had spent in the forests of Lindisse. "At last one night you rode the night-mare and awakened."

"You spoke to me as I speak now to Cadmar."

"Yes. And I believe wherever he is wandering, he hears you."

He shook his head and dropped his chin. "I asked him to stay here with me at Kilton, and now he may have been dealt his death-blow."

"He could have been killed in his forest retreat or on the road, and his death be wasted. Here he killed the man who speared Godwin, and so delayed Godwin's death long enough for you to kill the chief." I placed my hand over Gyric's. "At one time Cadmar cared much for Earthly fame. He is gravely weak from loss of blood, but like the true warrior he was he boasted once to me of his great might. He will live to hear his daring act sung of by the scop."

Gyric was silent a moment. "He told me long ago, the night of our hand-fasting, that you had courage to match your beauty. Do you recall that?"

Tears were in my eyes. "I recall every moment of that day, Gyric."

"I will tell him when he wakes that you have wisdom, too."

He lifted our joined hands and pressed them to his chest. My heart was so full I could scarce speak.

217

"You are the wise one, Gyric; you who have done so much to advise Godwin. Cadmar said it too." I glanced to the fire-pit where Godwin sat on a bench with a few thegns. "Tell me what will happen now, my love."

Gyric took a breath and let it out slowly. "Even our King is without a hall, all his estates overrun. I have thought much on it; I know Ælfred and his ways. We might send to him to join us here. But I have told Godwin that Ælfred is better off where he is, moving about the marshes with no fixed camp. If he and his remaining men come here, we are a fixed target for the Danes. It may take them time, but they will mass against us, and Kilton, King, and all be lost."

"And of Kilton?" All the folk of the village were once again gathered behind our walls, and all now knew that those were the last walls standing against the Danes in the Kingdom.

"With so many dead I do not think we could stand under another attack. But Worr is training up each able bodied man to fight. We will have a force, should Ælfred be able to make a stand."

Tho' our hardship was great in the weeks that came, we knew it was as naught to that suffered by the King and his household. Ealhswith his wife was with him, and their small children; they had escaped with their lives but little else and now wandered as fugitives living off the few folk whose trevs bordered the fen fastnesses. At Kilton our stores were low but so many had died that there was enough for hall and village too. The death of so many thegns and the great hurt to Godwin made it hard for any gladness to be felt when we gathered at night, and Dunnere began the breaking of bread with a special prayer for deliverance of our King and the sparing of the land. For days I would walk into the kitchen yard and be surprised again not to see some man or woman who had fallen, and Modwynn told me that Ceric tossed at night in his sleep. The bower house had been untouched, and save for the dark stain of blood from the small attack of two Summers ago, bore no sign of violence. Now that I was heavy with the child within me I was grateful for the rest it gave me.

Our one pleasure was seeing the small signs that gave us hope that Cadmar would live. One day his eyelids fluttered, on another his hand moved, he took more broth and ale more willingly. One morning I had finished checking his wound when he moved his foot. I stood up and looked down the long length of him. His eyes opened. Gyric was seated by his side and Cadmar lifted his hand and found Gyric's arm. Gyric seized it in his own and cried out, "Cadmar?"

Cadmar's eyes were dim and fixed, but I saw he squeezed the hand that held his. I moved closer.

"Tell me what happened," he asked, in a voice scarce above a whisper.

"Cadmar!" rejoiced Gyric, and I came and clung about my husband's shoulders.

"Tell me what happened," Cadmar repeated. "After I split his skull with my knife."

"I found a spear and drove it into the back of the chieftain's leg. He fell and I slit his throat with my seax."

A faint smile played around the monk's lips. "I am sorry I missed a good fight," he said, and fell into easy sleep.

When he awoke later both Godwin and Modwynn joined us at his side. "You live, my lord," said Cadmar, gazing with unblinking eyes at Godwin.

"Gyric saved my life when it was lost," he said in a low voice. "And you killed the man who took my shoulder."

"And my lady Modwynn, and the little lord?"

Modwynn laid her white hand upon the monk's brow. "We were spared, dear Cadmar. As we rejoice that you have been."

The warrior-monk sighed, and I thought only he and I and Gyric knew what was at the heart of that sigh.

At dusk a week later the horn sounded two short blasts from the ramparts, telling us that someone on foot approached our walls. We all lifted our heads and those of us who could moved forward out the doors and to the palisade gate. The wardman repeated his call, and Godwin, who could not climb, sent a thegn up to look. The man jumped down the last bit of ladder and came to Godwin's side.

"True, my lord. A single figure, cloaked, and walking slowly."

"Abroad now, and alone? I think it a trap. Did you see any sign of movement amongst the crofts?"

"None, my lord, tho' the light be fading."

Godwin looked around him. "Warenoth and Worr. Arm yourself and go out to meet this stranger."

Men around us muttered that this was a ghost come as omen of our soon end, and wondered if Dunnere should not be sent; but Godwin shook his head at such talk. The gate was pulled open the slightest span, and Worr and Warenoth, dressed in ring-shirt, helmet, spear and shield, passed out onto the red clay road, now nearly black in the little light. We stood clustered, watching. They neared the figure, and we heard them hail their warning. Then of a sudden the men began to run towards the figure, and we watched Warenoth, a big man, gather up the walker in his arms. Both men came as fast as they could back to the gate, Worr waving his arm and calling.

"Lady Edgyth! It is Lady Edgyth!"

Modwynn's hands flew to her lined brow. "Alive!" she cried, and clutched me tight as the whole yard exclaimed their wonder.

Now they were before us and the gate swung shut. The hood had fallen back from Edgyth's head and she smiled upon us, her grey eyes almost silver in the dusk. Her face was white and thin and her whole body looked as frail as a feather. She made a little gesture to be put down, but Warenoth strode to the hall with her, and not until a bench was set before the fire-pit did he relinquish his slight load. She kissed first Godwin, and rested for one moment her pale hand upon the linen wrap that bound his shoulder. Then Modwynn and Gyric were embraced and kissed. I hung back, taking in my hands the cup of ale that the steward had hastened to bring.

"Ceridwen, dear sister!" she greeted me, and my tears flowed down my face so that I must pass her the cup lest she drink them as well.

"You walked all this way?" demanded Godwin. Modwynn was sitting next her, chafing her cold hands and wrists.

"It is not far, years ago you and I used to walk out nearly so far for pleasure." She smiled up at him. "But as joyful as I am to be with you, I sorrow at seeing our village empty." Her

221

eyes rose to the wrap about Godwin's shoulder. "And this hurt to you."

In a few words she was told of the attack upon Kilton after the Peace had been made. "They came so sudden and in such force that if I had not been out with a few men hunting and thus surprised them from behind all might have ended badly. As it was I stand here before you only because of Gyric's hand."

Edgyth looked her wonder and her gratefulness to him, and stretching out her hand took his in her own.

"But how have you come to us thus?" asked Godwin. "The next day I sent two men to fetch you. They never returned, and so we thought the worst."

Edgyth closed her eyes for a moment. "I am sorry for the men you lost." She took a sip of ale and began. "The Danes did come to us, as sudden as they did to you. Our wardmen saw them, and some of our poor men fled at the start. Abbess Hilde gathered us together, and ordered the gates swung open lest the church suffer fire. We had but a moment to pray and bless ourselves. Abbess Hilde showed no fear and was ready to meet her death, and we tried to be upheld by her great courage. They galloped into the yard of the convent, hooting and yelling, and were met by our Abbess, who stood in front of all of us with her arms outstretched. Boldly she looked their leader in the face. He was a tall man, on a huge horse, and was I think surprised to meet naught but a group of woman and a few frightened serving folk. The men behind him laughed and whooped at the sight of us, and a few of them jumped from their horses and rushed towards us.

"Some of us were young and all knew what to expect from them. But their leader wheeled his great horse to stop them, and kept looking at Abbess Hilde and up at the wooden cross that tops the church. He spoke to his men, and they argued, and he spoke angrily and gestured with his spear at the cross, and at us.

"He turned and threatened some of his own men with his spear, and tho' they were angry they stalked off. They ranged through the store houses and took all our food, but their chief would not let them go into the church. Thus Mother Abbess' silver cross and chalice were spared. The whole time the chief stayed in front of us, as if to guard us, and when his men came back he questioned them and looked at the sacks of meal and all the hens they carried. He made them drop a small portion of the meal and a few hens so we would not starve. Then before they rode off, he marked a sign upon our gate, and made us understand not to wash it off."

"To keep other marauders away," said Gyric.

"Yes, I think it was just that. All of us expected death, and received mercy. There is good in some of them, after all."

Godwin finally spoke again. "Like as not he feared the wrath of God, seeing you as holy women."

At this Edgyth nearly laughed. "I am far from holy, but Abbess Hilde surely is. We all stayed as long as our food stores allowed, then went our ways. I know now that some of us went home to find nothing left." She looked around at all of us, and her pale face beamed. "In faith, whatever God intends for us, how grateful I am to be home."

When we had gathered again later that night I went to Edgyth, my great ring of keys in my hands. "These have been yours this many years, tho' they hung at my waist," I told her. "I welcome you back, Lady of Kilton."

Chapter the Eighteenth:
True Metal

SEED was sown, lest we live only to starve. A whole chain of boys ranged through the far orchards and into the forest, listening and watching, ready to alert the next with horn or shrill whistle should any intruders be spotted. In this way the village planted their seed-corn, but tho' the warming soil be soft and the blue sky pleasant, no sowing songs were sung as they went about this task. Thegns on horseback stood watchful upon the road, and those who walked behind their ploughs or with sowing-bag at waist glanced again and again at the walls before them and the trees behind.

Inside the burh yard Worr was training up all men found suitable to carry a spear. Yard workmen, serving men, and village men formed this new force. These were joined by ten slaves, mostly stable workers, who in thanks-giving for his life Godwin freed and armed. Few of his new force were as ardent as these.

Within the hall itself we were always kept busy. Of the score of thegns who had been carried injured inside, four had died of their hurt. Some who lived were hurt as grievously as Cadmar, and had always woman or boy at their side to tend them. Edgyth proved at once her value amongst them, and from her first day back she spent many hours checking the wounds of each and rifling the contents of the Simples chest and the stores of Berhtgit the herb-woman to compound remedies to ease pain and speed healing. She had learnt much from her time with the holy women at Glastunburh, and counted Abbess Hilde as a leech of great skill. She pounded dried leaves of sweet balm with boiled mare's milk and pressed the mass as a compress on the chests of those who rasped in their breathing from long lying still. She beat the white of a hen's egg with birch twigs, and spread it over healing sword cuts and spear gashes, and then laid spider webs over this wash to quell the forming of scars and make the skin less tight. She delighted Ceric by having him scout about the hall and bring her on two sticks the webs she sought. The wound through Godwin's shoulder was healing up, but the arm when she unbound it hung limp and useless at his side. He could not lift it, try as he may, and when with brow furrowed with pain and intent he failed, she rubbed the naked skin with sheep's fat pounded with cockle and yarrow. She then took the arm at the wrist and gently moved it up and down, across Godwin's chest and out again, so that he gritted his teeth and she must look only at his shoulder to keep the tears from her eyes. She did this each day and then bound the arm up close against his chest with a linen wrapper, and told him earnestly that the arm would once again serve him.

Cadmar was sitting up now, and was still my special charge. I took pains to care for him, for his life was dear to us all, and most especially to Gyric and to me. Edgyth looked at his wound for me, and praised my skill in sewing up the skin and keeping the gash free from heat, and she ordered for Cadmar strengthening brews to make thick his blood. One day I came into the hall and saw her kneeling at his side, and saw too the shaggy head of the warrior-monk bent in prayer, and knew they prayed together. From that day he became again less warrior and more monk, and spent time even in discourse with Dunnere, who before the attack he had through modesty or disdain not kept company with. But he in no wise became meek, and when he tried to stand and have the cut leg bear his weight, oaths poured from his mouth as from a tanner's. It rankled him that he could not move, and so counted himself useless to the burh, until Godwin had made for him a special chair in which he could sit with his hurt leg extended before him. In this he was carried to the yard and so oversaw the training at arms that Worr each afternoon schooled the village men in.

One forenoon I sat alone with the monk. Since he had awakened he was always hungered, and I had brought to him a bowl of thick wheat browis mixed with shredded pig. He sat sideways at the table, his wounded leg stretched flat upon the bench before him. After a time he lowered his spoon to the bowl and let it lie. I followed the gaze of his narrowed eyes and saw he looked at the upright timber to which I had been tied, and at the base of which he had fallen and nearly bled his life away. Singed and blackened thatch crowned the upright timber nearest the fire-pit, and tho' the hall was quiet, just then the morning of the attack seemed very close.

"When I saw you run towards me, I thought it was to kill me, and I was glad of it," I told him. "I thought Gyric already dead, and did not want to live as that man's captive."

He looked at me as if roused. "I ran to kill him, not you," he answered. "I knew your lord Gyric would be near to you, and when I saw you there had my best hope of finding him. But the Dane who seized you was an easy mark. A man who stops in battle to secure his booty rarely lives to enjoy it." He looked at me, and then lowered his eyes. "I have never killed a woman, even one who was trying to kill me. How much less could I slay the loved wife of my lord? 'Glad of it,' you say. Can you, Lady, who has so much, hold your life so cheap, and God's plan for it?"

I knew his words were not meant to shame me, but knew also he could not know how our beliefs differed. "I do not know about a plan for my life," I told him in truth. "I only know that in that instant I felt to die by a friend's hand was better than to live when all who I cared for were dead or enslaved."

His voice dropped as he answered me. "Forgive me, my Lady. I am no one to scold, after the life I have led. As I was falling I feared all was lost, and you and the boy still alive, and taken. I praise God for the safety of us all!"

I heard in these fervent words the torment he had in that moment suffered. I placed my hand over his own maimed right hand, but my words could not convey half of what my heart was feeling. "Cadmar, stay with us. Always. We have need of you here, of your steadiness."

He smiled. "In faith, Lady, even should you drive me from your door I could not leave now," he said, gesturing at his wrapped thigh. He blew out his breath and ended, "I have lived long enough to see the patterns in my life. First as a thegn at Sceaftesburh. That life ended for me with the death of my boys. I found a new life in the forest, which served me well for many years. Now I am called here. To remain with you at Kilton seems to be God's will."

I walked alone in the pleasure garden, restless and unable to stand at my loom. The heaviness against my ribs made all but simple walking unpleasant for me. I traced again the gravel paths lined with faded stubble, from which green shoots now showed. Then I felt a twinge, and then a growing dampness between my legs, and as I caught up the skirts of my gown and mantle the dribble grew and wetted my wool stockings through. So now at last the coming of the babe was upon me.

Within the hall sat Gyric, and Godwin, and Modwynn, and Edgyth, and now I must go there with my news. I had walked the same garden when Ceric had been ready to come, and had with joy and fear gone to the hall to tell Modwynn;

227

but now I stood joyless and mute upon the path. I was staring at the hall when its door opened. As if bidden Edgyth stepped out, and looked at me, and with a single glance read my face. She smiled and hurriedly turned back to the hall, and in a moment came back with Modwynn.

All was ready in the bower house, and still serving women came one after the other that afternoon, carrying armfuls of linen sheets and towels, copper basins, bucketsful of fresh water for the cauldron and many cakes of charcoal for the braziers. The floors had been laid with straw, and pottery jars of herbs brought by Berhtgit from her drying shed in the village covered the tabletop. Modwynn had told me this birth would be quicker than that of Ceric. She walked up and down with me and every time I felt a twinge I spoke aloud so that the herb-woman Berhtgit might take note of it.

At first the twinges were few, and far between, and the heaviness in my ribs was my greatest discomfort. Then the twinges grew longer, and the heaviness turned to dull ache in my back. Modwynn urged me not to lose strength, and gave me cup after cup of broth to spare me from weakness. At last I begged her sit herself, and Edgyth walked with me, arm about my shoulder, up and down. When the afternoon was far gone the herb-woman made up a pile of cushions upon the floor, and bid me kneel and lean into them and so rest; and in truth I could walk no further. This gave me some release, for the twinges were now pains, hot and sharp within me, like a band tightened and loosed about my belly and back, clenching and unclenching.

Trays with food and drink came. I could not eat; my bowels were not steady, but I begged Modwynn and Edgyth to go up to the hall to take their meal, where they would not have to listen to my groaning when the pain came. Berhtgit squatted down and lifted my gown, and urged them too to go, as the babe was far from coming. But leave me they would not, for which I was in secret gladdened, for tho' to suffer Edgyth's kind words and gentle touch was a kind of torment to me, yet her calm presence and the steady voice of Modwynn gave me strength.

Now both Edgyth and Modwynn walked with me, one upon either side, and we stopped often and I just leant against the table to rest. The pains grew sharp, and quicker, and at times I cried aloud. The pain would push inside me, sharper than I recalled from Ceric, and I would push against it until it laxed, and on and on in endless circle. As the pain grew larger my mind grew smaller, and I saw my wild mother's face before me, and keenly felt her wantonness as my own. Both Edgyth and Modwynn uttered prayers over me that the babe might be quick and hale, and all over soon; and I would have in my heart asked Frigg to speed me from this trial if I had thought I deserved her help. As it was I felt alone amidst these good women, and knew my shame added to my pain.

Edgyth boiled up dried juniper berries steeped in honey, which she said would help the child come, and I drank two strong cups full, choking on its masked muskiness. I knelt again against the cushions, and it eased the pain in my back for a time, but the pain kept moving, and so must I. I was so weary then that I could scarce rise. I wore naught but my shift now, for the room was blazing with warmth from the braziers, and washing-water stood steaming in the iron cauldron. Berhtgit peered between my legs for the one hundredth time.

Then came a clenching so hot and sharp that I near buckled to the floor, tho' both the herb-woman and Edgyth held me; and Modwynn stood and grasped both my hands and looked into my eyes and told me that the child was near. They lowered me gently to the birthing cloth so that my back rested upon the cushions, and held my shoulders as great waves of pain washed over me. I felt hands gripping my arms,

229

and thought Edgyth groaned as she heard me, but my gaze was fastened on the eyes of Modwynn and her voice strong and steady as she spoke to me unceasingly. Now the spasms came so quick they were one upon the other, and I could not so much push as just let the pain flow out of me before it came again. I had one arm reaching up, clasping onto Edgyth, and the other was held fast by Modwynn as she and Berhtgit knelt before me.

"Here, here is the babe," breathed Modwynn.

I felt a tightening and burning, and then a single great wave of pain that carried the babe out from me and into the world. I looked down to see the dark head emerging, turning to one side with a little shrug, and slip out on a river of wet into the herb-woman's waiting hands. A cry of joy went out from the women, and Modwynn proclaimed, "A man-child; just like Ceric," as she laid the glistening babe upon my weary belly.

It was the dark of the night, not yet dawn, and a serving woman went from the bower house to the hall to fetch Gyric. I heard the sound of his spear butt on the gravel path outside, and his anxious voice as he questioned the serving woman, and heard too the voice of Godwin. I put my hand on my new son, and sobbed.

Later that morning, when dawn had come fully, and the babe had been washed and swaddled, Godwin and Edgyth came with Modwynn richly dressed to the bower house. Gyric sat in the oak chair across from the dragon bed, where I now lay. The babe lay asleep under my arm.

Modwynn came to lift the bundle from me, as she had with Ceric, to place the child on Gyric's knee so he might in law accept him as his own. I lifted my arm to stay her as she came, and Gyric rose.

"Edgyth, come closer," I asked.

Gyric faced his brother and spoke. "We give this boy to Godwin, Lord of Kilton, and his wife Edgyth, to be their own son."

The smallest of gasps escaped Modwynn, and Edgyth reached out across the space to her husband. Godwin's face had gone white.

"Do you truly relinquish your claim on this child?" he asked.

I looked at Edgyth's face, lit with an inner light. I tried to steady my throat, swollen with tears. "I do relinquish him, with love."

Godwin looked to his brother, but seemed unable to speak.

At last Modwynn did. "Gyric, and you as well?"

He nodded his head, and said firmly, "Truly, he is Godwin's son."

"And so he shall be Godwin's son!" cried Modwynn, clasping her hands before her in joy.

Tears were starting in my eyes as I placed the babe in Edgyth's trembling hands. She wept, and held the tiny face to her own before passing him to Modwynn. Edgyth went to Gyric and clasped her arms about him and kissed him upon both cheeks, and kissed too his hands. Then she came to me and dropped down on her knees at the side of the dragon bed, the bed which had brought her naught but sorrow, the bed in which her new son had been conceived, and cradled my head in her arms and kissed me upon my mouth.

"May God bless you for this, Ceridwen!" she said, and could speak no more.

Godwin sat in the carved oak chair, and Modwynn placed the babe upon his knee. He laid his good hand upon the little one's head. He looked across at me, and his green-gold eyes burned. It took a moment for him to find his voice, and effort to keep it steady. "I accept this child as my own, and name him my son and heir."

So the bloodline of Godwin of Kilton would continue; and I bid them take the babe at once to the hall. Some babes had of late been born amongst the women of the yard, they might have their pick of women to suckle it. As they left, the babe began to cry, and my breasts ached, that had held him nestled there but once.

Tho' the boy was a hearty one, each day was so uncertain that Godwin did not wish to wait until Easter-tide to have him Christened, and bade Dunnere make all ready at the end of the month. They chose for name Edwin, an admixture of mother and father's name, as was custom. Despite her work about the hall Edgyth was never without the child, and at her side moved Hrede, who carried him back and forth between the kitchen woman who suckled him so that he was always within Edgyth's reach.

On the night of the naming-feast Gyric and I went to where they stood, the babe in Edgyth's loving arms. She had gained flesh and colour and looked young again. I pulled off the heavy braided gold bracelet that Godwin had pressed on my wrist my first day at Kilton.

"This is my naming gift to your son," I told them.

Godwin took it from my hands and held me in his embrace for one moment. Our eyes met, and he spoke low. "You are true metal, unalloyed," he told me.

Chapter the Nineteenth: Two Kings

WHITSUNTIDE approached, and down the red clay road galloped two riders from Ælfred. The fyrds of all the scattered shires of Wessex were massing around the King for a final stand against the Danish foe, and every man of Kilton who could march and bear a weapon was besought to join Ælfred at the hollow where Ecbert's Stone thrust into the air.

We had all waited and hoped for such a summons, for now we knew Ælfred believed he had men enough to re-seize his Kingdom, or die fighting for it. Godwin made haste to prepare men and stores for the ride, and one night called all of us from the high table into the treasure room. It was now the room in which he and Edgyth and little Edwin slept, for Modwynn had had a small bower built hard by the stone chapel for her use, so that the Lord and Lady slept as befit them amongst the burh's treasures.

Godwin looked at us all in turn as we came in. At his side stood Edgyth, her face mild and grave, and at their feet lay the cradle holding their sleeping son. First walked in Modwynn, and then Ceric, holding his father's hand and looking around with wide eyes. I came at their side, and then Dunnere helping Cadmar, who now walked with the aid of a crutch beneath his arm. Then came the older thegns Aldgisl and Byrnstan and Warenoth, and then Worr, who had lately been asked by Godwin to take a place at the high table.

"We ride tomorrow," began Godwin. "I take every thegn who is fit to fight, and all the men who Worr has trained. I leave you, Gyric, in command as my brother and heir, until my son be of age."

Gyric answered with resolve. "I pledge that you shall find all in good order when you return."

"I know that is true," said Godwin. "You, Cadmar, I ask serve as counsel."

The monk nodded his head in assent, and said, "I offer what I can."

Godwin glanced at the young thegn by Gyric's side. "Worr too will stay here; he is your man."

But Gyric shook his head. "I commend Worr to you. One good arm can turn a battle, and he wants to fight. He can track almost as well as Wulfstan did. And no one in all of Kilton rides so well as he. Should you need a fast rider, you will do no better than Worr."

Worr stepped forward to receive this praise, and Godwin nodded at him and said, "Then he fights with me."

The words spoken were simple and direct, as had been spoken often when Godwin had left Kilton in the keeping of his brother, but Modwynn looked with soft eyes at her eldest son as he stood across from her, his arm still wrapped close across his chest.

"Godwin," she asked, "how can you yourself fight, who cannot hold a shield?"

"How did Gyric slash a bandit upon the road? Or with spear kill the Dane who held my life-thread in his hands?" asked Godwin in return. "It can be done. My shield will be hung about my neck, and bound close to my body."

He turned back to the task at hand. "I leave Kilton with only ten thegns to guard it." He paused and looked around at each of us. "If we do not return, there is little I can offer other than you make your way to where you might take ship for Frankland. There is much treasure in silver, and some in gold."

Gyric held out his arm. "We are going nowhere. You will return, brother, and find your treasure and your hall awaiting you." And with that the brothers entwined arms in pledge that this be so.

So Godwin rode away, as he had many times over the years, only this time he rode not only with his thegns behind him, but with fourscore cottars marching with spears upon their shoulders. We all gathered to see them off; every man, woman and child left behind had someone dear to them in those ranks. When the thegns were all horsed Edgyth, Lady of Kilton, raised her little son in her arms so that his father might see him, and Godwin, sitting upon his horse with his arm bound tight to his chest, gazed down upon them and them alone.

On either side of the clay road the young grain was high and green, and in the orchards the apple blossoms already fallen to the new fruit that clustered there, and we looked long until the last men vanished through that distant line of trees.

That night the ten thegns left at Kilton joined at the high table, and as we ate not even the scop with all his skill could hide the fact that his voice as he sang to us echoed in the empty hall.

I had bid good night to Ceric in the little house where he slept with Modwynn, and walked across the gravel paths to the bower house. The folk of Kilton were already abed in their long houses along the wall. The thinnest of crescent moons shone above the pleasure garden, and the air was still. No night bird yet cried.

I bolted our door behind me and saw Gyric, sitting up in bed, and spoke to him so he knew it was me. His back rested against one of the dragon posts, and just above his head was the scar in the wood where he had driven deep Godwin's seax. I saw that rent in the wood each day, had run my finger across it, and knew that nothing could restore the wholeness of the grain. Yet deep as it was, it did not weaken the bed nor mar its beauty.

Gyric sat against it, his hand closed around the gold cross that lay upon his bare chest.

"It is so still," I said, as I slipped in beside him. "The hall nearly empty. And even the village folk are quiet."

"We are truly alone now, come what may," he said. "Are you frighted, my love?"

I thought on it. "No. I do not think so. We have been through so much, I do not think I am any longer afraid."

He turned to me and asked a question a warrior would ask of another. "But you wish to live?"

"Yes, yes," I answered quickly. "I wish to live, and to see you and Ceric thrive. I have always wanted life, save for one moment in the hall when I thought you dead."

He stretched out his hand to find mine and in his familiar gesture brought it to his lips. He kissed each of my fingers, and then my palm he pressed to his lips.

"I want life, and your happiness, Gyric. And for all to be well here at Kilton. And - I want to have a daughter."

He squeezed my hand, and I went on. "The hall needs a daughter, and a girl could give us such joy. Modwynn, too."

He still did not speak, and I could not read his face. "Is this what you wish, too?"

"Yes," he said. "I want you, and your daughters, and more sons too. I want to live long and well with you, and have as much of joy as I can." A smile bowed his beautiful lips. "I have proven to be hard to kill. This must be for a reason, and part of this reason must be my love for you."

Left as we were with few defences save the stout palisade walls, Gyric gave much thought to the best use of our resources. He determined that watchfulness lent a greater sense of safety to the burh and its folk, and with Cadmar set about devising a whole system of new ward-towers and out posts stretching far past the village, greatly exceeding the reach of the old. From these small towers a single watcher could see long distances and alert by whistle or horn any suspect movement. The forest too was covered, and wardmen stationed along all the forest tracks of size enough to admit of men travelling in groups. At one end of the pleasure garden and in the kitchen yard like towers were raised at the sea face, and always manned. Should we suffer another direct attack, the burh with its reduced stores and few men could not last long, but simply to know there would be greater warning of the enemy's approach shed some calmness on our days.

Cadmar himself oversaw the construction of these ward-towers, and since he could not yet ride, drove himself about in a small horse-drawn wain, ferrying timber and hollering commands. At night he made the table laugh with his jests and stories, and was ever of good cheer. Edgyth too was full of faith and gentle strength in these weeks, and made by her calm manner each day pass in hope of happy outcome. To watch her with Edwin, alight with joy in this babe, at times wrung tears from my eyes. Modwynn, seeing this, would come to me in private to comfort me for what I had forsworn, and it was my greater pain that she knew not from whence my true grief sprang.

When word came, we knew at once it was good, for from the outermost reaches of our ward towers came the two short and one long blast that told us the Lord of Kilton or one of his own men was near. Nearly a month had passed since Godwin had ridden off, and now came four riders, two from him, and two from the King himself. We could see the golden dragon banner of Ælfred a long way down the road, and even hear the shouts and calls of the men upon their horses. As they grew nearer to our walls they were joined by the wardmen themselves, who clustered around the horsemen and took up the cry. Godwin's thegns Aldgisl and Byrnstan flanked the two from Ælfred, and as they approached the gates Aldgisl looked down upon us and cried, "Victory! Victory and peace!"

Before he had even swung from the saddle he fastened his eyes upon the anxious face of Edgyth and said, "My Lord Godwin is well, Lady," and Edgyth and Modwynn embraced in joyful tears.

Now Aldgisl was before us and spoke to Gyric. "My Lord, your brother sends you greetings and these glad tidings. Know that he is well and that Ælfred, King has upon the field at Ethandun driven the Danish host from the field of battle. Guthrum retreated to the hall at Cippenham, and the King and his fyrd laid siege for fourteen days. On the fifteenth day Guthrum himself appeared to sue for peace, and the King reclaimed his hall and accepted the surrender of the Danish host."

Then followed such tumult of rejoicing that no further words could be heard, as all of Kilton pressed forward as if to try to touch the bearers of this good news. Gyric had clasped hands with Aldgisl and Brynstan, and Ceric was jumping up and down in eagerness and joy at his father's side as Edgyth and Modwynn and I laughed and wept in turn.

Once inside the quiet of the hall, the clamour of the yard shut behind us, the four riders told us over full ale cups the tale of the last weeks. One of Ælfred's men spoke of the meeting of the thegns of the two remaining ealdorman, Godwin and Odda, and how the men of Sumorsaet, Defenas and Hamtunscir massed together to form a single army behind their King.

"We locked shield with shield, shoulder to shoulder, and formed an unbroken shield wall that drove across the field at Ethandun. We shocked the Danes by our numbers; they thought Ælfred driven deep into hiding would never be able to marshal such a force behind him. The fighting was fierce, but at last they broke and ran. We pursued them back to their stolen hall at Cippenham, and made our camp before the walls, knowing our force was too great for them to be able to break through us and flee. We had then only to wait for their stores to dwindle, and at last Guthrum came out to us."

We all marvelled at this, and Cadmar and Gyric shook their heads. "But what proofs do they offer?" Gyric wanted to know.

The thegn held up a leathern scroll holder. "This is the greatest of them," he answered, and pulled from it a new inked piece of parchment. He lay it down upon the table before him, and began to read.

240

THIS IS THE PEACE THAT I, ÆLFRED, KING,

With my Witan bind and confirm with oaths with
Guthrum, King of the Danes, for ourselves and for our
subjects, both living and unborn, who care to have God's
favour or our own. That Guthrum shall take his men
and leave Wessex forever in Peace, and that the lands
we agree are now their own should be left uncontested.
That any hostages who remain on either side be given up
in good faith. In testament to his word Guthrum follows
with his act and has by the grace of God received Christ,
and the name of Ælthelstan, and I myself serve as his
God-father. And that his thirty chief men have followed
in receiving Christ through holy Baptism.

And here I sign my name, and what follows is the
name and mark of Guthrum and his thirty jarls who
make this Peace with me.

Ælfred, King of Wessex

Guthrum, King of the Danes of East Anglia

Orm of Jorvik

Ulf of Jorvik

Ari of Snotingahem

Sidroc of Lindisse...

That was I all I heard, tho' the buzz in my ears told me
the list of names went on. Sidroc lived, and was amongst
those who were now counted as the jarls of Guthrum, King of
the Danes, and had made his mark upon the parchment that
Ælfred's man read from.

At the hearing of these baptisms Dunnere cried out that
a miracle moved in our midst; and blessed aloud the name of

241

Ælfred, King; but most of us around that great table were as silent as me, thinking on all this.

Now Godwin's man, Aldgisl, spoke, and his plain, open face, creased with fighting and weather, gave weight to his words so that we none of us have doubt.

"All true; it is all true, and we four have witnessed this all with our own eyes, just as we stood in the shield wall. The baptisms took place near Æthelinga, and each man, re-born in Christ, donned his new linen tunic. And Ælfred gave rich gifts to Guthrum, and a fine gift each to Guthrum's jarls, and has fed and kept them at his hall at Wedmor. Our Lord Godwin sends us to request a certain sum of silver and of gold, and a number of fine things from his treasury, as he himself wishes to bestow gifts upon these men, and asks that we might return to him at Wedmor at once with the items he lists. We ride to tell you these things, and that soon the King and Godwin will ride with his guests here to Kilton, that you prepare for them." Aldgisl pulled a small fold of parchment from his belt, and handed it to Byrnstan. The younger thegn took it up and squinted at it, and began to read.

"The cask of silver pieces in the green chest; the wood casket which holds the gold neck chain and the pins set with garnets, the shoulder clasps of gold and lapis, the casket of carved ivory." He placed the parchment in front of Edgyth and Gyric and said, "This is what he asks for, my Lady, my Lord."

Gyric fingered the scrap as Edgyth looked down upon her husband's hastily inked words.

"His hand," she smiled, and passed it to Modwynn; and Gyric said, "You shall ride with these things on the morrow."

"I thank you, Lord," answered Aldgisl. "My Lord Godwin will be glad to have them, and has he himself received from Guthrum a necklet of gold." He looked around the table for a moment. "Also Sidroc of Lindisse, he that was here, gave to Godwin three horses, saddled and bridled, and an iron battle helmet chased with gold, and a pound of amber beads as large as hen's eggs."

Cadmar leant towards Gyric. "Is this the Sidroc of Four Stones, then that you spoke of?" Gyric said in a low voice, "Yes."

Cadmar considered this a moment. "He is shrewd, this Dane, to give especial gifts to Godwin, and thus strengthen the bond he has with you here."

For answer Gyric only nodded.

The talk went on for a long time after this, and the men told of how Ælfred, having forged this peace and won perhaps the greater victory of his bitterest enemy's conversion, now wished to take Guthrum and his men to the key burhs in the Kingdom of Wessex to celebrate the new pact they shared.

More drink and food was brought, and Gyric and Cadmar spoke to them of the month passed at Kilton. After a while I rose and went and looked upon the Peace parchment where it lay unrolled upon the table. It was well-prepared and well-inked, by a scribe who knew the great import of the words he wrote. At the bottom I saw the name of Ælfred, drawn by himself in his large hand; and by it the name Guthrum, smoothly written by the scribe, and next it the single letter G scratched into the parchment with force. Beneath these came the names of the thirty Danish jarls, unlettered all, who made marks by their names where they had been told to do so. Many of these were of the simplest kind, two lines crossed; but by Sidroc's name I saw he had drawn the rune Sigel ᛁ , meaning victory, to sound out the first letter of his name; and my finger reached out and touched the rune he had drawn.

The morning of their coming dawned fair and warm, and as promise of a fine day the Sun crept across the yellow sheafs of wheat bordering each side of the clay road. I glanced down that road early, not long after the Sun had risen, and looked at it empty and red in the slanted light, and thought of what it would carry to us within that day of return. We in the hall were kept much occupied with our preparation, but when the horn upon the ramparts rang out the two short and one long blast that told of the Lord of Kilton's coming, we streamed through the gates and took our places before the crowd. All of Kilton's folk lined the road through the village and to the burh wall. Many held aloft short branches of oak to greet their King and Lord, and were noisy and gleesome as they stood before their crofts and on the margins of the fields. All had donned their gayest clothing. I wore again my green silk gown, a gift so long ago from Ælfwyn's hand, for it was of all my gowns my favourite, and the one in which I felt most fully myself. Her silver brooch lay pinned at my neck, and around my brow circled the golden fillet.

Gyric stood at my right hand, with Ceric before us, and at Gyric's right stood Cadmar. Next him was Modwynn, and then Edgyth, beaming as she held Edwin in her arms. Ranged behind us were the ten thegns who stayed at Kilton, in their finest tunics and adorned with all the silver arm-rings and necklets each man possessed.

The procession appeared from out the orchards, and as it drew closer to the outlying crofts a cheer rose from the throats of the folk awaiting them. Ceric before us was wriggling in eagerness, and as the group came closer I told Gyric all as I saw it.

"They are riding in ranks of four. Godwin is at the far right, and next him is Ælfred, and next him must be Guthrum, and another Dane. They are all richly dressed. Ælfred looks stronger than I have ever seen. Godwin is smiling and talking and the others looking at him. His arm is in a sling and no longer pinned up close to his chest. He is on a new horse, not one of his own, big and black and with a long mane."

"What is Guthrum like?" he wanted to know.

I looked at the figure leaning forward across his saddle-bow. "He is older than I thought; a man of Cadmar's age or more, his hair and beard are all grey. He is of no great size. Around his throat is a huge gold necklet."

"And behind them?"

"There are many ranks of horsemen, almost a score or more. Then rows of men on foot. A string of horses being led. And lastly come four or five waggons, pulled by double horse teams." I brought my eyes back to the front of the procession. "The men riding are talking and laughing and looking out over the crowd to the walls. Some of them are our men, or the King's, but others are clearly Danes."

"Do you see Worr?" he wanted to know.

I strained my eyes to try to pick him out. "I do now. He is on the outside, about three ranks back, talking to a Dane. I think Warenoth rides on the other side." I looked again and saw that the Dane Worr jested with was Sidroc.

"Is he well? Is Worr whole?" asked Gyric, which forced my eyes back to the young thegn.

245

"Yes, he looks hale and hearty," I assured him.

Sidroc turned his head from where he sat upon his bay stallion, and his eyes swept the line of folk who stood before the huge gates. He found me, and held my gaze for just a moment. Then Worr saw us too, and raised his hand, which made me speak to Gyric. "Worr sees us, he is waving," and Gyric lifted his hand in greeting.

The front rank was nearly upon us now, and Edgyth moved forward as the men began to rein in. Ælfred and Godwin were smiling down at her as they swung off their mounts. The face of the young King, no older than Gyric, was battle-worn and drawn, the light blue eyes grave above his smile. Yet there was such quiet force in his manner and bearing that it seemed a glow of health lay upon his cheek.

Thegns and stable men came up to take the horses; and amidst the tumult of greetings and welcoming gestures Godwin was before us. He embraced first his wife, and placed upon his son's round face a kiss, and then held Modwynn with his good arm and kissed her brow as she clung to him. Then he took Gyric's hand where he extended it, and pressed his brother close to him, and said, "Never was Kilton left in greater danger, or in better hands. From the day I rode off I believed I would return and find you and Kilton waiting for me."

No tribute could be more justly spoken than this, but Gyric brought tears to my eyes as he answered, "I thank God for our deliverance, and for your life."

Then we were moving as one through the gates, and into the yard and to the scarred iron-strapped oak door of the hall, swung wide to admit us. All the tables were set up, and serving men waited at each with bronze ewers and basins so that our guests might wash their hands, and from the kitchen yard door came a line of serving men led by the steward, who

246

stood with fresh baked wheaten loaves piled high on platters. At the high table were set silver ewers of ale, for the mead was to be kept for the feast that night; but the ale was Modwynn's finest, that known as bright ale, which by long standing becomes mellow and clear. Godwin led his chief guests to the high table, Ælfred in the centre in the great carved chair, and Guthrum just at Ælfred's left, and Godwin at the King's right, and then many of Ælfred's own men, and so the tables filled. Each table had Danes at it, and thegns of Godwin's and of Ælfred's, and at each these former enemies sat as friends.

When everyone had a place, Godwin stood. He looked out over the expanse of his hall, filled now with his own men, the picked men of Ælfred, and ranged amongst them the most powerful of the Danes, lately his fierce foes. All looked back at him, and the Danes looked too at the wonder of the great hall of Kilton with its painted walls and precious glass casements.

"I welcome you to Kilton," he told them, "in fellowship and peace. And I welcome our two great Kings who sit amongst us, Ælfred of Wessex and Guthrum of Anglia."

Nothing Godwin could have said would have pleased them more. The Danes roared at hearing Guthrum named as equal to Ælfred, and the hall shook with their cheers and stamping of their feet. Ælfred rose now, and bid Guthrum do the same, and these two great war-chiefs raised their arms above the crowd to receive the homage of their warriors. Ælfred scanned the faces before him and began to speak.

"I give thanks for this welcome, and for the guiding hand of God Eternal who has brought us here on this day to sit as brothers. Let us in every action recall the sacred vows we have made to Him and to each other, and keep our time together here with joy and gladness."

247

The hall once again cheered, and then Edgyth nodded at me. She took up a ewer, and so did Modwynn and I; and Edgyth, Lady of Kilton filled first the golden cup of her King, and then of his guest, King of the Danes, and then of her own dear husband. Modwynn went to a second table with her ewer, and I to a third, and that is how I found myself swirling ale into the cup that Sidroc held before him.

We did not speak nor did I look at his face, but I saw glinting upon the wrist of his sword hand the silver disk bracelet before I moved on to the next man.

The king spoke more, and then Guthrum, in halting but well chosen words, spoke, and the men broke their fast with the loaves, and the hall grew loud with the sounds of talk and laughter. I sat at Gyric's side at the high table, glad at his gladness, watching him as he leant in to hear what Godwin or the King was saying, taking pleasure in the way he clasped his golden-rimmed cup. Across the fire-pit Worr sat at table with Sidroc, and Warenoth too, and the three were jesting with each other, and Warenoth pulled something from the bag at his belt to show to Sidroc.

Then Worr looked across at us, and said something to the other two, and raised his arm to me, and I said to Gyric, "Worr is coming to speak with you," as he crossed the floor to us. Gyric swung around from the table to greet Worr, and the two stood by the treasure room wall as Worr began to tell of the battle at Ethandun and the siege at Cippenham. In a short time Warenoth and Cadmar too joined in this talk, and mindful of our guests I took up the ewer in my hands.

I began at the high table, where Ælfred smiled upon me and Guthrum inclined his head and nodded, and then went to any man who held up his cup to be filled. I moved through the hall, and saw Sidroc sitting with another Dane, and then saw him lift his cup.

He held his cup close before him, and I bent and spoke near his ear. "There is a grove of pear trees near the forest by the road. I will be there just before Sun-down."

"I will be there, shield-maiden," he answered in a low voice.

Chapter the Twentieth: A Gift

LATE in the day when the crowded kitchen yard was filled with the hustle of the coming feast, and Godwin and Gyric and Ælfred sat with Guthrum in the hall, I went to the mare's stable and rode off at a walk through the gates and onto the clay road. Pasture land to one side was busy with men pitching hide tents to shelter our many guests, and waggons bordered the road. The lowering Sun, still strong, was slanting hard against the huts of the villagers as I passed the last of the crofts and then the apple orchards. I kept on, and reached the pear grove, and turned my mare from the road.

I went a little way in amongst the trees, and slipped off my mare and tied her to a tree stump. I walked slowly about the grove, waiting. Yellow pears lay nearly ripe in heavy clusters on the slender-leafed trees. Down in the pasture I could see many horses moving about, and upon the road oxcarts moved slowly towards the burh. A few horsemen rode up or down. Then a lone horseman made his way up the road, cantering through the red dust. As he neared us my mare raised her head and whinnied shrilly, and Sidroc's bay arched his glossy neck and called back. Sidroc swung down and dropped the reins behind him. He stood before me, and we beheld each other.

He had now thirty Summers, and was in the pride of manhood. Tall he had always been, but now his form had filled out, telling in one glance of his strength and vigour. He was a powerful war-chief, and a warrior of fame, and a winner of much battle-gain, and looked these things, all three. He wore clothes of skilful make, a tunic of finely spun wool of such dark blue to be nearly black, and upon this, a leathern tunic with scrolling designs cut into it. Over his leggings were leg wrappings of brown leather, and he pulled from off his hands short gloves of the same. Upon his left wrist was a heavy bracelet of gold, and upon the right glinted the silver disk bracelet. His hair was trim and even, and I saw at his left temple a strand of grey amongst the dark. His beard lay close to his face, and when he smiled at me the top of his scar went crooked.

I almost could not speak, seeing him there before me, and finally said, "You live."

He laughed. "Yes. I have not yet been called to the great hall." He gestured to the sky above us. "But I have seen many battles."

"And are untouched," I answered.

"The shield-maiden has not chosen me," he said quietly.

At this I smiled, and found my true voice. "How is Ælfwyn?"

"She is well. Busy. I built a second hall for my new men, and Ælfwyn and her mother run all with skill."

"She is as beautiful and kind as ever," I said for him, knowing it to be true.

He nodded. "She is a good woman."

"You will carry a letter to her from me?"

He nodded, but said no more.

"And little Ashild?" I asked.

He grinned. "She will be one to watch. She is as comely as her mother, and as crafty as her father. There is a boy, too now, who I named Hrald, the name of my father."

"I am happy for you, in both these children," I said. "And Ælfwyn's sisters? How do they fare?"

"The eldest wed Asberg two Summers ago. He wanted her enough to become Christian."

"Asberg?" I recalled his yellow hair and blunt, good natured face. He had ridden with Sidroc before to Kilton, but my sharpest memory of him was carrying the cocks that Yrling sacrificed at the pit of Offering at Four Stones.

"Yes. When she told me she wished to wed I set a high bride-price for her. The girl is nearly as comely as Ælfwyn and very rich. A few of my men who were wed wanted to send away their wives so they could marry her, but Ælfwyn would not allow this. At last the girl chose Asberg amongst them, but told him she would have him only if he became Christian. So he did. And they are happy enough, and even have a son now."

"And of Eanflad?"

He shook his head. "The little one. She still does not speak. She has grown, but is still not right. Last year I caught one of my men trying to force her, and killed him for it. Now the rest know to leave her alone. Once the priest tried to drive his Devil from her and frighted her so badly I nearly killed him too. She is left in peace now, at Burginde's side, and cares well for the little ones."

"She is like the daughter Burginde never had," I thought aloud.

He laughed. "Yes, and now that Burginde has grown so fat and wears so many brooches, she has need of younger legs about her."

The thought of this made me smile too. "You are very rich now," I said.

252

"Yes, I have won much booty, but I have not had time to look at it. There is in the treasure room at Four Stones six chests of silver and two small ones, filled with pure gold. Also I have two hundred head of horses; they are of the best." He looked across the expanse of the village to the burh and its timber buildings beyond. "But I do not have this rich land that Kilton has; he excels me in this. He has sheep and cattle to clothe and feed so many. His men too, are all good ones; I know this from Worr. Also his hall is finer. But I have enough."

I felt I could ask him anything and spoke so. "Are you done then, with war?"

"I will fight to keep what I have, but of treasure I am content."

His eyes told me he thought of more than silver or gold.

I asked now what only he could tell me. "Why did they do it, attack after the Peace had been made? Guthrum and his men swore on a sacred arm ring to leave Ælfred in peace, and then attacked. His vow was worthless."

His answer was quick. "He meant his vow, when he made it. That is why we swore so, each wetting with our own blood the silver arm ring." He pulled back his tunic sleeve on his left wrist and I glimpsed the new scar there.

"Then why this treachery? To have sworn so, and then to attack at so many burhs, kill so many folk."

"Guthrum meant to keep the Peace he swore to. This you must believe, only because I was amongst his men and saw and heard what followed. Not all of us agreed with this new Peace. Guthrum has much treasure and much land. His blood is cooling now, and he has had enough of war. Some of his men, the younger ones who have not been fighting so long, are still thirsty for treasure. There was much grumbling amongst them. We are many small war-bands come together to fight behind him, and he had no choice but to agree to one more try at winning all. Else some threatened to turn against him, and Guthrum would not risk losing what he has worked so hard to win."

"And you? Did you join in the attacks as well?"

"I did not. I was already back at Four Stones. But when I heard that Ælfred was massing a new force, I had to join Guthrum; he is my chief."

"Our losses here were very great. I myself was captured and many died."

He turned a little away from me and shook his head. "You do not know how I feared for you."

What I answered made him turn back. "You do not know how I feared for you."

Our eyes were fastened each upon the other's, and a slow smile spread across his face. I looked away beyond the line of the burh to where the Sun now was drowning in the sea.

There was more I wanted to know. "What will you do now, that there is peace?"

He lifted his hand towards the burh, and the men there. "We have pledged to settle what we have claimed, and share out the land amongst us. But it is not so easy for some. Of my men, a number have never farmed. They were trappers or fur-traders at home, and now they must work the land. Also we must raise many animals. For me in Lindisse, I must see that all gets done."

"You will be busy then," I said, thinking of the tasks that would fill the long years ahead.

"Yes," he agreed. "And it is sometimes harder to keep the good things you have than to win them in the first place."

"I know," I told him, and looked down.

"Guthrum, now, desires much: he wants to be like your King, win the regard of many people, and have coins stamped with his name upon them."

"Why did Guthrum become Christian?"

He thought a moment. "He had sworn to All-father and to Thor before Ælfred and his men. Kilton was there; he must have told you this. Then Guthrum was forced to break his vow to keep order amongst his own men. So the Gods were angry at him and gave the victory to Ælfred. There was a battle near Æthelinga, and the raven banner fell. It had been woven in a single day by Ragnar Lodbrok's own daughters, and had in it much force."

My face told him I did not know this name, for he went on. "He was a famed warrior chief, who won much glory in Frankland. But it was a king of Northumbria who killed him years ago, in a viper pit. Ragnar had daughters of great beauty and also great magic. All of us valued this banner and it flew always at war. It fell before Ælfred's men. When that happened, Guthrum knew he would lose. The Gods had turned against him."

I saw in my mind's eye this battle-banner captured, and thought of the women who had once woven it, much as Ælfred's wife had woven his own.

"Also, Guthrum has great man-craft; he thinks much, which is why he is a great chief. He knew that to submit to be baptized would have meaning to your King. Guthrum is weary of fighting and wants peace, and the best way to forge it is for each side to give the other some of what they most want."

I took this in, and then said, "You let yourself be baptized."

He shrugged. "My war-chief asked it of me. But it will take more than a new tunic to keep me from sacrificing to my Gods." He dropped his voice and touched his silver disk bracelet. "They have not failed me often."

He went on in a stronger tone. "And Guthrum took from his own treasure store to reward us, and Ælfred gave us gifts of great worth as his sign of peace."

I thought of the things Sidroc had presented to Godwin, and said, "The gifts you gave were very rich."

"It is good for a chief to be open-handed. Great ladies and goddesses too. Think of you; Kilton needed a son, and you gave him your own child."

There was no one else on Earth with whom I would share the coming truth. "The boy is Godwin's," I told him, and did not flinch.

He looked steadily at me for a moment, then lifted his face to the reddening sky. "I have always thought much of you, shield-maiden. Now I know that had you been born a man, you would be a king."

His eyes dropped to my face. "Will you tell me how this happened?"

I held the gaze of his dark blue eyes. "Yes. For a short time I forgot something you told me at table in the hall of Four Stones. You told me that no person can be first in everything, can possess all they wish to possess."

He considered a moment before he spoke. "And you have remembered this now?"

I nodded Yes.

He let out a low whistle. "You are like Freyja, a queen amongst goddesses. And had you stayed with me, become my woman, today I might rule over half this land."

A long moment passed, in which his eyes were fastened to my face. He did not smile or move, and then reached his arms to me.

"I ask now that you give to me freely what years ago I could have taken by force."

I raised my hand to halt his movement. "I cannot; a kiss is a pledge."

"Then make of your kiss a gift."

I could not refuse this, and now opened my palms to him. He took my hands within his own and brought them to his chest. For a moment he stood still, my hands clasped within his own, his eyes closed as he held them to his leathern tunic. Then he let go my hands and I stepped to him, and his arms crossed my back. Only once had he ever held me thus, before the fire-pit in the ruin that was Four Stones, but his remembered strength and stillness now surrounded me. He bent his face to mine, and his mouth sought my own.

In his kiss was great tenderness, and great passion, and the seven years desiring of me; and also in his kiss was he himself, the essence of the man Sidroc, heathen and warrior and man of goodness. Now as a woman I tasted him and breathed in his savour within the circling stillness of his arms.

257

We moved apart, and opened my eyes to find him gazing on me.

"You are a woman now, with a woman's wisdom. Having had your kiss, I will Offer to Freyja that it will not be the last. In this land or another, one day you will sit at my side."

I lifted his right wrist to my face. The bracelet he had once given to me bore the scars of the years he had worn it. Tears welled in my eyes and I kissed it, then clasped his hand in both of mine.

"I make you this vow, Sidroc. When my son Ceric reaches his twelfth year, I will send him to you. There is much he could learn from you. You can perfect his training. And, if you like...tell him of our gods. Ashild and he loved each other as babes. If when they are grown they find love together, it would bring Ælfwyn and me great joy."

I could not help but smile as I added, "He will pay a rich bride-price for such a girl."

Here I Rest my Hand   Ceridwen of Kilton

Ceridwen of Kilton

Calendar of Feast Days mentioned in the Circle Saga

Candlemas - 2 February

St Gregory - 12 March

High Summer - 24 June

St Peter and Paul - 29 June

Hlafmesse (Lammas)- 1 August

St Mary -15 August

St Matthew - 21 September

All Saints -1 November

Martinmas (St Martin's) -11 November

Yuletide - 25 December to Twelfthnight - 6 January

Anglo-Saxon Place Names, with Modern Equivalents

Æscesdun = Ashdown

Æthelinga = Athelney

Basingas = Basing

Caeginesham = Keynsham

Cippenham = Chippenham

Cirenceaster = Cirencester

Defenas = Devon

Englafeld = Englefield

Ethandun = Edington

Exanceaster = Exeter

Glastunburh = Glastonbury

Hamtunscir = Hampshire

Hreopedun = Repton

Jorvik (Danish name for Eoforwic) = York

Legaceaster = Chester

Lindisse = Lindsey

Lundenwic = London

Meredune = Marton

Sceaftesburh = Shaftesbury

Snotingaham = Nottingham

Sumorsaet = Somerset

Swanawic = Swanage

Wedmor = Wedmore

Witanceaster (where the Witan, the King's advisors, met) = Winchester

Frankland = France

Glossary of Terms

browis: a cereal-based stew, often made with fowl or pork

ceorl: ("churl") a freeman ranking directly below a thegn, able to bear arms, own property, and improve his rank

cottar: free agricultural worker, in later eras, a peasant

cresset: stone, bronze, or iron lamp fitted with a wick that burnt oil

ealdorman: a nobleman with jurisdiction over given lands; the rank was generally appointed by the King and not necessarily inherited from generation to generation. The modern derivative *alderman* in no way conveys the esteem and power of the Anglo-Saxon term.

frumenty: cereal-based main dish pudding, boiled with milk. A version flavoured with currents, raisins and spices was ritually served on Martinmas (November 11th) to ploughmen.

seax: the angle-bladed dagger which gave its name to the Saxons; all freemen carried one.

scop: ("shope") a poet, saga-teller, or bard, responsible not only for entertainment but seen as a collective cultural historian. A talented scop would be greatly valued by his lord and receive land, gold and silver jewellery, costly clothing and other riches as his reward.

thegn: ("thane") a freeborn warrior-retainer of a lord; thegns were housed, fed and armed in exchange for complete fidelity to their sworn lord. Booty won in battle by a thegn was generally offered to their lord, and in return the lord was expected to bestow handsome gifts of arms, horses, arm-rings, and so on to his best champions.

trev: a settlement of a few huts, smaller than a village

tun: a large cask or barrel used for ale

wergild: Literally, man-gold; the amount of money each man's life was valued at. The Laws of Æthelbert, a 7th century King of Kent, for example, valued the life of a nobleman at 300 shillings (equivalent to 300 oxen), and a ceorl was valued at 100 shillings. By Ælfred's time (reigned 871-899) a nobleman was held at 1200 shillings and a ceorl at 200.

Witan: Literally, wise men; a council of ealdorman, other high-ranking lords, and bishops; their responsibilities included choosing the King from amongst their numbers.

withy: a willow or willow wand; withy-man: a figure woven from such wands

About the Author

Octavia Randolph has long been fascinated with the development, dominance, and decline of the Anglo-Saxon peoples. The path of her research has included disciplines as varied as the study of Anglo-Saxon and Norse runes, and learning to spin with a drop spindle. Her interests have led to extensive on-site research in England, Denmark, Sweden, and Gotland. In addition to the Circle Saga, she is the author of the novella *The Tale of Melkorka*, taken from the Icelandic Sagas; the novella *Ride*, a retelling of the story of Lady Godiva, first published in Narrative Magazine; and *Light, Descending*, a biographical novel about the great John Ruskin. She has been awarded Artistic Fellowships at the Ingmar Bergman Estate on Fårö, Gotland; MacDowell Colony; Ledig House International; and Byrdcliffe.

She answers all fan mail and loves to stay in touch with her readers. Join her mailing list and read more on Anglo-Saxon and Viking life at www.octavia.net.

Made in the USA
Middletown, DE
05 September 2018